Tangled Echoes

TANGLED ECHOES (RECONSTRUCTIONIST 2)
Copyright © 2017 Meghan Ciana Doidge
Published by Old Man in the CrossWalk Productions 2017
Salt Spring Island, BC, Canada
www.oldmaninthecrosswalk.com

Library and Archives Canada
Doidge, Meghan Ciana, 1973—
Catching Echoes/Meghan Ciana Doidge—PAPERBACK EDITION

Cover design by Damonza

ISBN 978-1-927850-58-9

MEGHAN CIANA DOIDGE

Published by Old Man in the CrossWalk Productions
Salt Spring Island, BC, Canada

Author's Note

Tangled Echoes is the second book in the Reconstructionist series, which is set in the same universe as the Dowser and Oracle series.

While it is not necessary to read all three series, *in order to avoid spoilers* the ideal reading order is as follows:

Cupcakes, Trinkets, and Other Deadly Magic (Dowser 1)
Trinkets, Treasures, and Other Bloody Magic (Dowser 2)
Treasures, Demons, and Other Black Magic (Dowser 3)
I See Me (Oracle 1)
Shadows, Maps, and Other Ancient Magic (Dowser 4)
Maps, Artifacts, and Other Arcane Magic (Dowser 5)
I See You (Oracle 2)
Artifacts, Dragons, and Other Lethal Magic (Dowser 6)
I See Us (Oracle 3)
The Graveyard Kiss (Reconstructionist 0.5)
Catching Echoes (Reconstructionist 1)
Dawn Bytes (Reconstructionist 1.5)
Tangled Echoes (Reconstructionist 2)

Other books in both the Reconstructionist and Dowser series to follow.

More information can be found at:
www.madebymeghan.ca/novels

For Michael
without whom I'd still be entangled in darkness.

I never got involved in the dirt and the details of an investigation. I never let my preconceptions muddy a reconstruction. And I steadfastly refrained from ever allowing my past to dictate my future.

At least until the one person I couldn't lose went missing.

Because then I'd relive every dark moment of my childhood, confront every heartbreak, and even sell my soul if that was what it took to get her back.

Because I couldn't accept a future—not even a promised one of immortality and unbridled power—that didn't include one of the only two people I'd ever truly loved.

Chapter One

I was pacing. Again. Despite the early hour, my mind was already whirling with unarticulated thoughts and unanswered questions. The same as it had been for the past three months. That was why I was at the legal firm of Sherwood and Pine at eight in the morning on the eleventh of January. Seeking answers. For the seventh time.

Hence the pacing. And the ever-mounting frustration.

I strolled across the width of the brightly lit office for the umpteenth time, turning back at the front edge of the black leather sofa. Then, avoiding the matching set of chairs situated before the large oak desk inlaid with curly maple, I steadily wore the tightly woven beige carpet in the other direction.

I was aware that pacing made me appear weak, or worse, indecisive—though I was neither. Plus, the witch seated behind the desk wasn't paying any attention to me.

As it had been for every single one of our previous visits, Ember Pine's attention was riveted to the magical contract carefully laid out across her desk. I'd presented the magically imbued sheets of black-inked parchment to her three months before. Conveniently, her office was situated in a business tower a few blocks north of my apartment in downtown Seattle. Inconveniently, the only way she could read the document that had turned my entire life upside down was while I was in the room. The contract went blank if I was more than a few feet away.

Hence my perpetual pacing.

Ember's straight-edged nose was so close to the page she was holding gingerly at the edges that her bluntly bobbed dark-auburn hair brushed against it. Wary of disturbing the magic embedded within the contract, she'd worn cotton gloves during my first three visits.

She was murmuring quietly, peering through her gold-rimmed glasses from the tiny black lettering of the contract to her notes as she worked through what had to be her third pass on the document this morning.

Seven visits. Thousands of dollars in legal fees. My life in the balance. And evidently, the application for membership into the vampire Conclave—signed by my uncle and presented to me by Kettil the executioner in my bathroom at the beginning of October—was unbreakable.

Unbreakable.

As in, on pain of death.

Ember unfortunately hadn't been able to figure out yet whether that meant the demise of the signatories—aka Kett and my Uncle Jasper—or if it also included the only other names remaining on the contract—Declan and me.

I was seriously hoping for the former, blaming the vampire for this predicament almost as much as I blamed my power-obsessed uncle for offering up the entire Fairchild coven 'For Consideration.' Presumably that was to cement the deal, though he wanted the immortality for himself.

Speaking of being obsessive, I'd prepared for each of these meetings with Ember almost as carefully as I would have if I'd been about to come face-to-face with my maker.

Given the context of the contract, the dark humor of that sentiment wasn't lost on me. But nevertheless, I had smoothed my blond hair into the simple French twist I favored, double-checking that my nails were perfectly French manicured and that my navy-blue tweed sheath dress was pristinely pressed.

I hadn't seen the vampire since he'd given me the contract. And though I had no intention of reaching out to him myself, I kept expecting Kett to abruptly appear, demanding my acquiescence while I traversed the few blocks from my apartment to Ember's building.

And when he didn't, I ignored the nagging disappointment that lingered for the rest of the day.

I wasn't certain whether I wanted to confront the vampire and demand that he release me from the contract. Or if I wanted to offer him my lifeblood in exchange for an entirely new existence—and the chance to embrace who I was instead of who I thought I should be.

That quandary was my constant companion. And I had a terrible feeling that any notion of me having a choice in the matter was wishful thinking. So I forced my focus back on the present, where I was inherently more comfortable.

Even though this was my seventh time seeing her, it still appeared as if Ember had just moved into the corner office with its pretty peekaboo view of the water. Her degrees and artwork remained propped against the walls, ready to be hung except for the apparent lack of time and tools to do so. Instead of books and knickknacks, boxes cluttered the shelving matching the desk on either side of the sofa. The swanky space had apparently come with a recent promotion that Ember barely acknowledged, even when she'd been congratulated by a visiting senior partner during my second appointment. Given the state of the office, it was fairly obvious she hadn't fully embraced her new status within the firm.

The only personal item set out in the entire space was a framed charcoal sketch, which was placed facing outward on a credenza behind the desk. The arresting image had drawn my attention the first time I'd entered the office, and I still found it exceedingly difficult to tear my gaze away from it.

Rendered in smudged yet fierce and unfettered lines, the image contained behind glass was of Ember. Or, rather, a grisly depiction of her apparent death. Gouged throat, lifeless eyes, and all.

But even though the ghost of a smile on Ember's face—forever immortalized in charcoal—was haunting, I couldn't bring myself to ask her about the sketch. I had an instinctual sense that if I lowered the personal shields I diligently maintained, the sketch would be seething with magic. And it was rude to ask another Adept about her magic, or any magical items she possessed.

Though why Ember Pine would choose to display such a gruesome, foreboding image in a place of honor, especially when her prestigious law degrees were gathering dust in the corner, I had no idea. The gesture was completely at odds with the uptight, focused young woman I'd first met in the Academy over a decade ago and to whom Kett had directed me when he gave me the contract.

I was, however, completely certain it was absolutely none of my business.

Ember finally looked up from her notes, seemingly surprised to find me pacing rather than seated in one of the chairs before the desk.

"I've still been unsuccessful at finding another example of a contract with the Conclave," she said without any preamble. "Not in any of the vaults of any of the branches of Sherwood and Pine. Not even in the London office. And everyone knows that London is held by the oldest vampire in existence, along with his brood. His …"—she paused to scan her notes—"… his shiver."

"Not everyone," I said wryly.

Vampires were largely enigmas in Adept society. And though I might hopelessly wish that they had continued to remain a mystery for me—and for the only two people I held dear in this world—that was not to be. My name, placed without my permission on the contract now spread across Ember's desk, irrevocably associated me with the vampires—a part of the magical world universally feared and scorned by the rest of the magically Adept.

Ignoring me, Ember shuffled through her notes. "I've uncovered accountings of such contracts, though. Written histories. I apologize for it taking so long when you're on a relatively tight timeline, but I had to dig deep. Others have taken notes, though they had no more luck replicating the exact wording of the contract than I have."

One of the first things I discovered upon meeting with Ember three months ago was that the contract completely blanked out if anyone else touched it while I was more than a few feet away. The second unfortunate discovery was that no copies could be made, magical or otherwise.

"The senior partners are still incredibly excited about it," Ember said. "I've managed to contact every one of them, and from Washington State to New York to Amsterdam and London, they've all confirmed that it's unbreakable."

"But I didn't sign it!"

"Your coven leader must have a talent for true naming, then, or for tying spells to specific targets. Because usually the names have to be spoken out loud during the construction of a spell. Oh! Maybe he did evoke your names while he was inking them." Ember grabbed her pen and excitedly jotted down more notes to herself on a legal pad. "That's more of a sorcerer-held talent, of course. But the magic contained in the parchment, let alone the ink and the specific wording, is remarkable. So perhaps whoever drafted it aided your uncle with the binding."

I sat down, suddenly unable to keep pacing the office for another moment. Three months later, and I still couldn't believe that I was once again entangled in my uncle's machinations. He'd found a way to reach me, to rip away the freedom I'd sacrificed everything to obtain. He'd insinuated himself into my carefully constructed life simply by jotting my name on a piece of parchment.

The result of which was an offer of immortality. Of invulnerability. All I had to do was die, then give over my soul. Assuming such a thing existed. And if I said no? Or if I convinced Kettil, the executioner and elder of the Conclave, to pass me over? Then Declan—Jasmine's brother and the only other name not yet struck off the contract—would die and be remade in my place.

Or even worse, my uncle would finally surpass the limitations of his own mortality. Then the entire Fairchild coven would be vulnerable. He might even slaughter them all.

Not that the coven was my problem. Collectively, the members of my family had all made their own choices, siding with Jasper and maintaining their power base over the safety of their own offspring. Though in all fairness, perhaps they'd thought they could do both by sidelining Jasper, letting them keep their status within the Adept community unsullied.

Jasper's ability to ink a deal with the vampire Conclave proved just how shortsighted they'd all been. Again.

And Jasmine and Declan were still tied to the coven, as evidenced by both their names appearing on the contract. Though thankfully, Jasmine's name had been struck off by Kett last October. They were my concern. The only two people I truly loved.

After being remade into a vampire, Jasper's retribution for the past transgressions committed by the three of us would be cruel and prolonged.

"Wisteria?" Ember's tone indicated that this wasn't the first time she'd called my name.

I looked up. She held her pen poised over her notepad. "Is that a talent of your uncle's? True naming?"

"He has many talents," I murmured. I shook off my brooding mood, forcing myself to straighten my spine. For the seventh time, I tried to focus on asking all the questions that still remained unanswered. "Can I refuse?"

"I think that depends. Not outright. But as long as one of the two others remaining on the contract accepts, then yes. I believe so. But this is also binding to the vampire, Kettil the executioner ... which is a seriously fantastic name, by the way. You know that a kettil is a sacrificial dish, right? Used in druid rituals to catch the blood of their victims."

I moaned. It was a completely inappropriate display of emotion, but I just couldn't help it.

Ember bit her lip.

I breathed deeply, getting the dread that had tightened my chest under control. "You were saying? It's binding for Kett as well?"

"Yes." Ember shuffled back to the second page of the contract. "He's blood bound. He must remake a Fairchild witch. The division-of-power wording is specific and enforceable. As is the timeline." She glanced at her notes. "He has a little less than eight months to fulfill the terms. Did you get the sense that this was his ... Kett's choice?"

I shrugged even as I recalled Kett's odd demeanor—anticipatory, yet unsettled—when he'd delivered the contract to me. I pushed the thought aside. I had never needed to focus on the present more than I needed to that day. "So one of us will be killed within the next eight months?"

"Remade. But yes."

"It can't be my uncle. It just can't be."

"And this Declan Benoit—"

"No."

I said it sharply, but I didn't elaborate.

Ember nodded, returning her attention to her desk. "Do you mind staying a bit longer? Carmine Sherwood has a question about the specific language used in the transfer-of-power clause on the third page, but I wasn't able to get a precise copy of it last time. I thought if I skipped every second word, the magic might let me write out that much."

I nodded, barely listening to her. I'd spent two hours sitting around the offices of Sherwood and Pine two weeks ago while her three senior partners dropped by to read and touch the magically imbued parchment. They had tried having another person transcribe while one of them read it out loud, and were positively thrilled when the exact wording wouldn't stick to either a screen or a notepad. I was completely weary of hearing how beautifully constructed it was, what talent it would take to craft—and that it was utterly and completely binding.

Kettil, the executioner of the Conclave, was bound to remake a Fairchild witch. I was certain that Jasper assumed the witch would be him. But Ember and her associates had collectively decided that the addition of the appendix of names on the contract—the *For Consideration* section on the final page, which listed each and every Fairchild—was a clear indication that the Conclave wasn't so sure about admitting Jasper into their ranks.

Ember hadn't yet uncovered any indication of any similar stipulations among the notes she had found in her law firm's archives. Of course, without copies of actual Conclave contracts, the lawyers were being forced to make suppositions. And guessing made them and me equally uneasy.

My uncle might consider himself the most powerful witch in the Fairchild coven, but apparently the Conclave—or even just Kett—had other ideas. Or perhaps there were other attributes that vampires deemed worthy of consideration, such as personality, compatibility, and magical adaptability. Whatever the case, Kett must have spent years to assess, then eliminate, every name on the list except three.

Jasper.

Declan.

And me.

One of us was bound to call Kett our master. To be reborn through his blood, at least as I was able to understand it. To be an immortal creature of darkness. Forever changed.

My stomach twisted at the thought of Declan being ... warped that way. Misshapen. Altered irrevocably. Of the warmth of his skin being siphoned away until muscle and sinew turned to cold stone. Of his golden-hazel eyes flooded with the whirling blood I'd seen in the reconstructions I'd collected of the fledgling vampires last October. Of Declan being unable to be near anyone without wanting to tear their throat out, then consume every last drop of—

"Wisteria!"

Blinking my eyes rapidly, I became aware of my surroundings. I was still sitting in Ember's office, not facing my childhood-love-turned-vampire-fiend. A thin spiral of smoke was filtering up from Ember's laptop.

"Are you okay?" she asked.

As I nodded, I noticed that the glass had cracked across the charcoal sketch behind Ember. Obviously I'd become distressed, then lashed out with wild magic like some silly little fledgling witch. Many Adepts wielded magic that interacted badly with technology, but with my emotions running rampant lately, I was being unusually destructive. "I apologize."

"No worries. I'll bill you for it."

I laughed at her bluntness. Under completely different circumstances, the witch and I might have become unlikely friends. If either of us were the friend-making type.

"Oh, I had a photocopier brought in," she said. "Do you know what that is?"

"A machine or a person?"

Ember looked confused for a moment. Then she curled her lip at me and shook her head.

I was a reconstructionist. A magical photocopier, of sorts, though I copied residual energy left behind by Adepts, not pictures. Or, in this case, contracts.

"The machine," she said. "I've tried scanning and taking pictures of the pages, to no avail. But who knows? Maybe an old photocopier will work. Will you walk out with me?"

I nodded, gathering my purse, my cashmere scarf, and my navy-blue trench coat from the arm of the chair. Even though it wasn't a monogrammed model, the Louis Vuitton bag had been a misguided gift from an appreciative client many years before. I wasn't a fan of obvious labels, so it usually resided deep within my closet. My Dior briefcase was more circumspect—at least once I'd removed the decorative elements. But it had been returned to me by a Convocation cleanup crew last October, torn asunder by zombies and completely unusable. So I was stuck with the Louis Vuitton, which didn't hold half the items I usually needed to carry. I was thus lugging around two bags for work most days.

Fortunately, I was currently between contracts. Unconsciously flinging around wild magic potent enough to fry Ember's laptop from a distance made me a liability.

I strove to be professional and precise. But being offered immortality had completely eroded my sense of equilibrium.

Actually, it was the idea of my Uncle Jasper reincarnated as a vampire that terrified me. And being in a continual state of terror didn't sit well with me. Eventually, I'd do something about it—something I'd presumably spend the next twelve years of my life regretting in some form or another. Just as I had to some extent for the previous twelve.

I knew myself. I knew what I was capable of. And I had a sinking feeling that Kettil the executioner had gazed deeply into my soul, and the darkness he'd spied there was what made him decide to keep my name among those *For Consideration.*

In an effort to not become perpetually unhinged over my pending decision—or, to be completely extreme, my possible murder at my uncle-turned-vampire's hands—I added a set of cashmere-lined navy-blue leather gloves that rarely got worn to my outfit and braved the unusually cold weather along the waterfront. It wasn't quite the middle of January, but Seattle had already seen more snow than all the other years I'd lived in the city combined.

Passing my apartment building, I continued on to Pike Place Market, where I needed to pick up the free-range turkey I'd preordered for a belated Christmas dinner. Jasmine—who had spent actual Christmas eating tacos with Declan, then had been working an ongoing case over the New Year—was flying in to Seattle tomorrow. She would cook the meal while I hovered just outside the kitchen, so that I didn't accidentally ruin anything by short-circuiting a major appliance with my unpredictable magic.

I hadn't told Jasmine about the contract yet. I hadn't even hinted at it, even going so far as to encourage her to spend the holidays in Mexico with her brother when typically she would have come to me. I'd wanted to gather more information before I broached the subject. But, with everything as clear as I thought it was ever going to be—pending a conversation with the vampire Conclave, aka Kett—I was starting to feel guilty. I needed to have a conversation with Jasmine, and she in turn was going to have to talk to Declan. Unless he'd already been approached by Kett himself.

It seemed logical that after whittling his list down to the final three, the executioner would want to spend time with each of his prospective progeny. Hence involving Jasmine and me in his investigation of the fledgling vampires last October. So for all I knew, Kett could be having tea with Declan right at that moment. Though Jasmine's brother wasn't the crumpets-and-china type, and the vampire wasn't much of a conversationalist.

I didn't even want to ruminate on what possible activities a face-to-face meeting between the vampire and my uncle might involve. And really, such rumination was pointlessly disturbing. I'd have solid answers soon enough.

I allowed myself to meander through the long stretch of converted waterfront warehouses that made up the market, eyeing the items artfully displayed in the already-open booths. Pike Place was quiet this early on a Wednesday morning, and some of the vendors were still unpacking their wares. Hand-turned wooden bowls, letter-pressed cards, and iridescent glass vases gave way to gourmet beef jerky, jams and jellies, and bath salts. Then I was surrounded by flowers of all shapes, colors, and sizes. Perfectly put-together bouquets, ready to be displayed in homes all across Seattle.

There were more people in that part of the market, closer to the grocery and food vendors. The butcher's shop from which I'd ordered the turkey was about a half-dozen stalls away.

I paused, browsing through vivid displays of bundled mums, sunflowers, and gerbera daisies, and contemplated a dozen yellow roses for Jasmine's room, along with a secondary bouquet for the dining room table. If I could find one so late in the season, I could even pick up a small pumpkin and carve it out for a decorative vase. I still needed to purchase the fresh veggies Jasmine would need for the meal. A large butternut squash might do, though Jasmine would laugh at my feeble attempts at homemaking.

I caught the eye of the woman artfully cobbling together more of the bouquets that kept the deep buckets of water filling the four tiers of the flower booth well stocked. As far as I could see, no two of her arrangements were exactly the same.

"Something special?" she asked.

"Yes, please." I selected a dozen of the yellow roses, handing them to her over the rows of flowers between us. "These. And could you put together a large bouquet with sunflowers and anything red you have on hand? Roses, gerberas, mums? No baby's breath."

"Greens? Around the edge, like this?" She gestured toward a large orange-and-white bouquet near her.

"Yes, please."

She nodded, turning back into the booth to wrap the yellow roses in newspaper before dealing with my request.

My phone buzzed. I fished it out of my abnormally small bag, which I'd tucked underneath my arm, the Conclave contract stowed within its meager depths.

Glancing at the screen, I saw the name Betty-Lou and a picture of a hedgehog eating cheese.

Jasmine. She enjoyed remotely changing the picture attached to her number on my phone whenever she liked. Passwords meant nothing to a tech witch of her talent. But thankfully for me, those same skills meant I could use my phone without my volatile magic frying it. Also, she was a big fan of cheese.

Laughing under my breath, I tapped the screen to answer the call while covering my other ear against the general din of the market.

"Hey, babe," I said. "I was just buying you—"

A male voice interrupted me. "Jasmine's missing."

Even without my immediately comprehending the words, the harsh tone of the voice felt as though it sliced through all the vulnerable parts of my body—heart, throat, stomach. A rush of stark fear flooded through my system, weakening my limbs. I nearly dropped the phone.

Then I digested what he'd said.

"What?" I whispered, unable to step away from the flower booth, unable to do anything but painfully press the phone to my ear. "Missing?"

A void of utter dread opened around me, swallowing me—heart and soul—though my body remained mired in the mundane world.

"You heard me, Wisteria." He snarled my name viciously. "Get your ass on the jet and get here."

"Jet? Here?" Still unable to absorb what was being said—or who I was speaking to—I was simply parroting his words, Creole inflection and all. "Where? Get where?"

"You know where." He paused, then growled. "They won't talk to me."

"Declan ..."

The connection between us went so quiet that the sounds of the market filtered back into my consciousness. I glanced down at the screen. We were still connected.

I pressed the phone back to my ear. Questions, concerns, and more fear leaped to the forefront of my mind as it caught up with the present. Though I barely recognized his voice or his stiff inflection, this wasn't the first time I'd heard him utter that phrase. 'Jasmine is missing ...'

The first time had nearly gotten all three of us killed. The first time had changed our lives irrevocably.

The first time was the beginning of the last time I'd seen or spoken to him.

"Declan?" I whispered a second time, needing the confirmation.

"It's me," he said gruffly.

I nodded like an idiot, then forced myself to speak. "I'll text with an ETA."

"Do that." Then he abruptly ended the call.

I'd never heard him so angry.

No, correction.

I'd never heard him so angry at me.

His voice had been dark and terrible. Nasty. Nothing like I remembered him. But then, I hadn't heard him speak in over twelve years.

Jasmine was missing.

I tapped the screen of my phone, dialing a number I'd had no cause to use since I was sixteen.

An automated messaging system answered, reciting instructions. "Pickup location. Destination. Passengers. Time of departure. Method of contact."

"Seattle," I said. My voice caught in my throat so thickly that I had to force the next words out. "Connecticut. Wisteria Fairchild. Solo. Immediate departure. Text this number."

I ended the call, then stood in a state of utter numbness. Not seeing the market's other customers as they crossed in and around me, brushing against my shoulders.

I should have been moving, reacting. Fixing the situation. But I was trapped within a single breath, within a moment of complete uncertainty.

I was lost within the possibility of everything that might have befallen Jasmine. All the terrible things that could have happened without me having so much as an inkling that she was in trouble. While I'd been shopping for flowers and childishly fretting over a decision that would be made when it was time to make it, and no sooner.

Jasmine was in trouble. There were no other circumstances in which Declan would pick up the phone and call me.

Jasmine's phone.

He'd called me with Jasmine's phone.

She would never be parted from her phone, not while still conscious.

A deeper wave of terror flooded my system, waking me up from the stupor of my fear.

Fight or flight. Fight or flight. Fight or flight.

The flower-booth vendor was talking to me, holding my bouquets out. Not hearing her words, I reached blindly into my purse, pressing three twenty-dollar bills into her hand as I took the flowers.

"Hang on," she said, turning to her cash box to make change.

But I was already turning away, crushing the flowers to my chest and forgetting the turkey and all the other treats I'd been gathering.

I left the market, dashing across the cobblestone street instead of walking to the far corner and waiting for the light. I had to get back to my apartment. I had to keep moving.

I had just given my phone number to the Fairchild call center. I'd revealed the city in which I lived. Though honestly, I was sure my family had long known I was in Seattle.

I was going back.

I had sworn to myself that I'd never go back, not under any circumstances.

Fight or flight.

There was never any choice, really. Even after the adrenaline stopped racing through my system. Jasmine was the one thing … the one person I could never walk away from.

Even if it meant going home.

Even if it meant hearing the loathing in Declan's voice. Even if it meant seeing him look at me with the anger that was the foundation of that hatred.

Jasmine was missing.

I was going back.

Chapter Two

I arrived at my apartment completely unaware of the steps that had taken me there, or where I'd dumped the flowers en route. The city streets, the pedestrians—even my building's doorman, who must have let me in because I couldn't remember using my fob—were all a blur.

I'd been unconsciously propelled by an ingrained instinct to keep moving. Keep pushing forward. Until I found myself standing just inside my front door, staring down at the two packages sitting on my entrance table. A padded envelope and a large box wrapped in white paper.

The concierge never knew whether or not I was in town, so after someone calling up to see if I was home, any packages not needing signatures that arrived for me were unobtrusively placed just inside my apartment. Conveniently, the recently installed wards coating the apartment's walls and front door didn't repel or block nonmagicals from entering.

A small bowl—a pretty piece of indigo-dyed pottery—sat on the other side of the glassed-topped, metal-legged entrance table. A matching metal-framed mirror hung on the wall above.

I caught sight of my reflection. I looked … empty.

The bowl was for my keys, but I never used it. Jasmine did. Whenever she was in town, she would toss her own keys in the bowl. Usually she'd be laden with groceries and laughing about something as she came through the door—

Debilitating pain shot through my chest, but I fought to breathe against it. I forced my gaze away from the mirror. I forced myself to close and lock the door behind me, to remove my coat and scarf and carefully hang both up in the hall closet. I forced myself to deal with the packages, pushing aside the envelope as I tore open the wrapped box.

Allowing the white packing paper to fall carelessly to the floor, I opened the equally white cardboard box within, then unearthed a large, black, crocodile-skin briefcase from the reams of white tissue paper.

A notecard tucked within the paper shook loose, coming to a rest facedown on the blond-oak hardwood by my feet.

I stared dumbly at the briefcase. It was my bag. Or, rather, it was an exact replica of the bag that had been torn apart by zombies three months ago—zombies called forth and controlled by a necromancer trying to save her son's life. The signature chain and logo had been carefully removed, exactly as I'd done when I'd purchased the briefcase from the 2010 Dior spring collection.

I retrieved the notecard from the floor. It read:

> *I apologize that it took me so long*
> *to find a replacement.*
> *—K*

K for Kettil.

His handwriting was neat and precise, though heavy-handed enough to dent the thick linen card.

The briefcase was the third gift I'd received from the vampire since the incident in the graveyard. Since he'd presented me with the contract. As with the other two, my address had been carefully handwritten on the wrapping, with no sign of a return address or postage. Presumably, the vampire had the packages delivered by local courier, magical or otherwise. Kett had replaced my midlength, dark-navy Burberry heritage trench coat first. Then he'd replaced my teal pashmina stole—both of which had been shredded by zombie birds, then bloodied and grass-stained in a tussle with a fledgling vampire. And now he'd replaced my bag.

I'd had no other contact with him. I believed he was just trying to be considerate, rather than actively wooing me into an eternity by his side. But I still wasn't certain how I felt about accepting the gifts.

Except I desperately wanted the bag. I desperately needed the normalcy it represented.

Scooping the second package off the table along with the bag and my purse, I moved into the kitchen to deposit all three on the island. Dumping the contents of my purse on the white-streaked gray quartz counter, I set about packing the Dior briefcase. Then I crossed over to my pantry, retrieving my four pillar candles and the six three-inch oyster-shell reconstruction cubes I happened to have already made.

I owed Kett a thank-you note, though I had no idea where to mail it. Perhaps care of Jade Godfrey at her bakery in Vancouver.

Because I wasn't looking, I grabbed the second package that had been waiting for me at the door instead of the sunglasses case I'd been reaching for. I almost tossed the thick bubble-wrap envelope back on the island counter. But then I felt something inside it.

Something small. Sharp cornered, even through the padding. A cube.

I glanced at the label adhered to what appeared to be a prepaid FedEx envelope, not recognizing the handwriting. The package was small enough that it could have gone through the mail. And it wasn't addressed to me.

It was addressed to *The Conclave*. With my address.

My stomach soured. I ran my hand across the package, now feeling a full collection of tiny cubed shapes in the bottom right corner.

Without thinking through the ramifications of opening a package addressed to the vampire Conclave, I tore at the plastic flap. Ripping it open just enough, I dumped the contents on the counter.

I'd already known what it was. I'd already felt the magic through the paper and plastic. But my mind refused to believe, refused to accept what I was feeling. Not until I was confronted by the sight of Jasmine's gold necklace and its collection of twelve tiny oyster-shell cube charms.

My oyster-shell cubes. Shimmering with my magic. The tiny reconstructions that I'd collected for Jasmine's birthdays, one for each of the years since we'd made a bid for our freedom and lost our family in the process. Since I'd lost Declan. All the time that Jasmine had quietly and desperately tried to keep the three of us together, to keep us from completely unraveling.

I moaned, pressing my hand over my mouth as if I could contain the sobs of fear threatening to overwhelm me.

Jasmine never took the necklace off.

So what the hell was it doing in a package addressed to the Conclave and shipped to me?

I was shaking as I forced my hands and arms to obey me, digging into my new bag for my phone and texting Declan.

Where did you get Jasmine's phone?

I took a picture of the necklace and the envelope. Then I took another closer shot of the return address. A post office box in Connecticut.

Litchfield, Connecticut. The seat of the Fairchild coven.

I texted both pictures to Declan. To Jasmine's phone, which he had used to call me. Her phone, like her necklace, was something Jasmine would never be without.

My phone pinged with a text message.

>*Don't text me here. The phone might be cloned.*

I had no idea what that meant. But before I could ask for clarification, another text message appeared on my screen, this one from a number I didn't recognize.

>*It was mailed to me. Same return address. That's what brought me to Connecticut.*

Addressed to the Conclave?

>*Yes. Do you know why?*

Two things came to mind. The first was my direct connection to Kett by way of the Conclave contract. The second was the investigation Jasmine and I had conducted into the fledgling vampires. But how either of those things could have led to Jasmine being missing, I had no idea.

Except Jasmine wasn't simply missing. She'd been kidnapped, and the return of the cellphone and necklace were the kidnappers' first attempts at contact. Two obvious attempts to draw the Conclave to Connecticut, if not specifically targeting Declan and me.

There was a more obvious connection, though—one that pointed directly to my Uncle Jasper.

Obviously, Jasper knew that Declan and I were connected to the vampire Conclave, because he'd forged that connection himself when he put our names on his contract.

And the last time Jasmine had gone 'missing,' she'd been taken by our uncle.

It was an irrational and entirely circumstantial conclusion. But anger flooded through my system nonetheless, washing away the fear that had been threatening to immobilize me since I'd first heard Declan's voice. I applied my fingers to my phone.

I'm on my way.

I clipped Jasmine's chain around my neck, carefully tucking it underneath the front of my dress. Then I shoved everything else into my bag. Practically running, I crossed through the living room to my bedroom, then threw together a carry-on suitcase packed with the warmest items I owned.

Those included a matching set of royal-blue cashmere knitwear—a lace scarf, hat, and wrist warmers that had been a series of gifts from Pearl Godfrey, the head of the witches Convocation and Jade's grandmother. I rarely wore those treasured hand-knit items in order to keep them in pristine condition. But I had a feeling I would need all the comfort I could collect to face the next couple of days.

A text message pinged through on my phone.

> *Collingwood airfield. ETA 10:30 AM PST.*

Declan must have had the plane en route to me already, or it had already been somewhere on the West Coast. I consulted my map app. Collingwood was apparently a private airport just outside the city. Trust the Fairchilds to never mix with mundanes if they could help it.

I texted the concierge, requesting a taxi. Then I added toiletries to my suitcase before grabbing a three-quarter-length black wool coat that I only rarely wore, leaving my trench coat in the closet. I locked the door behind me and ran for the elevator.

In the cab on the way to the airfield, I finally calmed down enough to think through the possible implications of receiving—and opening—a package addressed to the Conclave.

Kett was the executioner and an elder of the Conclave. Whoever had mailed the package must have known that I had some connection with the governing body of the vampires—as did Declan. But they must not have known that we were in contact with Kett specifically. Otherwise, the parcel most likely would have been addressed to the vampire directly.

So was Jasmine's kidnapping more about her connection to the Conclave, rather than my connection to Kett? I normally would have assumed that the ongoing case she'd been working on over the holidays was an investigation for the witches Convocation, but Jasmine was open to freelancing. And last October we'd both worked for Kett—or, more specifically, for the vampire Conclave itself.

So if Jasmine had been working for the vampires—maybe even all these past months since we'd worked with Kett—I had no idea how many Adepts she might have come into contact with. Or how many might consider kidnapping her in order to get the Conclave's attention. Or simply as a response to the Conclave's investigation. Because it would be so much easier to hunt and capture a witch than to face the executioner himself.

Jasper being involved was an easy conclusion to jump to. And it was one that needed to be at the forefront of any investigation I attempted to mount. But I reminded myself that I had no evidence of his involvement other than my belief that at some nebulous point in the future, it would come down to me against him—again—in a confrontation that would most likely cost me my life. And I wasn't keen on sacrificing myself without cause.

My name on the Conclave contract, and Kett's unconfirmed preference for me, might force that confrontation sooner rather than later. But for now, I needed to approach the situation as rationally as I could.

The obvious thing to do would have been to contact Kett for clarification. Except I didn't have his phone number. I contemplated texting Pearl Godfrey for the vampire's contact information, which she could get from Jade. But I wasn't certain who I wanted to involve before I had more information. For all I knew, Declan was overreacting. Perhaps some idiot had stolen Jasmine's phone and necklace, then had decided to play a terrible prank on us.

But I knew that Jasmine had Kett's cellphone number. She'd been texting with him back and forth during the case we'd investigated with the executioner.

On a hunch, I opened the contacts on my phone, scrolling through the list of work-related acquaintances I'd been accumulating since I was eighteen. When I came to the Ks, I found a Photoshopped picture of Chuck Norris and a tub of peanut butter.

I snorted. Only Jasmine could have accessed my contacts and inserted the photo—referencing a conversation about the vampire's confusion over the phrase 'gargling peanut butter'—along with Kett's cellular number.

Even possibly kidnapped and in danger, my best friend could still make me laugh.

I texted Kett the picture I'd taken of the envelope, along with the closer shot of the return address.

I waited for a few moments, phone in hand, just in case the vampire replied quickly. Then, as the cab pulled into the parking area of the private airfield, I double-checked that the volume was up as high as it could go and tucked the phone away in my bag. I didn't need to risk compromising the electronics with my currently volatile magic.

Whether or not vampires were involved in Jasmine's disappearance—Kett or anyone else—didn't matter. Declan had called.

Even after twelve years, even after leaving him alone and severely wounded in a hospital bed without a word of farewell, he would have known that all he had to do was call. He knew that I'd do anything within my power to help him or Jasmine.

And though my family's reaction to my return with Declan at my side might be fierce and bloody, he was no longer a practically orphaned sixteen-year-old boy at their mercy.

I had to trust that together, we would find Jasmine.

And God help whoever had her, or whoever had hurt her.

Twelve years ago, we three had broken the most powerful witch in the western hemisphere. Literally. We broke Jasper's back because he had threatened more than simply our safety or our lives. He'd tried to take Jasmine away from us.

And there was no rule or moral code we wouldn't break for each other.

Because we three were more than family.

We three were bound by blood, forged by terror, and united by magic.

I knew that sitting while not being able to do anything useful through a five-and-a-half-hour flight was going to be excruciating. Thankfully, the jet was waiting for me at the airfield, departing just moments after I was on board.

Equally thankfully, I didn't recognize a single member of the crew, and I was relieved to not be bombarded with questions about my extended absence from the coven. After settling on a chicken salad and the timing of my dinner, the stewards were politely solicitous, leaving me alone in the eight-seat passenger cabin.

Since I'd last used the Fairchild jet, it had been upgraded from a Learjet to a Challenger 350, custom decorated in beige leather, glossy woodgrain paneling, and metal trim throughout. Of course, the high-end technology—touch screens, HD monitors, and so forth—that was now literally at my fingertips meant little to me, though I plugged my phone in to maintain its charge.

I had randomly selected a seat near the middle of the cabin, knowing that even on a flight across the country, my magic wasn't powerful enough to affect the engines. The wide seat was fully reclinable and came with a footrest, but I remained upright, staring fixedly out the window as if watching the world roll by could somehow force the plane to go faster.

My phone pinged with a text message after we'd been in the air for about thirty minutes. I'd been about to resort to requesting a magazine to keep myself distracted.

I expected the text was from Declan, who I'd sent my estimated time of arrival once I'd confirmed it with the steward. I was due to land in Connecticut shortly after 7:00 P.M. EST.

But it was Kett, requesting more information about the picture I'd sent him while in the cab.

>*When did you receive this?*

I immediately texted back.

About an hour ago.

>*I'm six hours away.*

I'm not home. I'm on the jet, heading to Connecticut.

>*Litchfield?*

Yes. Was Jasmine working on a case for you? Tracking Nigel's maker?

It was nothing more than a guess that Jasmine's apparent kidnapping might be related to the events that had accumulated in the deal I'd clumsily brokered between Teresa Garrick and Kett last October, with Nigel's immortal existence and Ben's life in the balance. Nigel's one and only stipulation had been for Kett to avenge his death—the first one, when he'd been remade against his will. Then Nigel had given up his immortality to spare Teresa's son, Ben. If Jasmine was working for the Conclave, she might well have been helping to track down Nigel's maker.

>*You opened the envelope. Do you have it and its contents with you?*

I stared down at the series of text messages on the screen of my phone. The vampire never answered questions straight up. I hadn't yet figured out whether he was just constantly playing games, or if he simply deemed some responses beneath him. However, I had no patience for either option with Jasmine potentially in jeopardy. So I ignored him in turn and went on the offensive.

When was the last time you saw or heard from Jasmine?

He took long enough to answer that I thought he might have dropped the conversation. I was tempted to text back something along the lines of *two can play the 'ask another question instead of answering' game*, but I was pretty sure I'd made my point. Something about interacting with the vampire made me snitty and childish. Which was disturbing, since he was interested in possibly making me his child. Or remaking me.

>*New York. Twenty-three days ago.*

New York? Jasmine hadn't mentioned being in New York to me. Her text messages had been sporadic the last few weeks, but I'd assumed that had been because of the holidays.

>*What was in the package, Wisteria?*
Jasmine's necklace.
>*The one that held the reconstructions?*

Yes. No message.

>*The message was clearly articulated.*

My stomach squelched with fear. I didn't need Kett confirming my concerns. Not until I'd gathered some sort of actionable information.

>*Why are you heading home?*

The return address.

That was a lie of omission. I'd been heading home before I'd received the package, but I didn't want to mention Declan yet. I didn't want to open up any discussion with the vampire that included Jasmine's brother.

>*I will find you.*

Now why did that sound like a threat?

I had the immediate urge to text back and tell Kett to not track me down, but the Conclave's name on the envelope completely voided that option.

>*Text me if your investigation leads you elsewhere.*

>*Please.*

I wondered briefly how difficult it had been for Kett to type out that last word. Then I chided myself for being uncharitable as I texted back.

I will.

Kett dropped the conversation after that, and I returned to staring out the window at the miles and miles of cloud shielding the earth from my view.

I brushed my fingers across one of the two tiny reconstructions attached to the platinum bracelet I wore perpetually on my right wrist. Magic hummed underneath my fingertips. My magic, in the reconstructions—along with what I assumed was some sort of combination of Kett's power, Jade's alchemy, and my magic embedded in the bracelet's tiny house, fence, and tree charms.

I hadn't removed the bracelet since Jade had altered it in the kitchen of her bakery, arming me against vampires—or fledgling vampires at a minimum, along with Kett specifically—for my peace of mind. But I wasn't interested in contemplating the magical artifact at the moment. Instead, I reached for the magic contained in one of the tiny reconstructions, effortlessly pulling a glimpse of a nine-year-old Jasmine from it.

Believing that I would never return—that I would never see Jasmine or Declan again—I had collected two reconstructions before leaving Litchfield for the last time. One was of Declan by the lake. And the other was of Jasmine in the orchard, the day the three of us became a family. The day we'd learned that no one would ever protect us, unless we protected each other.

I spun the reconstruction magic underneath my fingers, watching Jasmine throw her head back and laugh at something either Declan or I had said. Her blond curls danced around her head, her vibrant blue eyes flashing with humor.

Then I let the reconstruction wink out. Staring at it too long wasn't emotionally healthy, and all I really needed was a glimpse to buoy me. Reconstructionists could easily get obsessed with watching their recreations—as addicted to that magic as a witch could get to black magic or blood magic.

I'd spent every moment of the past twelve years of my life striving to live in the light. To be useful. To contribute to the greater good. Content to be a cog in the operations of the Convocation.

And now I was flying into the darkness I'd barely escaped the first time. Literally and metaphorically. It would be after sunset when we landed, and Declan's obscure statement of 'They won't talk to me' could mean only one thing.

Even if Jasper wasn't involved in Jasmine's kidnapping, I was going to have to confront at least some of the members of my family.

But first, I'd have to face my childhood sweetheart, who had every reason to hate me.

He was waiting for me as promised, standing near a beat-up black Jeep with Connecticut license plates. He'd parked a few feet away from the hangar at the Fairchild's private airfield in the middle of Litchfield, Connecticut. I stumbled upon seeing him while exiting the jet, grabbing for the railing at the top of the metal stairs as subtly as I could without betraying my reaction—or tumbling all the way down.

From that breath onward, I saw nothing in those moments of my arrival that wasn't him. I didn't know if it was snowing or if the moon had risen. I didn't hear the polite goodbye the steward offered. I didn't feel the cold, though I probably should have put on my cashmere hat instead of leaving it in my suitcase. I had changed into a royal-blue merino sweater and navy-blue herringbone slacks on the jet.

Declan.

Age twenty-eight.

His dark-brown hair was cropped short, but it was still wild. Untamed. His bronzed skin was darker than it usually would have been this time of year—twelve years ago, at least. Perhaps he'd been in Mexico for longer than just Christmas with Jasmine. Brushed-metal sunglasses hid his eyes, even though it was after seven in the evening. He was wearing a long, custom-made black leather jacket that had taken a beating, probably on many occasions. The jacket came down to the top of his heavy work boots, but I could see the dark jeans he wore through slits in the side seams. Even from a distance, I could sense that the jacket was layered with a multitude of spells, but only because I couldn't resist taking a peek at his magic through my personal shields.

He looked nothing like the boy he'd been. Yet my heart knew him in an instant.

I took a step down, then another, carefully descending the stairs. As I drew ever closer to Declan, I visualized my magic building up all around me, enforcing the personal shields I usually held in place effortlessly. Nothing about this day, or this meeting, or about finding Jasmine was going to be effortless. So just as I created reconstruction cubes, pulling them layer by layer out of crushed oyster shells, I gathered my magic tightly around me.

Declan and I were no longer friends. Technically, we weren't even blood related. And, leaning against the front grille of the Jeep with his arms crossed and a deep glower etched across his face, the discontent he radiated made that even clearer.

This wasn't a reunion of long-lost lovers.

Another member of the flight crew had already brought my suitcase to the bottom of the steps, standing beside it politely while I finished descending.

"Thank you," I murmured, taking the handle he'd extended for me.

Then I crossed the tarmac, intending to greet Declan politely, then climb into the Jeep. I'd be poised and professional, as always.

Except as I drew near and Declan unfolded his arms, straightening to his full height, I didn't pause and offer him a cool smile.

Drawn almost against my will, I closed the space between us. Abandoning my suitcase, I reached forward and up, touching the arms of his sunglasses, then lifting them up and away from his golden-hazel eyes.

I just wanted to look at him for a moment. I just wanted to see him as he was, not as he had been. I knew every curve of his sixteen-year-old face. That boy was forever captured in the reconstruction I wore on my wrist, hidden among the charms of my platinum white-picket fence.

But the Declan before me was a man. Taller—well over six feet—and broader through the shoulders. His face was constructed out of sharp edges. A long-healed scar twisted from his right ear down the side of his neck.

"Wisteria," he said, growling his irritation. But not touching me or batting my hands away.

"I've missed you," I said, knowing it was absolutely the wrong thing to say.

Declan frowned, then turned his head, pulling his sunglasses away from my loose grip.

I stepped back, but only because I was worried he'd push me away. I was certain that I would completely shatter if he ever touched me in anger.

"You hold your magic oddly." His accent was thicker, as if he'd spent time in his native Louisiana since I'd seen him. His tone was blunt, just on the edge of nasty. "Confined. To your eyes and the palms of your hands."

I turned away without answering, reaching for my suitcase. He grabbed it before I could, then opened the passenger-side door for me as he carried it around the Jeep. I climbed in as he stowed it.

By the time he slid into the driver's seat, I had my shields fully in place—magically and emotionally.

"Where are we going?" I asked, trying again for my well-rehearsed professional tone.

"Christ, Wisteria. You show up—"

I interrupted him before he could get heated, deliberately enunciating the question a second time. "Where are we going?"

Declan swore under his breath. Something in French, or his Creole version of it.

I didn't understand the words, but I got the tone. I folded my hands in my lap as if supremely patient. Then I looked out the window.

It wasn't snowing. The ground was bare, in fact, which was at complete odds with my childhood memories. Or at least the ones I hadn't locked away and hoped to forget.

Declan started the Jeep. "Grey's," he said. "Fairchild House."

Grey Fairchild, Declan and Jasmine's father, was a distant cousin of mine in addition to being my uncle. When he'd married Dahlia, the least powerful of the Fairchild siblings, he'd brought money and business sense to the union, rather than powerful or unique magic. Though he hadn't needed to adopt the family surname, as my father had.

"I tracked Jasmine there based off the last text messages on her phone, but I can't get through the wards without blowing the entire place up. And yes, I did ring the bell."

"Dahlia was in residence?"

Declan snorted. "What do you think?"

Dahlia, Jasmine's mother, had adamantly refused to set eyes on Declan after Jasper revealed his existence, having gone to New Orleans and returned with the nine-year-old boy. Apparently, even nineteen years after discovering she had a stepson only two months older than her own daughter, she still blamed Declan for Grey's indiscretion.

It had never been made clear to me if Grey had known of Declan's existence, choosing to ignore his son even after his magic had proven a disappointment to his mother. Jules Benoit had been seeking a daughter—a female descendent who carried the ancestral power of the dark arts and necromancy, not a son who wielded witch magic. Declan had been left to the care of his elderly maternal grandfather as a result, who then died. Leaving Declan abandoned without home or money, and with no way to contact his mother or any other family members.

"Who knows you called me?" I asked.

"No one."

"Who knows you have Jasmine's phone?"

"Whoever answered the front-gate intercom at Grey's but didn't bother to let me in, and whoever they've told."

"So they know Jasmine is missing."

"They know I think she's missing. But you know how much value the Fairchilds place on my opinions."

"Did you keep the envelope the phone was sent in?"

"The box. Yes." Declan's tone was still tense. "From FedEx, like yours. No residual magic, and a tracing spell didn't lead anywhere."

I glanced over to him. Tracing spells were delicate magic, requiring precise and finely tuned casting. Declan's magic was not attuned in any of those ways. At least it hadn't been twelve years ago.

He twisted his hands on the steering wheel under my gaze, spitting out extra information. "A friend cast it before I left New Orleans."

The word 'friend,' begrudgingly uttered as if it were necessary to shield the other caster's identity from me, knifed through my belly. I knew Declan wasn't a monk. In fact, based on the bits of information I picked up among Jasmine's general but constant chatter, I was fairly certain he tore through sexual partners, leaving a wake of broken hearts across the years that separated us.

Still, his guarded tone spoke volumes about a witch 'friend' who'd tried to help him track Jasmine before he'd even thought to call me. That indicated a relationship of some depth. But Declan was free to love whomever he wished.

Just because I was incapable of doing so had no bearing on the situation.

I fiercely held on to my cool facade, turning my gaze back to the road before us. "We should compare the packaging."

"Already done," Declan said. "Both were prepaid. No way to tell who dropped them off, at least by any means at my disposal. We could try to track down the PO box, but tracking Jasmine's movements might be quicker."

My stomach soured, though I'd already suspected that the post office box wasn't a lead either of us would be able to take terribly far. I wasn't a trained investigator. I had no skill in magical or mundane means of tracing or tracking, and if Declan had ever managed to focus his magic enough to take up that line of work, Jasmine never mentioned it. Investigation was her forte.

The sky was dark blue, slowly deepening to black. Neither the stars nor the moon had made an appearance yet. Streets, sidewalks, and front yards slipped by on either side of us. Again, I saw no evidence of snow.

I almost opened my mouth to make some comment about the unusual weather, but then decided that Declan wasn't likely to lower himself to chatting benignly with me.

From the private airfield, it was a fifteen-minute drive through a mostly residential area to Fairchild House, where Grey and Dahlia had resided for as long as I'd known them. Their estate shared a property line with Fairchild Place, my parents' residence, with both properties occupying five acres in the center of Litchfield. My Aunt Rose resided fifteen minutes to the south, while Fairchild Manor—Jasper's residence, assuming he was still there—was fifteen minutes to the north.

The Fairchild coven owned large swaths of land throughout the state, most of it acquired centuries before and now operated through various corporations and different branches of the family. The town of Litchfield had been founded in the early seventeen hundreds and was set in a landscape of rolling New England hills and woodlands across which early American architecture was predominant.

"What did you mean when you said the phone might be cloned?" I asked.

"That they might have copied Jasmine's phone so they could monitor it," Declan said. "Send it to me, then track my response through it."

"But you used it to call me."

He glanced over at me briefly, quickly returning his gaze to the road. "I didn't know if you'd answer if you knew it was me."

I wasn't certain how to respond, because I had no idea what I would have done if his name had appeared on my phone.

Declan tersely redirected the conversation. "What's the connection to the Conclave?"

"A case Jasmine and I were working on together in October."

"With the necromancer and her son?"

I nodded, once more thinking back to that night in the graveyard and the deals that had been cemented there. Jasmine must have filled Declan in on the details of the investigation. "I have no idea how that would come back at us, though. Especially with you involved."

"We were the only two mailing addresses in Jasmine's phone."

I glanced over to Declan, but he kept his gaze glued to the road. He'd taken off his sunglasses at some point, as if wearing them earlier had been an extra layer of protection from me. But they were too dark to be practical while driving.

I thought about mentioning the Conclave contract stuffed into my bag, sitting on the floor now beneath my legs. Except Declan wouldn't need to ask why the packages containing the phone and Jasmine's necklace had been addressed to the Conclave if he knew of that tenuous possible connection through Kett and me to Jasmine's disappearance.

And I wasn't ready. I wasn't prepared to tell him that Jasper wanted to be a vampire. That if Kett didn't select our uncle, either Declan or I were next in line to be turned into an immortal, invulnerable, blood-crazed monster. Sitting barely a foot-and-a-half from him for the first time in over a decade, I just couldn't admit that a vampire saw something in me. Something that made offering me eternity by his side a possibility.

Of course, Declan could have been hiding all that from me as well. I had no way of knowing whether Kett had presented him with the contract months ago.

"Did you know Jasmine was in New York?" I continued the conversation as if I hadn't just been sitting silently with too many thoughts whirling around in my head.

He nodded. "On a case."

"Then she came … here?" I subbed the word 'here' for 'home' at the last minute. This place wasn't home to any of us anymore.

"Apparently."

"She was supposed to come to me this weekend, for a late Christmas."

"I know."

Silence fell between us again. I wondered if his 'friend,' the witch who had cast the tracking spell, had also spent Christmas with Declan and Jasmine. Then I refocused on our surroundings, not allowing myself to wonder any further. Large hedges and gated driveways slipped by my window. The area was starting to look familiar, which made me realize that Declan was taking the longer route into the neighborhood of Litchfield's larger estates. Avoiding driving past my parents' property.

The Fairchild siblings—Violet, Dahlia, Rose, and Jasper—lived in fairly close proximity, but they had never been particularly interested in seeing each other outside of coven business. At least that had always been my impression. But I had no idea how that dynamic had shifted after Jasmine, Declan, and I tore through their carefully projected facade.

My mother, Violet, was the eldest of the siblings, and a potion master. Her salves and draughts—the regulated ones, at least—were exceedingly sought after and commanded a hefty price. Not that the Fairchilds needed the extra income.

Rose, the healer, born second, sat on the Convocation. Dahlia, Jasmine's mother, was proficient at charms and wards. And Jasper was the youngest and the most powerful. He commanded the coven's magic, controlling the blood ties that bound us together. As a teenager, I had believed there was no spell he couldn't cast. No assault he couldn't withstand.

Until we three had turned on him.

Twelve years later, I had no idea what had become of his magical capacity, except that he apparently retained a talent for true naming, the ability to tie another person to a spell without their knowledge or permission—or to a contract, in the case of Declan, Jasmine, me, and presumably every other member of the Fairchild family.

I toyed with the platinum charm bracelet on my right wrist, finding a touch of comfort there—both in the reconstructions I carried of Declan and Jasmine, and in the protective magic that Jade had imbued within the bracelet. Unfortunately, I had no idea whether the magic I'd successfully wielded against a fledgling vampire was going to be any help against the elder witches I was about to confront.

We pulled up to the front gates of Fairchild House and stopped. The estate was the smallest of the properties in terms of acreage, but it might have been the most richly appointed. The narrow grass frontage and sidewalks were edged by a low stone wall that was topped by a tall wrought-iron fence. The imposing Georgian mansion beyond was symmetrically arranged around its crowned and corniced front entrance. It stood at the far end of a long, perfectly straight drive lined by ornate lampposts whose white globes shone in the evening light.

"They've rebricked the driveway," I said.

"New security since the last time you were here, as well," Declan said. "Cameras." He pointed to the top of the gates. "Motion sensors."

"That's awfully mundane of them."

"Jasmine's work. Trying to prove her worthiness. As always."

I didn't answer. I knew that the security system couldn't stop me from entering the grounds. Even with the electronics warded by Jasmine, I could easily short-circuit all of it with my magic. But I needed a closer look at the wards.

Declan pulled ahead but didn't bother to turn into the driveway, rolling the Jeep to a stop a few feet away from the gates. Shifting my gaze out the side window to eye the wrought-iron fencing, I laid my right hand on the door handle, gathering my bag in my left.

"I've missed you too," Declan whispered.

I stilled, remaining turned away from him. Though it was a sentiment I'd offered earlier, I wasn't certain how to respond now that he'd reciprocated. I wasn't certain how to broach everything that needed to be said with my next breath.

He opened his door and stepped out of the vehicle, breaking the moment. I followed without trying to recapture it.

We needed to find Jasmine. If we were lucky, she'd be in the house and completely unaware that we thought she was missing. Dahlia was more than capable of vindictively withholding that information, especially from her husband's illegitimate child.

But even as my mind framed that possibility, I knew it wasn't at all logical. Jasmine wouldn't have gone this long without checking in with one or both of us, with or without her phone.

Still, it was each tiny glimpse of hope that would keep me moving forward, preventing me from simply crumpling into a heap of despair. So logically or not, I would cling to that hope while searching for other possibilities, other clues. I would do that over and over, and the trail would lead to Jasmine in the end.

Chapter Three

Buttoning up my long wool coat after carefully rearranging my lace scarf, I stood before the high gate with Declan just behind my left shoulder. It had actually been cooler in Seattle, which didn't line up at all with my expectations—but which also wasn't remotely relevant to our current situation.

Fairchild House, however, looked exactly as I remembered it. Winter-bare maple trees lined the straight drive up to the roundabout entrance of the stone mansion. Ablaze with light, the stately six-bedroom house looked utterly inviting. It was the residents who were off-putting. The white window trims and shutters stood out in the evening light as though newly painted. Smoke curled from three of the house's six chimneys.

I raised my hand, reaching toward the buzzer attached to the stone pillar on the right side of the gate. But then I hesitated.

"They didn't even answer you?" I asked without looking away from the house. "When you buzzed earlier?"

"They listened."

I pushed back the right sleeve of my coat, flicking my wrist a few times so that my bracelet settled across the back of my hand.

"How many times have you been here?"

"Jasmine used to sneak me in on our holiday breaks."

"Otherwise you stayed at Fairchild Manor? With Jasper? Or did you go to Rose's?"

Declan shrugged instead of answering.

I raised my right hand, palm facing the invisible wall of ward magic that stood about two inches away from the wrought-iron gate. Declan wouldn't be tuned to his stepmother's wards. In fact, it wouldn't have surprised me to learn that Dahlia had added extra layers of magic to her protection spells with the specific intent of keeping Declan from ever setting foot in her home.

My palm met with resistance. I pressed against the magic. It blocked my advancement, though it didn't try to grab or expel me.

"Are you going to knock?" Declan asked, sounding mildly amused.

"I am."

I gathered my right hand into a fist, channeling all my anger and frustration into the bracelet-turned-magical-artifact on my wrist. Though it had been years since I'd deliberately wielded my magic in any way other than creating reconstructions—except when tussling with a fledgling vampire—it was the perfect time and venue for a test of whether or not I could wield the magic contained within the platinum trinket willfully.

Perhaps it wasn't Dahlia and Grey's fault that I was in Connecticut. They might have known that Jasmine was safe and sound, but were simply too mired in the past to share that information with Declan, causing him to leap to conclusions. Perhaps it was someone else altogether who was playing with us.

Or perhaps this was just the first step toward a confrontation with Jasper that I had always known was coming.

But none of those possibilities would hold me back. I had chosen to remove myself from the Fairchild sphere of influence, but not out of fear for myself.

I'd left to protect Declan and Jasmine.

Our elders were contemptuous, power-hungry snobs, willing to feign ignorance of the dark deeds that had shaped our childhoods because it suited them to do so. Jasmine might have been willing to set that aside in order to maintain a relationship with her parents and our Aunt Rose. But I wasn't.

Not bothering with any of the niceties that were expected of a witch requesting an audience with an elder of her coven, I punched the ward blocking our entrance with the magic I'd gathered into my fist. Once, twice, three times, I assaulted Dahlia's carefully constructed shields.

Ripples of blue gossamer spread outward from each blow, reverberating across the length and breadth of the magical barrier standing between me and the answers I sought.

"Well, that's one way of knocking." Declan's cadence deepened and lengthened, as it used to do when he was pleased. Or when he was preparing to do bodily harm. Apparently, he hadn't completely changed.

I pivoted, slamming my open palm onto the buzzer. "This is Wisteria Fairchild. You will open the wards, granting entry to me and Declan Benoit, and then you will answer our questions." My haughty tone intensified, sounding nothing like my poised, professional self. "Or I'll tear it all down."

I slammed my palm against the buzzer a second time. Then, with a sharp pulse of my magic, I intentionally overloaded its electronics.

Declan chuckled under his breath. He was juggling three small, smooth stones in his right hand, each one feeling as if it contained a tiny burst of his magic.

I took three deliberate steps to my left, standing directly in front of the gates.

"One," I said, raising my voice but not shouting.

The ward magic standing between me and the house shifted. The gates began to open.

Declan swore something nasty, quietly. When we were younger, he'd never spoken in his native Creole. Over all the years that Jasmine had given me his address so I could mail Declan his birthday reconstruction, I couldn't remember any of them suggesting he'd gone back to Louisiana. Of course, I also had no idea if he'd ever received or opened those packages.

As we waited shoulder to shoulder for the gates to creep open, I wanted to ask after Declan's mother and whether or not he'd tracked her down. But the question was too intimate—and would have been so even under different circumstances.

We didn't huddle in the orchard grass anymore, hidden from the stars by the boughs of fruit-laden apple trees. Whispering secrets to each other.

Down the long drive, the front door of the stone mansion opened. The inside light setting the stained-glass sidelights ablaze spilled across the front steps, golden white. A tall blond woman stepped out, appearing to be in her early forties though I knew she was a decade older.

Dahlia Fairchild.

Jasmine's mother. The youngest of the Fairchild sisters. Ward builder and charms maker.

My aunt was dressed from head to toe in deep cream, wearing a silk blouse, wool crepe pants, and low-heeled shoes. A three-strand pearl necklace stood out against her lightly tanned skin. She glowered in our direction, crossing her arms against the chill.

I didn't take a single step until the gates had fully opened. Then, with Declan following, I walked up the drive briskly, maintaining eye contact with Dahlia the entire time.

An equally tall man stepped out behind her, running his hand casually through his lighter blond hair. His pleased smile was in complete contrast to his wife's hardened demeanor.

Grey Fairchild. Declan and Jasmine's father. By blood, at least. Overseer of the day-to-day business of running the various Fairchild corporations and business interests.

"Rudeness doesn't become you, Wisteria," Dahlia said as we drew close.

I didn't bother answering, pausing only when we reached the base of the stone steps leading up to the entranceway. From this vantage point, I could see the massive crystal chandelier centered within the sweep of the foyer stairwell.

"Dahlia Fairchild." I acknowledged my aunt first, then glanced over at Grey. Declan and Jasmine's father was more casually dressed than his wife, wearing a brown crew-neck sweater and black slacks. "Grey Fairchild. We have questions pertinent to our investigation."

Dahlia jutted out her chin. "How dare you speak—"

I interrupted her smoothly. "I believe I've already made it obvious what I will or will not dare to do. On more than one occasion."

I let the heavily implied threat settle between us.

Grey glanced uneasily at Dahlia.

My aunt dropped my gaze, turning back into the house without another word. She hadn't acknowledged Declan at all.

Another wide grin spread across Grey's face. His hair had lightened and thinned with age, making him appear to be his natural age, somewhere in his midfifties. Apparently, he didn't subscribe to my mother's age-defying potions. "We were just having an after-dinner drink."

"We aren't staying," I said. "We're here on business."

"Yes. You've made yourself clear, niece." He stepped to the side, indicating the way into the house.

I climbed the steps, passing Grey and crossing through into the foyer. Light-gray marble spanned the entranceway, leading to the drawing room on the left and the front parlor on the right. A sweeping staircase of dark wood cut through the center of the house. Antique glass sconces adorned the walls, bestowing the entrance with a soft haze of warm light.

I heard, rather than saw, Grey clap a hand to Declan's shoulder.

"Son."

I didn't turn back to gauge Declan's response. I didn't want to see more pain etched across his already perpetually tense features. But for all I knew, maybe he had forged some sort of relationship with Grey after all the years that had passed.

I continued through the entranceway, knowing that Dahlia would be pouring herself a second—or third—glass of Chardonnay in the drawing room. I had three questions to ask. And, depending on the answers, I wanted to be gone before she had a chance to pour her next glass.

Removing my coat and carefully folding it over my left arm, I double-checked that Jasmine's necklace was hidden underneath the lace scarf Pearl Godfrey had made me. Whether or not my aunt and uncle knew it, the fact that I wore a gift from the chair of the Convocation held sway in this house. For good or evil, depending on everyone's individual mood.

Despite my bluff at the gates, Dahlia could physically remove Declan and me from her home with a flick of her wrist. Power plays would get me only so far with my family. As soon as I stopped either amusing or intriguing them, I'd have to ante up. The Fairchilds weren't known for their attention spans. Jasper and I were the exception.

I wasn't comfortable comparing myself to my uncle in any way, but it was the truth—and quite possibly the reason Dahlia had allowed us onto the property so easily. For fear that what had happened to Jasper could also happen to her.

It was a concern I'd encouraged twelve years ago, when punishment was to be meted out over Jasper's fate. A narrative I'd built that went beyond the actual capacity of Jasmine, Declan, and me to create any sort of real chaos. And I still believed that it was my hastily strung-together accounting that had kept Declan alive.

One of us had needed to be punished for what we'd done to Jasper. Declan was the easiest target, forever the outsider. I'm not sure it even crossed our parents' minds to believe me, to side with us over their coven leader. At sixteen, Declan had no hope of standing alone against even a single elder Fairchild, let alone the entire coven.

So I'd made a deal. And now, more than a decade later, I was just as desperate to get out of Connecticut with Jasmine safe as I was to escape without the details of my peace treaty crumbling under reexamination.

A fire was crackling away in the large white-brick fireplace that occupied the far wall of the drawing room. The wood-framed sash windows on either side had been opened to counter the heat. Dahlia prowled back and forth within a few feet of the flames. The cut-crystal wineglass in her hand reflected the fire, filled with blood-red wine that glowed as if teeming with potent magic. Apparently, Declan's and my arrival called for something more substantial than Chardonnay.

I didn't bother setting down my bag or my coat, choosing to stand just within the seating area. The antique furniture hadn't changed since my grandparents had occupied Fairchild House. Cleaning charms, wielded specifically by Dahlia, maintained the upholstery, the carpets, and the wooden floors. Or at least such charms had been used for the past twelve years.

For centuries before, brownies had kept the Fairchild houses tidy and our tables filled with food. The members of that rare race of the Adept weren't servants, however. They chose whom to align themselves with—usually a bloodline, but occasionally a specific area or parcel of land, regardless of who its owner was. Often, the responsibilities for maintaining estates would pass down from generation to generation.

The mostly unseen presence of brownies was considered a blessing, and their magic was symbiotic. They kept our homes, even fortified our lands—and in doing so, they maintained their connection and place with the magical world.

But Jasper and I had severed that connection. No brownies would ever tie themselves to a Fairchild again.

Grey swept past me toward a sideboard laden with crystal decanters filled with wines and spirits of various hues, partially jostling me out of my tainted recollections. From the corner of my eye, I saw Declan leaning in the archway behind me, not entering the room.

"Without Bluebell, we might all be dead. Jasmine, Declan, and I," I said, aware that I was lashing out at myself more than anyone else in the room. "Or starved, at a minimum."

A vicious snarl flashed across Dahlia's face. Grey raised a cautioning hand in her direction, holding sterling silver tongs and a single cube of ice aloft in the other hand.

I hadn't meant to be so confrontational, so up front. Not right away, at least. But the comment had slipped out, just as my magic had been doing for months.

Directness wasn't a trait encouraged at Fairchild family gatherings.

Dahlia regained her composure. In response, Grey turned back to the sideboard, ignoring the decanter of wine and pouring what I assumed was a scotch on the rocks instead.

"We know what you hold to be true, Wisteria." My uncle's tone was patient, almost warm, but definitive.

"Yes," Dahlia said with some heat. "We know exactly who to blame."

Her eyes darted toward Declan for a split second, then she immediately locked her gaze to me instead.

I smiled smugly.

She narrowed her eyes at me.

I carefully schooled my expression. Dahlia was still scared of Declan. Good.

"When was the last time you saw Jasmine?" I phrased the first of my three questions as politely as I could, knowing that Grey and Dahlia should have answered it when Declan asked them hours ago.

"Monday. Two days ago." Grey matched my smooth tone. "She stayed for the weekend."

"She was in Litchfield on a job?" My second question.

"Visiting her parents," Dahlia said. "Is that so difficult for you to understand?"

I almost answered snottily, but for the sake of expediency I opted for my third question instead. "Where did she say she was going when she left?"

They glanced at each other.

"To see you," Grey said. "For a belated Christmas celebration."

He was lying.

Witches weren't natural lie detectors. Not like werewolves, who could hear the slightest increase in another creature's heartbeat. But Fairchilds didn't hesitate before speaking.

"She wasn't planning to be in Seattle for three more days." I waited for either of them to respond.

They didn't.

Declan snorted. "Let's move on, Wisteria. This didn't matter to Dahlia this morning, and it won't matter now. Jasmine will have stayed in her room. You can look for residual to reconstruct."

"You won't be performing any magic in this house," Dahlia blurted out.

"No?" Declan took two measured steps into the drawing room, deliberately casting his gaze around. "Who's going to stop me from finding Jasmine? You?"

"She's not missing," Grey said irritably. "You know she's off with some … boyfriend."

"Without her phone?" I asked.

Grey's brow creased with the first hints of worry.

"I repeat," Dahlia said. "You will not be casting in this house."

"She will, stepmommy dearest," Declan said. "And if you want to try to stop her, you'll have to go through me."

"I'll throw you out, you ingrate," Dahlia spat. "Long before you can cast a single counterspell."

Declan flicked something at her in response. Dahlia shrieked and spun away, sloshing her red wine across her cream silk blouse and pants.

Whatever Declan had thrown landed in the fireplace, then exploded harmlessly with a shower of sparks. "Try me," he said. "I always thought this place could do with some updating."

"That's enough," Grey said sternly. Then to my surprise, he turned to Dahlia. "From both of you. It's past time to be done with this nonsense."

Dahlia sneered at her husband. Though to judge by her body language, she was more livid about her outfit than by his words.

"Wisteria," Grey said. "Please feel free to search any room of the house you deem necessary." Dahlia opened her mouth to protest, but he cut her off. "I believe you need to change. Then perhaps you can fill me in on whatever information Declan provided you this morning. About our supposedly missing daughter?" He placed heavy emphasis on the word 'our.'

My aunt lifted her chin defiantly.

I turned away from their escalating argument, swiftly crossing out of the drawing room before I got entangled in it any further.

Declan was a constant reminder for Dahlia of Grey's infidelity. But having known of his existence for almost twenty years—and not divorcing Grey—it seemed more than past time for her to let it go.

The same logic didn't apply to the grudge I carried, though. Leaving Jasmine, Declan, and me to the mercy of Jasper's so-called training was another matter altogether.

Crossing through the entranceway, I quickly jogged up the foyer stairs toward Jasmine's bedroom on the second level. For a brief moment, I thought Declan might not follow me, and I wondered if I should be worried about him bringing the house down on our heads. But before I was halfway up the stairs, I heard his heavy footsteps behind me.

I couldn't imagine what being in the house and talking to Dahlia with any sort of civility was costing him.

Actually, I couldn't imagine what calling me had cost Declan. My betrayal was much more destructive than that of a father and a stepmother who'd never even pretended to love him.

I had loved Declan beyond anything and everything. And I'd still walked away.

Oak hardwood inlaid with walnut ran throughout the upper levels of Fairchild House. The bedrooms branched off from the top of the stairs along a central corridor, with guest rooms at the front and family rooms closer to the rear. Jasmine's room was on the far left, beyond the main bathroom.

Tugging the first of my pillar candles from my bag, I pushed open the door to her bedroom. Crossing through to the window without bothering to glance around, I immediately placed my green candle—for earth—on the north-facing desk.

Only then did I notice the piles of electronics occupying every surface in the room. Multiple laptops were stacked on the white-painted antique desk. Tablets and cellular phones were tucked among rows of fantasy and sci-fi titles on the built-in white-painted bookshelves. Monitors and computer towers had been haphazardly stored in the corners of the walk-in closet, which stood with its paneled doors ajar as if Jasmine had grabbed something from within its depths, then left in a hurry.

I spun around, scanning the pink and green decor of the room.

Declan paused in the doorway, watching me.

Jasmine had never bothered to redecorate, simply layering more items on top of the colors and fabrics she'd selected for the room as a teenager. Electronics also littered the white canopy bed and its side tables, most of them in some state of dissection.

"Was … is she … building something?" I asked, retrieving my three other candles, then leaving my bag and coat tucked out of the way on the deep windowsill.

Declan shrugged.

I stepped to my right, skirting the edge of the large rug that ran underneath the bed, then placing my blue candle on one of the side tables. Blue for water.

"What do you need the candles for?" Declan asked.

"For my circle."

He snorted. "You know this room. You know this house. Use the walls as your edge, the wards as your final boundary."

"My collections are contained. Precise. Without flaw."

"Yeah. I get that about you now."

If we were still nine years old, Declan would have just called me a scaredy-cat. If we were still nine years old, I would have effortlessly proven my magical prowess to him, then laughed when he begrudgingly acknowledged my superior ability.

But we weren't nine. And adults didn't goad each other into botched castings.

I eyed him without speaking, maintaining as much poise as I could given the circumstances.

He frowned, crossed his arms, and didn't bother me any further.

Nudging as much of the technology to the outer edges of the room as I could move easily, I placed my two remaining candles—red for fire at the south, white for air at the east. There was a chance that the reconstruction I was about to cast would damage Jasmine's devices, but I hesitated to remove them from the room because I wasn't sure what, if any, clues I was about to uncover. My spell would call forth only residual magic. If Jasmine had interacted with something nonmagical, I might not be able to piece together what was happening if I couldn't get a visual sense of what she'd been working on.

I knew without bothering to drop my personal shields that the entire room would be coated in layer upon layer of Jasmine's magic. Despite living with Declan and me at Fairchild Manor from the ages of nine to sixteen, this had been her bedroom from the moment of her birth. If she'd been here within the last few days, I would need to extricate that point in time from years of older residual impressions.

I retrieved my lighter from my bag, expecting Declan to make some crack about me using nonmagical means to light my candles. He didn't.

Pacing the room in as much of a circle as I could, including crawling across the bed, I lit the pillars one by one.

Declan snorted.

"This is Jasmine," I said snootily. "The bed might be important." I instantly regretted the words, which I realized made it sound as though I considered Jasmine promiscuous.

"Please," Declan said. "She's not going to bring anyone here."

"No. She wouldn't."

I'd forgotten that discussing Jasmine with Declan wasn't a betrayal. He loved her as much as I did. In fact, for both of us, Jasmine might be the only person in the world we truly loved. Unless my cousin had been unnaturally circumspect about Declan's personal relationships, or lack thereof. Unless the 'friend' he'd mentioned so guardedly earlier was more than a casual entanglement.

I stood facing the doorway, as close to the green candle as I could get without standing on the desk. I raised my arms at my sides, palms forward. Then I pushed my magic around and through the circle with which I'd encompassed the bedroom.

Declan gasped involuntarily as the magic brushed by him in the doorway. He took a step back into the hall.

Within my circle, various streaks of light-blue witch magic danced around just about every item in the room, though the bed and the path to and from the door were more intensely tinted. The residual had always been present, but I'd remained blind to it until I had the protection of my circle. I didn't like seeing or feeling magic involuntarily, because it meant the wielder was powerful enough to get past my ever-present personal shielding.

Jasmine had spent countless hours in her bedroom. The house itself had been occupied by generations of witches stretching back close to two hundred years. The land itself had belonged to the Fairchilds since before the United States of America was founded.

I beckoned the residual layers forward, sifting through the tinted magic in search of the most recent impression. I could easily spend hours calling forth moment after moment, watching Jasmine grow and mature. Seeing all the moments she'd spent without Declan or me at her side.

Invading her privacy.

But I was seeking immediate answers, so I coaxed forward what I determined to be the outermost layer, hoping it would reveal a glimpse of Jasmine's most recent visit.

Within the circle, the magic eagerly reformed. The light in the bedroom shifted, brightening. Whatever was about to replay had occurred during the day.

A half-formed image of Jasmine suddenly appeared in the doorway, like a ghost standing before Declan, who still stood a step beyond the edge of the circle.

Within the reconstruction, my cousin strode backward into the room as the scene was revealed in reverse.

"I've got her," I said. "Not sure how recent it is yet."

Declan pressed his hand against the side of my circle, tapping into the reconstruction without asking. Without needing me to guide him. His intense energy momentarily destabilized my magic, but I was able to smooth the flow quickly.

We'd had the same mentor. We'd had the same lessons, before it became obvious in what direction our talents lay. Or, in Jasmine's case, didn't. Both Declan and Jasmine could probably attempt to cast a reconstruction themselves, though it wasn't likely they'd be successful. However, that meant Declan could tap into my casting, just as Jasmine could play the reconstructions I sent her for her birthday.

"What is she doing at the desk?" Declan asked, calling me back to the scene still playing out in reverse before me.

Within the reconstruction, Jasmine was seated at the desk, typing on her laptop. I couldn't see much of the screen from the side, but I didn't bother trying to change the angle of the reconstruction. Technology and magic didn't mix, so even with a perfect view, it was unlikely I'd be able to pick up much detail of whatever text was flowing across the screen at the behest of Jasmine's fingertips.

"Looks like she's sending an email," I said. "I can try to zoom in on the reconstruction when we play it back."

Jasmine's brown leather satchel had been dumped across the desk beside her, as if she'd tossed it with some force. A few items had spilled out. Her face was tense, drawn. Darker blue magic glowed from underneath her dark-brown sweater, around the area of her heart. She was still wearing her necklace with the reconstructions. I had to stop myself from reaching up to touch that same necklace currently tucked under my sweater.

"She looks tired," I murmured. "Drained, really. Pale. Maybe even angry."

"She was home," Declan said. "Can you blame her?"

"And the items on the desk, spilling out of her bag ..."

"I can't see any of that from here."

I leaned along the edge of the circle, pressing my hip against the end of the desk and gingerly placing my palm on the windowsill for support. I hadn't left myself much space to move, knowing that I could manipulate the magic in the playback and wanting to capture as much detail as possible with my first pass.

A lipstick, Jasmine's phone, and what appeared to be a hotel key card lay next to her satchel.

"Do mundanes use those key cards, like the ones you get in hotels, for anything other than hotels?" I asked.

Jasmine suddenly shifted back from the desk, moving backward as she reverse-pulled her laptop back into her bag and slung it over her shoulder. Then she crossed—again walking backward—out of the room.

That was quick. Why take the time to come upstairs and get set up at the desk, then leave again so quickly? Had she received some sort of information, in an email or a message on her computer, that motivated her departure?

Declan hadn't answered me about the key card.

I glanced through the circle at him. His blue witch magic surrounded him in a halo, with lightning strikes of darker blue throughout. I'd involuntarily looked at Kett through a reconstruction circle once, and the red-and-black cloud of seething magic that had encompassed him still haunted me. That glimpse of the dark power surrounding the vampire had made me exceedingly certain that I never wanted to look at another Adept through the boundaries of an active circle again.

But Declan wasn't just another Adept.

He was staring back at me, waiting for something.

I looked away, pressing my palms against the edge of the circle and commanding the reconstruction of Jasmine to play again. This time, it played out front to back.

Jasmine entered the room, practically throwing herself down on the swivel desk chair. Again, she appeared tired, even frustrated. She pulled out her computer.

"Show me the screen of the laptop," Declan said.

I shifted the magic of the reconstruction, trying to zoom in on the laptop. But as I'd expected, the screen was blurry.

Declan grunted. "Probably an email. And the key card?"

I shifted the reconstruction further, zooming in on the items on the desk.

"Unmarked. At least on the side we can see," he said. "And you're right, I have no idea what else it could be used for other than a hotel room. You're going to have to recast, dig deeper."

Ignoring him for a moment, I watched the rest of the reconstruction play out, seeing nothing that hinted at the reason for Jasmine's abrupt arrival and sudden departure. I allowed the circle to fall dormant before me, thinking.

"You have Jasmine's phone," I said.

"So?"

"So she banks online, or through an app on her phone. If she checked into a hotel a few days ago, it would show on the Visa she uses for work expenses. She was in Litchfield on a job."

Declan snorted. "Not visiting family?" he said mockingly.

"It's the wrong time of year for one of her biannual pilgrimages to purgatory."

Declan's face twisted with some strong emotion I couldn't wholly identify. It wasn't anger. Pain-filled frustration mixed with amusement, perhaps. He stepped farther back from the magic I held at the ready, leaning against the far wall of the corridor before he retrieved Jasmine's phone from his pocket.

I closed the circle. I could recall it instantly if needed, and I didn't want to risk damaging Jasmine's cellular. It was one of our only links to her.

"I need a password to get in," Declan said, staring at the screen. Apparently he'd found the banking app. "It's not the same as the one I used to open the phone."

"It's … it's the important one," I said. I found myself stumbling over the words, stumbling over reminding Declan of our connection, which Jasmine had immortalized in the form of a tattoo on her lower abdomen. "Or some version of it. Her tattoo."

Declan didn't lift his gaze from the phone, tapping his thumb across the screen a few more times. He nodded, indicating he'd opened the app.

He scanned the screen, scrolling. "Fairhaven Hotel."

"Fairhaven?" I asked mockingly.

He snorted, tapping the screen again and scrolling some more. "Grey's newest project. Looks like it's about ten miles away."

"Why would she need a hotel room when she was spending nights here?"

"New boyfriend?"

It was my turn to scoff. "Who she brought to Litchfield? To what? Ease into introducing him to Dahlia and Grey?"

"Maybe."

"Without telling us first?" Uttering the word 'us' and including Declan in that thought felt achingly and impertinently familiar. We weren't an 'us,' except when united by Jasmine.

He finally lifted his golden-hazel gaze to meet mine. "No."

"Well, it's the only clue we have." I moved through the room to snuff the candles out and let their wax harden. "Other than the packages that neither of us can trace any further. Not without bringing in an investigative team, at least. And we'd need more evidence to get the Godfreys and the Convocation involved."

I didn't bother collecting the reconstruction in a cube. We either had a lead or we had nothing. I also didn't voice my still-unverified certainty that Jasper was involved. Declan would have had no problem believing our uncle was at the heart of Jasmine's possible abduction—and would have had even less problem confronting Jasper about it. But supporting evidence was a necessity if we wanted to actually find Jasmine without dying in a hatred-fueled blaze of vengeance.

"You'd bring in the Godfreys? Here? You have that sort of ... relationship with them?"

"I believe so. Pearl Godfrey would come. Or she'd send a representative. A skilled investigator, at least."

Declan laughed harshly. "That sounds like an excellent idea. Finishing what we started twelve years ago." But he sobered quickly, glancing down at the phone in his hand. "But I'm not sure it gets us any closer to finding Jasmine. Not quickly. Too much protocol."

I nodded, moving swiftly around the room to collect the candles, my bag, and my coat. Pearl Godfrey would come to Connecticut if I asked. The elder witch might even skirt procedure for me. But she couldn't just blithely enter Fairchild territory and start asking questions.

And the reality was that I didn't want her asking questions. Truth had a way of getting tainted and tarnished around Fairchilds, and Pearl Godfrey wouldn't appreciate that kind of runaround. Just as she wouldn't appreciate the picture my family would paint. Of Declan, of Jasmine, and of me.

She might even believe the elder Fairchilds over the three of us. And even if she didn't, an insidious seed might still be planted. An idea that I wasn't to be wholly trusted.

"We go to the hotel," I said, as if I hadn't been standing mute in the doorway while my mind worked through all the implications of expanding our investigation. "If we confirm anything, then we figure out who to involve. Rose, most likely."

"Rose," Declan sneered, crossing his arms. "Because she's been so helpful in the past."

My heart pinched. Without thinking, I stepped forward to lay my hand on his forearm—wishing as I did that I could do more, that I could take his pain away with my touch. I would take it all, everything that had ever afflicted him, and hold it in my heart if it would alleviate his misery.

He dropped his arms, pushing away from the wall and striding down the hall toward the foyer stairs.

"I don't need your pity, Wisteria," he said without looking back. "It's useless to me."

I just stood there, mute in the center of the hall with my arm extended. Rooted to the floor.

He glanced back. "Just like all the guilt couching your every word. It's absolutely useless."

Pushing through the low ache of dread that had been dragging on me for most of the day, I raised my chin archly. "Well, I do loathe being useless, don't I?"

"Right." Declan nodded curtly. "Good that we got that out of the way."

"Indeed." Then I strode toward and past him without another glance. My heart felt heavy, crammed into my chest like a piece of lead. But since that was how it always felt, ignoring it was second nature.

Descending the stairs swiftly, I left Declan in my wake. Because that was where he wanted to be, after all.

Chapter Four

My mother was standing in the foyer, glaring up at me as I descended the stairs.

Her deep-burgundy ribbed knit dress fell to midcalf. A black-printed silk scarf was artfully arranged around her neck, and her wrists and fingers dripped with jewelry—most of which contained hidden compartments for her deadly concoctions and restorative salves. Her blond hair was swept back from her face in a sleek coil. She hadn't aged a day in the twelve years I'd been gone.

But then, she wouldn't have. Violet Fairchild was the most highly regarded potion master in all of North America, if not the Western world. And that wasn't simply due to the Fairchild reputation.

If the family hadn't already been filthy rich after generations of dominance within the Adept community, the profits from my mother's concoctions would have easily maintained all four of the family estates. And that didn't include any of her off-the-books brews. If any member of the Convocation—excluding Rose—ever set foot in my childhood backyard to see the range of poisonous and illegal magical flora that bloomed there, the Fairchild reputation would be completely sullied. Rather than simply tarnished by rumors, and by my defection.

"Wisteria." My mother acknowledged my entrance frostily, then raised her light-blue-eyed gaze over my head, curling her lip derisively.

Declan's footfalls behind me became weighted as he deliberately clomped down the polished walnut treads in his heavy boots.

My mother lowered her gaze to meet mine again. I quashed the smirk that had risen at Declan's impertinence, pausing at the base of the stairs.

"This is a sight I never thought I'd see," Violet said. "We had a deal, Wisteria."

"Are you here to enforce it?" I asked, sounding deadly even to my own ears as I laid my wool coat over the banister. Then I deliberately pushed back the sleeves of my sweater and resettled my bag on my shoulder.

My mother's gaze fell to the bracelet on my right wrist. She frowned. "Our judgement never extended to you. Or Jasmine."

Declan landed heavily to my left, standing shoulder to shoulder with me. "And why was that, Auntie Violet?" His Creole-tinted drawl was deep and deliberate.

"You are no nephew to me, Declan Benoit," my mother said, uttering his name as if it might be a curse.

A motion to my left drew my attention. Declan was rolling a series of stones in his right hand, magic sparking off the obviously spelled rocks.

I glanced up at him.

He was glaring at my mother as if she were the root of all evil, which she wasn't. She was simply a self-centered megalomaniac—though the same could be said of almost every Fairchild. But even if Declan wasn't likely to throw the first spell and initiate the fight, his expression was more than enough to get a rise from my mother.

And for a moment, I thought about letting go.

I thought about allowing everything I held so carefully contained within me to slip away, throwing away my years of careful living, ending all our familial strife in one fell swoop. And taking everyone with me.

My mother took a measured step back, almost pressing against the double entrance doors behind her. But her gaze rested on me, not Declan. She wasn't fearful, but I could see her furiously reassessing the situation.

She was most likely deciding whether or not she could take both of us at once, knowing that we were immune to just about anything she could throw at us. Because she'd made us so. But I was certain, mother or not, that Violet Fairchild always held back a few of her nastier tricks.

"You might want to cap that, Wisteria," Declan said. "Before you trigger the wards."

Magic. He meant my magic.

I became aware that I was holding my hands before me, raised as if to pummel anyone within reach. The bracelet on my right wrist was pulsing with power.

"Don't you tell my daughter what to do," my mother snapped.

A Fairchild's priorities were never skewed by logic. The outsider—Declan—was always going to be the bigger threat.

"We've gotten off to a rough start." My Aunt Rose bustled into the foyer from the drawing room, pressing her clasped hands to her chest. She was wearing a pretty silk dress speckled with periwinkles. And she looked old. I'd seen her in passing at a Convocation function only a year before, and she'd looked older then, with thick white streaks throughout her blond hair. But still not as dreadfully thin and sallow-skinned as she appeared now.

"Rose," Declan said. Her name sounded as though it had been pulled from him in shock.

So I wasn't the only one who'd noticed the stark transformation.

Rose flapped a hand at Declan, crossing to place a kiss on his cheek. He obligingly leaned forward, tucking his spelled stones in his pocket. Despite her wearing kitten heels, he still towered above her.

Then Rose stepped past Declan, pulling me into a hug I didn't want. A touch of her magic danced across my shoulders and the exposed skin of my neck. It felt wrong, off somehow. But I wasn't sensitive enough to understand how or why.

I glanced at Declan over Rose's head. The concern I felt was also etched across his features.

Excepting Jasmine, Rose was the closest person either of us had to a caring family member.

My father, Slate, strode into the foyer. He was dressed in casual pants and an open-collared blue pinstriped dress shirt. After glancing my mother's way with a frown, he crossed to greet me. "My girl!"

I instinctively thrust my hand forward, palm facing his chest.

He faltered, looking momentarily pained.

Rose clucked her tongue, but she didn't comment on my behavior.

Dahlia and Grey were hovering in the archway to the drawing room.

Heat flooded my cheeks as embarrassment flushed through my system. And all of a sudden, I felt childish and unsure. Ungrateful, spoiled, and disrespectful. It was an ingrained reaction to being faced with my family, clashing now with my sense of self, my sense of morality. Everything felt tangled and tight within my chest.

I needed to not be there. I needed to be anywhere else except surrounded by my family.

"We were just leaving." Declan's voice was a low, threatening growl. "But Violet appears to be blocking the door."

"We just wanted a word," Rosc said. Her tone was thin and needy. "We ... we believe this could be an opportunity—"

"Jasmine is missing," I said. I grabbed hold of that reality, using it to anchor myself within the present.

"Oh, really." Dahlia sighed dramatically. "Of all the games—"

"It's time for you to return to us, Wisteria," my mother said, though she didn't sound terribly pleased at the prospect.

"Yes," Rose said, patting my arm. "Balance must be restored for the coven to—"

Declan's laugh cut Rose off midsentence. His humorless outburst was riddled with disbelief and edged in anger.

"You can leave any time you wish," Dahlia snarled at her stepson. "In fact, Wisteria knows better than to bring you here. Or to be seen with you at all. Evidently, twelve years is too long for a prissy princess to keep her word."

Silence fell across the foyer. I could actually hear a clock ticking somewhere nearby, but I couldn't visualize one within my memory of the house. I'd been avoiding this moment, this inevitable confrontation, since the day I left Litchfield. But with Declan and I returning, I should have expected it.

Declan slowly and deliberately turned to face me. His leather coat brushed my leg.

I met his steady, searing gaze. He was no longer the boy I'd dallied with by the lake. He was no longer the broken boy I'd left in the hospital.

"What does she mean?" Declan asked. Barely suppressed thunder rolled through his words. Sparks of his magic rained down from his clenched hands.

I didn't answer him. The situation was about to spin out of control, and I was dreadfully certain that Declan and I couldn't fight our way past four Fairchilds at the height of their powers.

"It was always going to come to this," I murmured.

"What does she mean?" Declan asked again, enunciating each word pointedly.

"Absolutely nothing, Declan," Rose said gently. "Tempers are high."

"Oh, please, Rose," my mother said. "Why do you insist on treating them like idiot children? They never were such creatures. Well, Wisteria wasn't. Dahlia is simply reiterating what you already know. After what you did to our brother, Jasper, putting him in that godawful wheelchair, you are no longer welcome in our homes. Wisteria was to never have any contact with you. That was how she bargained for your life, Declan. How did you think you walked away unscathed twelve years ago?"

"We just didn't think you'd leave too, Wisteria," my father said. "We never wanted to lose you."

"After I put Jasper in the wheelchair," Declan said, speaking slowly as if he was piecing something together while glancing around at all the elders in the room, "you were all scared of me. That's why there was never any retribution other than sending me away to school."

Dahlia started to snarl something, but Grey placed a cautioning hand on her arm.

Declan looked at each of them again, finally locking his gaze to Rose's over my head until our aunt guiltily looked away.

Then he laughed harshly, as if coming to some realization that pained him. "If I could put Jasper down at sixteen, just think what I could do to all of you now."

As if on cue, the four elders stepped slightly away from each other, fanning across two sides of the foyer.

That strategic move made the stairs at our back a defensive nightmare. If spells started flying, we'd have to shove Rose down or drag her with us into the parlor.

I glanced at Declan. He was smiling so grimly that the expression was almost fiendish. Everyone surrounding him was blond and perfectly poised. Even visually, he was an outsider. A malignancy that demanded to be removed.

"If we fight them, we'll never find Jasmine," I whispered. "Even if we win, we won't walk away unharmed. What will her kidnappers do? Wait around while we heal?"

"Kidnappers?" Dahlia scoffed. "She's off screwing some sorcerer or shapeshifter."

The sconce nearest to her exploded, raining glass shards across the marble floor.

All eyes turned to Declan, their collective glare redoubled.

He shrugged. "Wasn't me."

One by one, all the elders looked at me. Uneasy frowns furrowed their brows.

"We were just heading to a hotel to follow up on a lead," I said stiffly. "But perhaps we should just cut through the pretense and head straight to the manor."

"Hotel?" Grey echoed.

"Jasmine wasn't staying in a hotel," Dahlia said.

"Jasper isn't at the manor ..." Rose's whisper cut through all the other posturing.

My knees went weak at her words.

"Excuse me?" Declan snarled. "Where else would he be?"

"He winters at one of the family properties," Violet said smugly. "For the heat. Because of what you did."

Slate glanced at Violet, frowning. "He was just here—"

"For the holidays," Violet snapped. "What does that have to do with anything?"

My father's frown deepened. "Under the circumstances, with Jasmine missing—"

"Jasmine isn't missing," Dahlia said. "This is ridiculously contrived. Another bid for attention by Miss Too-Good-to-be-a-Fairchild." She waved in my direction. "Jasmine goes weeks without checking in."

"With you, maybe," Declan said.

I didn't respond. Much to my own surprise, I was relieved rather than scared. If Jasper wasn't in town, then his connection to Jasmine being missing was tenuous, and I might actually get out of Connecticut without facing him.

Apparently, I was a coward after all.

I grabbed my coat off the banister, folding it over my left arm and leaving my right hand and bracelet exposed. Then I walked slowly but deliberately for the door. Declan fell into step behind me.

My mother crossed her arms, defiantly cocking her hip into my path.

As I drew closer, I locked my gaze to hers. "That day in the hospital, when I discovered that you all knew ... that you knew everything he'd ever done to us and that you accepted it without question. That you thought it was simply the proper way of training us, the way it had always been done."

"That's not true," my father said to my left.

"Shut up, Slate," Declan snarled.

"That was the day you ceased to exist for me," I said. My voice was steady, though my hands were shaking. "The day I realized you never were my mother. My protector. That you were incapable of the love that requires, and that you would never be capable of holding me in your heart above all else."

My mother's expression became questioning, almost troubled. "It can't have been that bad."

"Move aside."

"It can't have been," she said, glancing over my shoulder to my father for support. "And if it was, you never made it clear. You never—"

"Move aside or I'll move you, Violet." I was trembling suddenly, but not with fear. I was infused with anger and frustration desperately seeking an outlet.

The stained-glassed sidelights on either side of the door cracked.

"This is insane," Grey said from somewhere behind me. "This can't continue."

My mother reached for me, then. As if she might be able to hug me, hold me, and siphon all my pain away.

Either that or she was about to poison me.

My father—his face stricken with concern—grabbed her upper arm and physically dragged her away from me.

I reached for the ornate knob, opening the door and stepping through it without another word.

Declan matched me step for step down the long driveway, his leather jacket billowing out like a protective sail behind us. Even without my coat on, the starlit night was oddly balmy. Or perhaps I was simply overheated.

"They're still in the doorway," he murmured. "Watching us."

I didn't answer. The gate swung open silently before us, remotely triggered. As I crossed onto the sidewalk, the property's wards slid across my skin, allowing me passage without resistance. I kept my mind carefully blank, thinking about nothing other than getting away unscathed. Well, getting Declan away unscathed. Poised for something more … ready to fight if necessary.

But they let us walk away with the final word. An action unheard of among the Fairchilds, except for Jasper or me. My uncle and I were the only ones who were patient enough to seek revenge rather than immediate retribution.

Declan quickened his step, crossing in front of me to open the passenger door of the Jeep. I stiffly slipped my coat on, then climbed in without comment.

He jogged around to the driver's side, climbing in and starting the vehicle at the same time. Then he cranked the heater, sending an initial blast of chilled air throughout the interior. I gathered the lapels of my coat tightly at my neck, waiting for the engine to warm up and the heat to kick in.

I could feel Declan looking at me. I gazed resolutely out the windshield, not wanting to talk. Just needing to stuff my damaged soul back inside of me. I had to shove it down deep to continue functioning. I wasn't ready to discuss anything. I wasn't certain I ever would be.

He chuckled quietly. "I'd forgotten what it felt like to be backed by you. By your magic. Though you hold it too tightly now. That's why it keeps getting away from you."

"It doesn't keep getting away from me," I said waspishly.

Declan snorted, then checked his mirrors and pulled the Jeep away from the curb. "Put on your seatbelt."

I obeyed him wordlessly. But my brain was in overdrive as the interior of the Jeep started to warm. What if I'd missed some obvious clue because I was so obsessed with Jasper's villainy? Some clue that might have led us to Jasmine immediately, and let us avoid the fruitless confrontation with our parents?

"We could have taken them," he said. "Even without Jasmine."

"We are what he made us," I murmured, unable to check the pain threaded through my words.

"That always bothered you more than it did me."

I didn't answer. I didn't have an answer.

It wasn't altruism that had sent Jasper to New Orleans, looking for Declan the summer before we all turned ten and started our training. No, our uncle had a long-term plan. A plan that was ruined when Declan and I inadvertently forged a greater connection. Then we turned what he'd created against him when he tried to take steps to put us in check. Steps that would have cost Jasmine her life.

The power of three, Jasper had called it. And Declan hadn't cared that he was being used, because he'd been abandoned and was living on the street. Because Jasper—or rather the brownie, Bluebell—fed and housed us. Because Jasper had given him Jasmine and me when he'd had no one.

"But what I'd really like to know," Declan said, ignoring my silence, "is why they think it was me who took Jasper down." His voice was silky smooth, deceptively sweet.

I glanced at him. He met my gaze briefly, then looked back at the road.

The headlights of the Jeep cut through the night as we drove past gated estate after gated estate. I leaned back in the seat, allowing the blasting heat to melt the remnants of all my fear and frustration away.

Declan didn't press me further, which was good because I suddenly realized I was exhausted. The dashboard clock read 8:37 P.M.

"What did they mean the coven was unbalanced?" I murmured, feeling myself drifting while I sifted through the conversation we'd just been subjected to in my head.

"Do you doubt it?"

"Yes," I said, giving in and closing my eyes. "Why now? They've been without the three of us for over twelve years. Why would it be unbalanced now?"

"I don't give a shit."

"No. Why would you?"

"You aren't going to answer my question, then?"

"You already know the answer, Bubba." I whispered his nickname, speaking to the version of him that I still held in my heart even after all the years that had passed. Even after all the loathing he'd leveled my way for the last hour and a half.

He didn't respond.

And I fell asleep like that, comforted by the heat and the moving vehicle. Momentarily safe in Declan's presence.

I actually napped for the fifteen minutes it took to drive to the hotel we'd tracked Jasmine to by way of her Visa statement. Dealing with my family was apparently exhausting. But no matter how Declan felt about me, I knew I could trust him without question.

Feeling refreshed and alert, I woke as Declan turned off the Jeep. He'd parked in the far corner of an exterior parking lot, wedged between a hulking Hummer and some low shrubbery that hedged the property. The nose of the vehicle faced the brightly lit portico entrance of a sleek luxury hotel.

The Fairhaven Hotel was shiny and new, its tinted windows appearing almost black in the dark and rising upward for at least fifteen storeys. The lower levels were set aglow by golden-tinted spotlights angled up from the landscaping and down from the lower roofline. The site was brashly modern, as if New York had bled over the state border and planted an outpost. Even without being sure of our exact location, I could see how the hotel completely clashed with the general early-American feel of the town around it.

"It's very ... glossy," I said. "For Litchfield."

Declan folded his arms across his chest. "Glossy is what Grey does best."

"Along with dragging the Fairchilds into the twenty-first century."

Declan snorted. Then a comfortable silence fell between us as we sat in the warm, dark interior of the Jeep, watching the entrance as a small number of vehicles came and went from the parking lot.

At the center of the ground floor, two uniformed doormen chatted just inside the automatic glassed entrance doors, greeting guests as they entered or exited. The lobby stretched beyond the front doors, extending back through the hotel with a seating area and a fireplace in the middle. The reception desk and the elevators were likely farther along, but I couldn't see them from our vantage point. A restaurant occupied the ground floor nearest to us, while the opposite front corner appeared to be devoted to an expansive lounge.

I stepped out of the Jeep, pausing to button up my coat. Declan also exited, remotely triggering the locks.

It was colder, finally, and the cool air felt like an assault to the exposed skin of my face and hands. Regardless of the legendary Seattle rain—and with the exception of the cold snap the city was currently experiencing—years spent mostly on the West Coast had made me a fan of milder weather. But now the chill invigorated me. I quickly stepped across the parking lot to the sidewalk that ran the length of the restaurant, moving toward the hotel entrance.

As I passed, I scanned the candlelit tables beyond the lightly tinted windows for familiar faces. I didn't expect to see Jasmine dining on lobster and sipping champagne, but being thorough kept me focused on the task—and not thinking about Declan following me like a dark guardian shadow.

We made a sharp visual contrast. Unshaven and darker-skinned, he would have pulled people's attention even without his ankle-length black leather coat. Whereas I most likely looked as if I'd just dashed out for a brisk after-dinner stroll.

I strode through the sliding doors into the front lobby, offering the doormen a polite smile. Then I watched their courteous expressions turn into frowns as they took in Declan behind me.

I continued through the lobby, taking in the decor of gold and black. I passed the entrance to the fairly busy upscale lounge, then the empty seating area arranged around a sleek, black-tiled gas fireplace. Nearing the registration desk, I offered the clerk the same smile I'd offered at the door. She immediately stepped forward.

"I'd like to place a call to Jasmine Fairchild," I said, channeling all the Fairchild sense of entitlement that I could. "She's expecting me."

"Of course," the clerk said amicably. Her fingers danced over the keyboard of her desktop computer. "If you will just step over to the courtesy phone …" She gestured toward a mirrored sideboard to my right.

"Thank you," I said, already turning away. As I neared, the courtesy phone rang. I picked it up.

Declan settled his shoulder against the wall to my left, facing the front doors and the entrance to the ritzy lounge.

"I'll put you through," the clerk's voice said in my ear.

I didn't bother thanking her a second time. The line went quiet.

"You really think she's just lounging around in a hotel, eating bonbons while someone rips off her phone and necklace?" Declan's voice dripped with sarcasm while he continued to scan the area behind me.

"I thought I might have been able to see the screen when the clerk opened the guest file," I said. "Or that if she asks me to leave a message, she lets the room number slip."

The phone on the other end started to ring.

"And," I continued pointedly, "we now know Jasmine hasn't checked out."

Declan didn't respond. Which was fine. When he was snarky, he wasn't a terribly interesting conversationalist.

As the phone continued to ring in my ear, I slowly scanned the reception area, noting the bank of elevators to the far left. Then I pivoted, scanning the entrance and the quiet lobby a second time. General chatter and faint music wafted in from the lounge.

Two vampires—a male and a female—walked through the automatic sliding doors.

"Holy hell," I said, spinning back to face Declan.

"What?" He glanced around behind me.

Apparently he hadn't spotted the two predators prowling their way through the lobby. But then, if I hadn't spent quite so much time with Kett three months ago, I might not have immediately noticed their 'otherness' either. But now I couldn't unsee it, noting it in every deliberate step they took.

The clerk interrupted the phone still ringing in my ear. "She doesn't seem to be answering. Would you like to leave a message?"

"Let's give it five minutes and try again," I said.

"Of course. I'll ring through in five minutes."

"Thank you."

I hung the phone up.

"Two vampires," I whispered, risking a glance over my shoulder.

The vampires in question had paused in the empty seating area around the fireplace. "They appear to be waiting for something … or casing the hotel. A man and a woman. By the fireplace."

Declan frowned, eyeing the two over my shoulder. The female sat down, flicking a neatly folded newspaper off the two-seater, square-sided black leather couch before settling in. Her dark hair was slicked back in an intricate braid, skewered through at intervals with what appeared to be shards of bone. She was dressed in sleek black leather pants, a sheer, banded top that exposed everything except her breasts, and an ankle-length mink coat. Her lipstick was blood red against dark skin.

The ivory-skinned male with short, spiked, dark-brown hair was sporting black-framed, gray-tinted sunglasses, dark-washed jeans, what looked like a black-printed rock band T-shirt, and boots that had never spent a minute on a construction site. He braced himself against the black slate fireplace surround, leaning toward the fire—rather obsessively for a vampire for whom flames could be deadly.

"Please," Declan scoffed. "Wannabees, maybe."

Completely in contrast to the business-casual attire of the other hotel guests, the two dripped of money and sex, moving languidly and barely bothering to conceal what they were. Thankfully, the lobby was fairly empty, but if they wandered into the lounge, they would likely create a stir even among those who couldn't see that they were vampires.

"Look closer," I snapped. "Watch how they move. Take a peek at their auras." I wasn't about to look at them without my personal shields firmly in place. But since Declan hadn't just spent far too much quality time with an ancient vampire, he would have no issue with doing so.

Though even without seeing their magic, I could tell at first glance that they were younger than Kett. Way younger. The clothing alone gave them away. Though obviously, they weren't mere newborns. From what the executioner had told me, fledgling vampires could have slaughtered every human in the hotel and still not sated their bloodlust.

Declan simply didn't know what he was looking at.

"They were just joined by a third," he said.

I glanced over my shoulder again. Another vampire had approached the first two, gesturing emphatically with her hands. The first two didn't appear at all moved by whatever she was saying. Her shag-cut hair was shiny black, bone straight, and obviously dyed. Her skin was olive toned, and seeing her alongside the darker-skinned female, I wondered whether vampires grew paler with age.

The new arrival's fingernails were at least an inch long and painted a purple so deep that it could have been black. Below a thin black turtleneck and a calf-length black pencil skirt, she wore silver-buckled boots with four-inch silver spiked heels.

"She's not even trying to pass," I murmured.

"Three vampires in Litchfield, Connecticut," Declan said. "Are you sure? I expected …"

"Blood-red eyes? Fangs? Deathly pale skin? They're young."

The phone began to ring. I picked up, going through the motions again of calling up to Jasmine's room, though I didn't expect her to answer.

"Three vampires," I said, keeping my back to the predators and my voice as low as possible. Whatever argument they were having by the fire was escalating, but I couldn't hear what was being said. "In the same hotel as Jasmine."

"Jasmine's dating a vampire," Declan said. "Maybe that guy? Though I suppose it could be one of the women. I never ask for details. I can't keep track."

I bit off a retort about his hypocrisy, focusing on the pertinent part of his revelation. "Jasmine's dating a vampire?"

"Yeah. Though I'm not sure dating is the correct term."

"Since when?"

Declan eyed me. "You really don't know?"

The clerk said something over the phone that I didn't quite catch.

"No message, thanks." I carefully replaced the phone in the receiver. Then, thinking quickly through all the possible implications of Jasmine dating a vampire, I pulled my phone out of my bag and texted Kett.

Why are there three vampires in Litchfield?

A response appeared on my screen almost immediately.

>Three vampires. Together?

Does this have something to do with Jasmine?

>You've disturbed a nest in Connecticut? That's very unlikely.

As I'd expected, he didn't offer any response to my query about Jasmine. The vampire clearly enjoyed with-holding information. He was even more controlling than I was. But I kept my mouth shut to protect those I loved, while he seemingly did so to cement his position of power over every situation.

We're in a hotel lobby. Fairhaven Hotel.

>We?

Declan.

>You traced Jasmine to this hotel?

She's registered.

>Stay away from the vampires. They won't know you're under my protection. You have no proof other than your word.

"Who are you texting with?" Declan asked irritably.

"Kett," I said. "The vampire who hired us last October."

I assumed that Jasmine must have mentioned having worked with the executioner when she'd told Declan about our investigation into Teresa, Ben, and the fledgling vampires. Either that, or Declan had been approached about the Conclave contract and was keeping it from me just as much as I was keeping it from him.

And who else would Jasmine be dating? Some random vampire? Or the vampire she'd practically thrown herself at a few months ago? It pained me, actually, that she hadn't mentioned she was seeing Kett in a nonprofessional manner. But then, I hadn't told her about the contract either.

"He says to stay away from the vampires," I added.

"It's terribly sweet of your boyfriend to be concerned about us." Declan's sarcasm quickly turned menacing. "But this is witch territory. We've tracked a missing witch to a hotel occupied by vampires. You do the math."

I didn't correct Declan on his boyfriend assumption, choosing instead to lay a cautioning hand on his arm and adding the sums as I tallied them out loud. "What do you think three vampires are going to do if confronted by the two of us?"

"I don't know about you," Declan said, breaking my hold with a tug of his arm. "But from me, they'll run."

"I've just been working with a vampire," I said, keeping my tone even and professional. "Trust me, the Academy is ill informed when it comes to vampire lore. Or perhaps even deliberately misleading."

Declan locked his dark, angry gaze to mine. "Perhaps you are the one lacking information. About me."

I kept my eye contact steady, but as nonconfrontational as I could. "The only way to destroy vampires is to cut off their heads. In this case, we'd need to do all three at once. Then set them on fire. Remembering that they move quicker than your eye can track, and can break every bone in your body with a twist of the wrist."

Declan's gaze flicked over my shoulder to the vampires still congregated by the lobby fireplace. "Sunlight … wooden stakes … holy water …"

"Not if the vampires are older. And only when wielded by a necromancer of power, plus I think the stake needs to be silver to be truly effective. And no."

Declan's expression blanked.

Then the skin between my shoulder blades started to itch. "We've drawn their attention."

"Yes," he said. "They're moving this way." He slipped his hand in his pocket as if readying one of his spells. "Toward the elevators."

We couldn't get into a magically fueled fight in the lobby of a hotel filled with mundanes. Not only would doing so expose Adepts to the world at large, but I was fairly certain Declan and I wouldn't survive it. My offensive power was limited. And despite the boost the dowser had given my bracelet, I had no idea what the trinket would do against three of the immortal undead.

"Meet me in the parking lot," I said, peeling away from the sideboard and leaving Declan behind.

"What?" he hissed after me.

Head held high, I strolled toward the trio, who were now standing before the bank of elevators. They were already watching me.

Putting a slight sway into my hips, I tugged my cashmere lace scarf away from my neck as if I were sweltering. Touching my exposed skin in a light caress, I then smoothed my hand up and over the back of my French twist.

A wolfish grin spread across the male vampire's face.

A few feet away from them, I deliberately flicked my gaze to each of the females in turn. The darker woman was regarding me coolly, and a sneer had spread across the face of the vampire with the purple nails.

I dropped my gaze as if suddenly overwhelmed by their presence—so that I could unobtrusively glance at the security panel that controlled the elevators. The guests' key cards would confine access to the common areas and the specific floor of the room assigned to each individual in the hotel. The eleventh floor was highlighted on the security screen.

I continued onward, sauntering past the vampires as the door to the elevator opened. The male leaned forward as if to smell me. I practically brushed him with my shoulder.

I held my breath. If he was planning to grab me and haul me into the elevator, I wouldn't have any time to react.

He let me pass.

I glanced back over my shoulder. The male vampire was still watching me, holding the elevator door open with one hand. The other two were waiting within.

Channeling Jasmine, I grinned at him saucily and winked. Then I turned my back on him.

He chuckled huskily. "Witch," he said with some satisfaction. I couldn't place his accent.

"What did you expect?" one of the females snapped. Her voice was American, through and through.

The elevator doors closed. I continued down the hall, pushing open a set of exterior doors that led to an outdoor courtyard and a side parking lot.

I had just completely baited three vampires, and my heart rate wasn't even elevated. So much for following Kett's advice.

Chapter Five

"What the hell was that?" Declan snarled.

I had circled around from the courtyard on the far side of the hotel through the parking lot. Declan was waiting for me, leaning against the nose of the Jeep.

"Eleventh floor," I said, completely composed in the face of his temper. I preferred to not waste my time with bullies, but Declan would have had no way to know that about me.

I crossed to his side as I snugged my cashmere scarf to my neck and rebuttoned my coat. I contemplated grabbing my hat out of my suitcase as I turned to gaze up at the hotel.

Declan grunted something I didn't catch, then crossed around to the driver's side of the Jeep. After digging around behind the seat, he produced a set of binoculars.

"So we just hope they haven't closed the curtains?" he asked snidely.

I shrugged. "And that they're not on the other side of the building."

"Idiotic," he muttered, looking through the binoculars.

"Then we find our way up and start knocking on doors." I was scanning the windows on the eleventh floor, most of the rooms still with their curtains open and appearing empty. TVs were flickering behind a few drawn blinds as well.

"Nothing." Declan lowered the binoculars after a cursory pass. "Is it my turn to tell you to wait while I stalk off and do something completely stupid now?"

"I'll come with you," I said, blithely ignoring his interpretation of my actions. That vampires were either staying at the hotel or meeting someone there was disconcerting—even without factoring in Jasmine's disappearance. And the odds that my cousin wasn't somehow entangled in whatever had drawn the vampires to Connecticut seemed astronomical.

And as such, moving continually forward no matter how thin the lead might be was my only defense against the dread of losing Jasmine—and the agony of being back in Connecticut.

I stepped into the shadows along the edge of the parking lot, Declan at my heels. We circled the hotel property as slowly and unobtrusively as possible. A fence and what appeared to be a massive mechanical room hampered us on the east side, so we backtracked to get around it. Declan took the lead, pausing every so often to gaze up at the hotel and count floors.

Halfway around the building, nearing the courtyard through which I'd exited after my reconnoitering pass of the elevators, the skin between my shoulder blades started to itch.

Someone magically inclined was following us. Or something.

I glanced quickly over both shoulders, seeing only a smaller parking lot to my right, partially filled with cars, and low shrubbery running the length of the fence to my left.

Knowing that any predator who could hide from my sight would most likely have excellent hearing, I slowly reached forward, brushing my fingers against the back of Declan's neck in warning.

He spun around, shoving me behind him while pulling some sort of long, dark object from the inside of his jacket. From the way he held it, it was some sort of weapon.

I tripped over the curb at the edge of the parking lot, tumbling sideways into the low bushes that bordered the property.

Magic exploded, ringing through every one of my senses. Momentarily disoriented, I clamped my hands over my ears, peering up at Declan. He was standing over me, holding what I recognized now as a wooden blasting rod—and looking vaguely confused.

He'd obviously just discharged the weapon. The rune-carved, tapered rod was eighteen inches in length and maybe two inches thick—and similar to the rods Jasper had taught Declan to carve out of maple and ash branches. They were a focus and repository for his unusual witch magic, which had asserted itself while we were all in our midteens. Carrying the rod with him was likely one of the reasons he wore the long leather jacket. But why Declan would need easy access to that sort of firepower, I had no idea.

I cranked my head to see what he'd aimed for.

A white-blond, exceedingly pale vampire was standing a few feet from us, gazing down at his chest. His three-quarter-length black cashmere coat was on fire.

Kettil, the executioner and elder of the Conclave. Apparently, he'd been skulking along the fence line a few steps behind us. And Declan had hit him directly over the heart with whatever explosive spell he'd channeled and amplified with the blasting rod.

Kett casually patted at the flames on his chest, reducing them to embers, then putting them out. Crisped flakes of his jacket and the sweater he was wearing underneath it fluttered down to speckle his high-sheen leather boots. Underneath the ruined sweater, his exposed chest appeared completely unscathed. His skin practically glowed in the moonlight.

I scrambled to my feet, brushing as much dirt and decomposed bark mulch off myself as possible.

The vampire glanced my way, then locked his silvered gaze on Declan, who still held the blasting rod between them. "It takes more than that to kill me."

"I could always push you into a volcano," Declan said with darkly tinted amusement, as if he attempted to take down ancient vampires every day.

"That might do it," Kett said, dispassionately continuing the insane conversation. "Provided I couldn't crawl out quickly enough, and that you wielded enough power to move me in the first place." He curled his lip with a hint of humor. "I know of fifteen beings with such power. Those who could do so, though perhaps not without dying themselves. And nine of them wouldn't bother. I'm nothing to them."

Declan snorted derisively.

I felt a little light-headed. The situation was about to tip over the edge into something terrible, and I wasn't sure I knew how to defuse it.

"You, I could kill with a mere thought." Kett's tone turned stomach-churningly ominous.

"Declan Fairchild," I blurted out in desperation, quickly forcing myself into a more formal tone. "Witch, nephew of Rose Fairchild, healer of the Convocation. Brother of Jasmine." I gestured toward the vampire seemingly carved out of marble. "Kettil, elder and executioner of the Conclave."

Kett held out his hand.

Declan switched the blasting rod to his left hand, grasping the vampire's hand without hesitation with his right.

As they clasped, sparks of Declan's magic cascaded from their mutual grip.

Kett chuckled.

Declan grimaced ruefully. Then he threw his head back and laughed.

They dropped the handshake. Apparently, measurements had been taken, assessed, and accepted—length, width, and power of thrust. They were both acting ridiculous.

"Took you long enough," I said snippily.

"I was aware of where you were at all times," Kett said.

"Because you're tracking me?"

"Do you doubt it? Though a blood exchange would make that easier."

"What the hell?" Declan took a step forward, placing me behind his left shoulder.

Kett didn't take his gaze off me, though his lip curled upward.

"He's playing you, Declan," I said. Then an idea hit me so hard that I could barely believe I'd only just thought of it. I stepped around Declan, charging into Kett's personal space, suddenly and viciously angry. "Tell me this isn't a test!"

"It isn't a test."

I shoved my finger against his exposed chest. My knuckle cracked painfully, but I ignored it as magic gathered around the bracelet hanging from my wrist. "Tell me this isn't a test for Declan."

"A test of what?" Declan echoed behind me, sounding as pissed as always.

Kett regarded me for a moment. Then he offered a hint of a smile. "This isn't a test, Wisteria. I know what Jasmine means to you." He lifted his gaze to take in Declan over my shoulder. "Though I have done nothing to contrive the situation, I will take full advantage of observing the Convocation's most sought-out extraction specialist."

I pivoted back, looking at Declan in disbelief. His face was a cloud of emotion—anger and frustration warring with underlying concern.

"Extraction specialist?" I asked.

Declan only shrugged in response.

"I don't even know what that means."

"It means I like to blow shit up, Wisteria," he said. "That's not news to you."

"No, it isn't," Kett said smoothly. "What is news to Wisteria Fairchild is that you're working for the Convocation at all. You and Jasmine. You are an interesting trio. I look forward to seeing all three of you in the same space."

I eyed the vampire. "Don't be creepy, Kett."

He laughed quietly.

"What have you and Jasmine been up to?" I asked. "Tracking Nigel's maker?"

"Indeed."

"And it brought her here?"

Kett lifted his gaze to the hotel. "Apparently. Though she didn't share whatever drew her home with me."

"And how exactly do you know each other?" Declan asked. "I'm sure the Conclave's executioner has better things to be doing than hanging out with a couple of low-rank witches."

I glared at him for the 'low rank' comment, but neither Kett nor I bothered to answer his question.

"They're on the eleventh floor," I said. "At least they went up there about twenty minutes ago."

Kett nodded.

"Do vampires often stay in hotels?" I asked.

"Follow me in two minutes," he said. Then he disappeared.

Declan flinched. "Jesus Christ!"

"It's a trick," I said with an offish wave of my hand. "He just moves quickly and uses the shadows to his advantage. He doesn't teleport or anything."

Declan was staring at me as if I'd gone insane. I waited patiently, expecting to be bombarded with questions.

But he only opened his mouth, then shut it. Twisting away, he ran his hand through his hair before finally speaking. "So this is the vampire Jasmine is dating, then?"

"I'm not sure. We'll have to ask him."

He turned back to stare at me, as aghast as he was frustrated. "The executioner of the Conclave."

"Yes."

Declan raised his left arm, still holding the blasting rod. The runes etched along it were glowing a faint blue. "I hit him. I wasn't trying to kill anyone, but that blast, point-blank like that, should have taken him down."

"Yes."

"Are you dating him?"

"No. He'll get pissy, though, if we don't follow in exactly two minutes. All right?"

Declan didn't respond.

"Declan. Jasmine might be in the hotel, and—"

"Yeah, yeah. Fine. Let's just follow the uber-powerful vampire into a hotel filled with vulnerable humans."

"The three vampires already in there are the only ones we should be worried about. At least for right now."

I stepped past him, swiftly crossing through the courtyard toward the side door I'd exited twenty minutes before.

Declan matched me stride for stride. "He's different than them."

"Older," I said. "More powerful."

He didn't comment further.

I paused before the glassed doors of the side entrance, checking my reflection and confirming that I was tidy enough to be wandering around the hotel without drawing attention.

Inside, the doors to the nearest elevator opened and Kett stepped out. He was already looking our way, expectant. His ruined sweater had been swapped out for a dark-green T-shirt. The damage to his black cashmere jacket was less obvious.

Declan reached around my shoulder, opening the door before me.

I stepped through, murmuring polite thanks as I did so.

The elevator door closed behind Kett, who waited for a moment to give us time to traverse the hall. Then he turned and tapped a white plastic key card against the security panel, punching in the eleventh floor.

I didn't ask where or how he'd sourced the room key. Because I knew he wouldn't bother answering anyway, deeming the question either beneath him or the answer obvious.

I stepped up beside the vampire, facing the elevator and waiting for it to return. Declan stood shoulder to shoulder with me, his gaze fixed to the vampire on my other side. Kett remained still, staring straight ahead rather than up at the numbers flashing above the door.

"You got the bag," he said. His tone was hushed, almost intimate. Perhaps even slightly anxious.

"Yes," I said. "I … it was waiting for me this morning, along with the package addressed to the Conclave. Thank you."

"It took me a while to source it."

"Yes. It's from the 2010 collection. I appreciate your time."

Kett nodded sparely. I caught the movement in my peripheral vision as the elevator doors slid open before us.

We entered in silence. After a moment, the door closed behind us. There were no room number buttons on the inside panel, only a display declaring the eleventh floor as the next stop. It made perfect sense given the security features the hotel employed for the elevator system. But for some reason, it made me exceedingly aware of the confined, almost suffocating nature of the space around me. I was hemmed in, with Declan on my left and Kett on my right.

"Breathe," Kett whispered.

Declan looked at him sharply.

I wrapped my hand over top of my coat sleeve, feeling the bracelet underneath dig into the skin of my wrist. "Did you find them?" I asked, keeping my thoughts focused on the task ahead.

"No," Kett said. "But they've been here."

"And Jasmine?"

"Not that I picked up."

The elevator doors opened, and Kett stepped into the corridor.

"We're just supposed to follow him around?" Declan asked, too loudly.

I stepped out of the elevator as Kett reappeared at the end of the hall, pausing for us to catch up. At least, that was what I assumed he was doing.

"Since he's the invulnerable one," I said to Declan, "following behind is prudent."

"He could be leading us into their lair," Declan said, stepping in front of me to stop my forward progress without touching me.

"The ones we saw aren't his ... nest mates," I said, stumbling over the proper group noun for vampires.

"And how do you know?" Declan asked. "If you aren't seeing him? Because you sure as hell aren't friends."

I gazed up at him. I understood he was angry with me. And that he was frustrated by the situation and the lack of information. But we needed to be moving forward, not arguing over small details in the middle of a hotel corridor. "Why are we here?" I asked pointedly.

"Don't school me, Wisteria."

"Then stop demanding to be schooled."

Declan glared at me. I held his gaze steadily, but every tense second that I did so, my mind screamed for me to soothe his anger and placate his concerns.

Except I needed him focused and angry, and I had no actual answers with which to soothe him.

He dropped my gaze. "Fine. I'll back you."

I nodded and stepped ahead.

He whispered something harsh under his breath. It sounded like, "As always."

My heart sank in my chest, and I almost faltered. No matter what I said or didn't say, it seemed I couldn't help but hurt Declan. And Jasmine. Both of them always wanted answers and assurances I couldn't give. I knew that Jasmine would have said that wasn't true, and that all she wanted was to be let in, to participate in our relationship as an equal. But I never knew what to do with that statement.

I squared my shoulders and strode forward to the vampire waiting for me at the end of the hall. He was emulating a statue as he was prone to doing—and most likely listening in on everything and everyone in the nearby rooms, in addition to the argument between Declan and me.

Kett rested his silver-blue gaze on me as I paused beside him, raising his eyebrow. "Ready now?"

Even I could hear the mocking in his tone.

"Are the vampires near?" I asked.

"I believe they've left, or they are elsewhere in the hotel," Kett said. "I'll let you into the room, leaving you to your reconstruction while I search further." He shifted his focus to Declan. "I assume you are somewhat capable of watching over the reconstructionist while she works?"

"Yeah," Declan said sarcastically. "Somewhat capable."

I ignored him to question Kett. "There's magic within the hotel room to reconstruct?"

The vampire nodded as he continued down the hall, finally pausing to slide his key card into the door lock on room 1115.

I was feeling slightly disoriented now that we were inside, but I was fairly certain we hadn't scanned the windows on this side of the hotel yet.

Kett opened the door, stepping partway in and flicking on a light.

"Kett," I whispered, my words momentarily catching in my throat, "is there … blood? Jasmine's blood?" Tears welled behind my eyes, but I held them back fiercely.

Kett brushed his fingers against my cheek so lightly and quickly that I saw the movement only as he withdrew his hand. "I would have prepared you," he said, "if that were the case."

I nodded, reaching for and pulling a candle out of my bag. I needed to focus on collecting clues rather than my fundamental fear that Jasmine might be injured or dead.

"I'll be back before you're done," Kett said. Then he disappeared from my sight a second time.

Declan darted forward, stopping the door with his foot before it closed. Then he gave me a withering look. "You aren't dating the vamp. Right."

He stepped inside the hotel room without waiting for me to answer. I almost admonished him about possibly contaminating the reconstruction I was about to collect. But then I reminded myself that I knew the tenor of Declan's magic almost as well as I knew my own.

Room 1115 appeared to have been recently cleaned. Declan crossed the length of the small living area, tugging the curtains closed. The decor was modern, echoing the black-and-gold palette of the lobby, though less intensely. The bed, pillows, and shams were swathed in white cotton linen with black piping. A muted gold duvet was neatly folded across the end of the bed. Two side tables, a desk, a sideboard for the TV—all stained a dark walnut—and a black, square-edged chair all made for nothing out of the ordinary in the room.

Except for the large pocket of residual magic occupying the space between the foot of the bed and the TV.

I glanced into the bathroom, noting the sparkling chrome faucets and the perfectly fluffed, folded towels. Then I stepped halfway into the room, following Declan as I held my right hand out to the magic hanging in an invisible cloud three feet off the ground.

Declan glanced at me. "I felt it too."

I nodded, not surprised. He'd walked right through the residual.

"No one has been here since housekeeping cleaned this afternoon," I said, tugging the rest of my pillar candles free from my bag and placing them around the room one by one.

Declan frowned. "Except the vampires, you mean."

"Well, no one who leaves fingerprints. Or footprints, for that matter."

Declan glanced at the tightly woven, light-beige carpet beneath our feet. "Don't mythologize them, Wisteria. They aren't gods. Any dirt they picked up outside would have been scuffed off in the lobby before they even hit the elevators."

"No, they aren't gods," I said agreeably, circling the room a second time to light my candles. "Just immortal and invulnerable. And possibly playing some game with the Conclave that Jasmine has gotten mixed up in."

"And why is that exactly?" Declan asked pointedly.

I stood at the base of the bed with my back to the curtained windows and Declan. Without answering him, I raised my palms toward the residual magic and closed the circle I'd paced out.

"Does it have something to do with the case you worked with her in Astoria?" he asked.

"Perhaps." Keeping my attention on the interior of my circle, I coaxed the residual forward. It revealed itself as a swirl streaked with teal blue. "Witch magic," I said, identifying it by color and tenor. "But I don't think it's Jasmine's."

Declan stepped forward, standing beside me and pressing his hand to the invisible edge of my circle. As he had in Jasmine's bedroom, he tapped effortlessly into the reconstruction I was collecting.

"Copper's," he said thoughtfully.

"The magic belongs to a witch named Copper? You know her?"

He nodded. "Proficient in charms."

"And tracking spells?" I asked, clumsily tying the conversation back to the witch who'd tried to track Jasmine on

Declan's behalf when he'd received the cellphone. The witch he'd hesitated to mention.

"Yeah," he said begrudgingly. "And tracking spells."

"Spells she sells? Specifically to Jasmine?"

"I think this was part of a set of spells she gave Jasmine as a Christmas gift."

My heart sank. Part of me had been hoping that the residual witch magic wouldn't be tied to Jasmine.

"Call it forth, Wisteria." Declan's voice was demanding, but then his tone softened slightly. "The vampire said Jasmine hadn't died here."

"No," I said tightly. "He just said there wasn't any blood."

Declan glanced at me, concern overriding his seemingly perpetual gruffness.

"The vampire," I said pointedly, "has a certain way of phrasing things. Or of not speaking, actually. I'm sure you'll pick it up soon enough."

"I don't plan on getting to know him as intimately as you obviously do."

I matched his offish drawl. "Well, I certainly don't know him intimately enough to pick up his magic in a circle not of my own construction with a single glance. I'm guessing Copper is proficient in more than just spells."

Declan curled his lip at me. Then he snorted. "You can't be jealous, Wisteria. Just because you don't want me in your life, it doesn't mean I have to be celibate."

I opened my mouth to retort, but he leaned in to me. He was close enough that his breath stirred the hair at my temple that had worked its way out of my French twist.

"And I'm definitely not celibate." There was a deep layer of loathing laced through his innuendo.

I met his gaze, completely weary of his incessant hostility. Jasmine might be dead. I could be about to reconstruct the moment of her death.

"Shall we continue, Declan? Or shall we waste more time while you snarl and strut? You've made your feelings known, from the moment you first called. But then, I've known how little you ever truly loved me, at least beyond the bonds that Jasper forced upon us, for a very long time now."

Declan stilled, eyeing me darkly. "I could say the same."

I shrugged as if it all meant nothing to me. I was back in Connecticut for Jasmine, not for some long-lost lovers' reunion.

He nodded stiffly, then returned his gaze to the circle.

I didn't bother trying to figure out what he was thinking. I wasn't a teenager anymore, desperate for someone to love me. I was an adult who wore her white picket fence on her wrist, knowing she'd never have any part of what it represented. I'd arrived at that resolution years ago—and having Declan by my side again made it that much more painful, but not any less true.

I called the residual magic in the circle toward me, speaking out loud for Declan's benefit as I would have for any other investigative partner. "No other magic in the room, just this pocket. Jasmine must have not stayed here at all. There aren't any personal items."

Declan grunted, acknowledging me but not contributing his own observations.

The residual magic resolved into a flash of movement, coming back toward us from the door. Multiple people, but moving so quickly that I couldn't track them without slowing the reconstruction down. I couldn't modify the initial manifestation while I collected it, though. I had to wait for whatever scene I'd captured to play out backward. Then I could pause and enhance it.

Jasmine appeared in the center of the room, her back toward me. Her dark-blond hair was a cascade of curls across her shoulders. She was wearing dark-blue jeans and a three-quarter-length brown suede jacket I'd never seen before.

She was also surrounded by three vampires. The two females from the lobby, dressed as Declan and I had seen them, along with a ruddy-haired male in pale-blue jeans and a long-sleeved dark-brown henley. I didn't recognize him as he pulled Jasmine toward him, then set her on her feet. Or, rather, as he picked her up and tossed her sideways in reverse.

"They grabbed her," Declan said. He was gritting his teeth.

I nodded, trying to keep calm. "I'll slow it down for the next viewing. But ... we know she's alive."

"She was alive."

"She is alive," I said, gaining confidence as what appeared to be a conversation played out backward before us. "They want something from the Conclave. They kidnapped her. But she's just a bargaining chip."

"Why can't we hear what they're saying?"

"Backward? Just wait for the playback."

A pool of magic flowed out around Jasmine, as if she'd just triggered a spell. It matched the tenor and color of the residual I'd felt when entering the room.

Then the reconstruction winked out.

Declan stumbled, pressing against the circle for a second before steadying himself. "What the hell was that?"

"That was all there is," I said, gathering the magic to me a second time.

"Three vampires and a witch, and that was all you picked up?"

"Vampires don't emanate magic the same way other Adepts do," I said, keeping my tone crisply professional. "If magic isn't directly involved, as in a confrontation, then there won't be anything for me to collect. I'm not a sensitive."

"I know you aren't," Declan said. "But you are tuned to Jasmine."

"And she wasn't doing anything magical until the moment she dropped whatever spell she got from your friend, Copper." Unintentionally, I enunciated the word 'friend' with too much emotional distaste for my own liking.

Unfortunately, Declan picked up on my annoyance, choosing to smirk knowingly at me instead of correcting or confirming my impression.

I looked away. Declan wasn't a crack in my armor. Rather, he and Jasmine—or at least my love for both of them—were my armor against everything terrible in the rest of the world. And as such, my well-honed emotional shields apparently couldn't keep him out. Still, I had a feeling that spending enough time with him would build up my resistance out of self-preservation, if nothing else.

I could only be hated to my face for so long without shutting down completely.

But the thought of becoming emotionally numb to Declan made me profoundly sad. Ignoring the heaviness settling in my chest, I focused my attention back on the dormant magic in the circle. I skirted around the edges of my barrier along the front of the TV cabinet until I stood with my back to the door—a vantage point that would allow me to see Jasmine's face without playing with the magic too much.

Declan was watching me closely, but he lifted his hand to the circle without comment, maintaining his position on the other side of the room and giving me some much-appreciated space.

"Ready?" I asked. My heart felt as though it was lodged in my throat. But the only sure way to get it loose was going to be watching three vampires kidnap my best friend, then finding the next clue.

Declan nodded.

I called the magic forth. It collected at my bidding, resolving into the moment before a spell was set off within the reconstruction. A cloud of teal-blue magic appeared before us, though it was most likely only visible from within the circle. To my eyes, at least.

"A reveal spell," Declan muttered, picking up the tenor of the magic before I did.

The light in the room shifted, becoming more concentrated around the desk where a lamp was illuminated next to a laptop.

Jasmine appeared, surrounded by the three vampires—the two females from before and the male I didn't recognize. She looked tired, but determined.

"The dark-haired vampire is missing," I said, smothering the well of emotion that came from seeing Jasmine surrounded by vampires with a cool-headed assessment of the scene. "And the room isn't as tidy. The magic feels relatively recent, but we'll have to look for other clues as to when this occurred. Last night or the evening before, perhaps."

"And what was she trying to reveal with the spell?" Declan asked. "Were the vampires cloaked? Is rendering themselves invisible something they can do?"

Jasmine shifted her gaze past the vampires until she was looking directly at me. As if she could actually see me standing before her.

"No," I whispered, as my belly hollowed. "Me. She was trying to see me."

"That doesn't make any sense—"

"Wisteria." Jasmine spoke within the reconstruction.

The three vampires whirled around in a blur of motion, their surprise turning into frowns when they apparently saw nothing and no one behind them.

"You've got this, babe," Jasmine said, continuing to speak to me as if I were in the room with her. "They're looking for Kett, because we're looking for them."

The olive-skinned vampire in the long pencil skirt and the four-inch silver heels snarled. "Who the hell are you talking to?"

Jasmine sneered at her. "You can't kidnap a Fairchild witch without retribution."

"Are we kidnapping you?" the ruddy-haired vampire asked with amusement. His accent was melodic.

"He sounds Irish," I said out loud, desperately trying to glean each and every clue as it was revealed.

"Could be Welsh," Declan said. "I had a couple of buddies from Wales in school. I've worked with them a few times since."

"There's a secondary glinting around them," I said, pausing the reconstruction for a moment. "Hints of blue in her aura." I pointed to the olive-skinned female, then to the male. "White, or maybe silver around him?"

Declan didn't answer.

I thought about the magic I'd seen gathered around Kett when I glanced at him through my reconstruction circle. Blue witch magic had been pooled in his palm. "Secondary powers? Like they were Adepts before they were remade?"

"Does it matter?" Declan asked impatiently. "Just play it through."

Understanding his frustration, I let my hold on the magic loosen, allowing the scene to continue.

Jasmine lifted her hand, dramatically pointing her finger toward the hotel door, toward me. "I call forth vengeance. She'll come with thunder and lightning at her right, and blood and fangs at her left. She'll come for you." She locked her fierce, blue-eyed gaze on the male. "She'll come for you, Yale Evans, maker of Nigel Farris."

Jasmine paused for dramatic effect as the two female vampires looked at the male in unison. The smirk had been wiped from his face.

"Who the hell is she talking about?" the darker-skinned vampire in the long mink coat asked him. Her English was also accented.

I glanced at Declan. "Spanish? Latin American?"

He nodded.

"No one," the vampire who Jasmine had identified as Yale Evans said.

Jasmine laughed. "Even vampires need bank accounts and credit cards, Yale, sire of Nigel."

"Don't call me that," he snapped. Any charm he'd been putting on earlier had evaporated with his mounting anger.

Jasmine looked back at me—or, rather, to where she knew I'd be standing in order to view the reconstruction. "Come get me, Betty-Sue. Thirty-three point three percent sign dash BBB three asterisks."

"She's just talking gibberish now." The olive-skinned vampire moved in a blur, retrieving Jasmine's laptop, satchel, and phone.

Jasmine, effortlessly robbed of her possessions, lifted her chin defiantly.

"You'll answer my questions one way or the other," Yale said.

"My name is Jasmine Fairchild, witch, niece to Rose of the Convocation, of the Fairchild coven." Jasmine recited her credentials with no emotion. "I'm in the employ of Kettil, the executioner of the Conclave. Walk away now and you might survive. Or at least get a chance to explain your actions. I'll make a phone call." She looked pointedly at Yale and sneered. "Nigel's sire."

Yale moved so quickly that Declan flinched. The vampire grabbed Jasmine around the neck, lifting her chin with his thumb and looming threateningly over her.

My chest tightened. She was baiting him deliberately. It was completely stupid, but Jasmine understood that I needed residual to reconstruct in order to retrieve the clues she was leaving. She wouldn't have known how long the magic of the reveal spell would linger, but goading the vampires into action would trigger their magic in a way that would have let me call it forth.

She curled her lip at the vampire poised to break her neck. "Stop trying to ensnare me, you cheap knockoff."

Declan groaned at the insult.

"Fairchild witches aren't so easily taken," Jasmine said.

"I don't see you putting up any sort of defense," the dark-skinned vampire sneered.

Jasmine, her head still awkwardly cranked backward by Yale, angled her gaze in my direction. She smiled knowingly. "Betty-Sue is so going to kick your asses."

"Stop looking over there," Yale snarled. Then he flung Jasmine away, tossing her into the arms of the mink-swathed female.

The vampires exited with Jasmine in a blur of motion, passing through the barrier of the circle into the hallway behind me. The magic within the reconstruction dissipated.

My legs gave out. I crumpled to the ground, staring at the empty space where Jasmine had just been standing. "She expected me to be here. She expected me to come."

"Of course she did," Declan said. "Just like she assumed I'd be with you. The idea that we'd band together for her goes without question." Then he strode past me and into the corridor. "I'll look for residual in the hallway."

Barely hearing Declan, I remained on my knees. I was out of my element—and quite possibly completely mishandling the entire investigation. This was the reason there were rules about investigators being personally involved in their cases.

"She expected me to find her," I murmured. "She thinks I can take on three ... four vampires."

Declan stepped back into the room behind me. "She doesn't expect you to fight them in hand-to-hand combat, Wisteria. Get off the floor."

Automatically obeying the tone of command in his voice, I gathered my feet underneath me though I didn't stand. "Thunder and lightning," I said. "That's you."

"Obviously."

"Blood and fangs."

"Kett." Declan spat the vampire's name with derision.

I smiled. I couldn't help it. Both Declan's instinctual loathing of Kett—of anyone who might threaten his sister—and Jasmine's outrageous behavior in the face of her own quite-possibly pending death were just so perfectly them. The 'them' that filled me, heart and soul.

I straightened, crossing the room to grab one of my oyster-shell cubes from my bag. I needed to shake off some of the self-doubt I had about my own abilities—by doing what I did best.

"After I collect this, I should reconstruct the hallway," I said, placing the cube in the center of the dormant circle. "If possible."

Declan nodded absentmindedly. "What was that 33 percent stuff?

"Her password." I called forth the magic within the circle a third time, so that I could channel it into the cube at my feet. "To follow the money."

"They took her laptop."

"So they did. But we just need to access her remote backup."

There wasn't enough residual magic in the corridor for me to reconstruct, though presumably the vampires must have traversed the hallway multiple times. So I collected my candles from the hotel room while Declan methodically searched all the drawers, then looked under the bed for any other clues.

"Why were they here tonight at all?" Declan said, scanning the room one last time. "Why come back?"

"To leave this," Kett said. He appeared beside us suddenly, holding a letter-sized envelope.

Declan flinched, began to snarl at the vampire, then checked himself. He took the proffered envelope, pulling a folded piece of paper out through the torn flap.

"I'd like to view the reconstruction," Kett said to me.

"What the hell is this?" Declan snarled in Kett's face as he thrust the paper and envelope in my direction. "Jasmine is being held as what? Collateral? A bargaining chip? What the hell have you gotten my sister into, sending her after them with no assurances of your protection? Leaving her at the mercy of your own kind?"

Kett stilled in that way he did. As if he had gathered all his magic tightly around him, and was about to rip out Declan's throat.

Panic flooded through me. I involuntarily crumpled the note in my hand without actually seeing what was written on it.

"Well?" Declan asked snidely. "What have you got to say for yourself, vampire?"

"Please," I whispered. "Please. Don't."

Kett's gaze flicked to me. His silvered eyes held no hint of red, yet I understood how angry he was.

"Don't what?" Declan asked. "Don't illuminate me? If you want my help, Wisteria, you've got to stop keeping goddamn secrets."

I tore my gaze from Kett, meeting Declan's scowl with as much composure as I could summon. "You know Jasmine makes her own choices."

"Influenced by him!"

Declan thrust his finger in Kett's direction. I waited a breath, but the vampire thankfully kept his gaze on me rather than amputating the offending digit.

"Shouting is not the way to deal with this situation, Declan," I said.

"Maybe if you gave a damn about anything, Wisteria," he snarled, "then maybe you'd understand the need to fight for it."

Anger replaced the wash of panic that had kept me rooted to the carpet. I stepped closer to Declan. He stumbled back from whatever he saw on my face, raising his hand as if to hold me off or grab me.

"Perhaps if you took a moment to listen, Declan," I said. "Perhaps if you took a moment to consider and absorb the situation, you wouldn't need to bully all the answers out. Perhaps then you wouldn't be so quick to condemn the rest of us for trying to maintain some sense of equilibrium."

Declan clenched his jaw in frustration. Then he stormed out of the room without another word.

I pressed my hands to my heated face, meeting Kett's gaze. He raised an eyebrow, tilting his head slightly.

"That was ... I was ... " I murmured. "That was possibly an overreaction."

"You were lovers," Kett said. "I wasn't sure. Is that the root of the schism in the Fairchild clan? I'm not well-versed in modern-day society, but given that you're not blood related, that would seem to be an extreme reaction."

Not answering him—mostly because the story was too convoluted to tell concisely, but also because it was too intimate a topic—I dropped my hands and crossed to the desk to retrieve the reconstruction from my bag.

Kett was beside me before I placed the magic-filled cube down on the desk. He reached out, hovering his fingers over the bracelet on my right wrist. And for a brief moment, I almost leaned against him for comfort.

"Will Declan Benoit stand between you and your future, Wisteria Fairchild?" Kett's whispered breath brushed against my temple.

I stared down at the two tiny reconstructions nestled with the charms on my bracelet. "What future?" My question was tinged with more grief than I wanted to admit. "The one defined by the contract with the Conclave?"

Kett moved his hand away from my bracelet without answering.

I glanced over at him. "You haven't crossed Declan off yet."

"I haven't."

"But you have investigated him?"

"Not as thoroughly as I scrutinized you." The vampire's tone was almost playful.

I looked away from him. There wasn't anything fun about the situation, not with the contract or with Jasmine missing.

"You are exceedingly shaken by Jasmine's disappearance," Kett said. "Both of you."

"Her kidnapping. And yes."

"Show me the reconstruction." He placed his fingertips on the edges of the cube.

Placing my fingers opposite his, I triggered the magic it held. But I couldn't rewatch the scene myself. Not yet. I was too riled up.

Staying close by so I could stop or retrigger the play-back if Kett desired it, I retrieved the note from the vampires that I'd inadvertently crumpled and dropped. Smoothing the paper out on the desk, I noted that it was embossed with the hotel's logo, and handwritten in a barely discernible scrawl.

We have your witch.
Tell us where to meet you.

I pulled out my phone, finding the picture I'd taken of the FedEx envelope and comparing the handwriting of the label to that of the letter. It wasn't a match. Though that didn't mean much with at least four vampires involved.

I cast my gaze around the desk, finding the folder that contained the hotel's complimentary paper, envelopes, and a pen. It was the same paper, the logo identical. I flicked on the desk lamp and held the top sheet up to the light, so that I could see impressions denting its otherwise blank surface. One of the vampires we'd seen in the lobby must have written the note while we were skulking around outside, trying to peer into the hotel's windows.

I picked up the pen and wrote my own note on the blank sheet.

Fairchild Park
Care of Rose Fairchild.
– Wisteria

I glanced over at Kett. He'd finished watching the reconstruction. He read my note, then plucked the pen from my hand, adding a short dash and the letter K underneath my signature.

That initial was an exact replica of the initial beside each of the names that had been crossed off the contract I was still carrying in my bag. Just written now in black ink, rather than blood. Blood would probably get the other vampires' attention, but it seemed unlikely that an elder would leave random samples around for his enemies to collect. Though perhaps such forms of malicious blood magic were a witch thing, not a vampire thing.

"Do you know any of them?" I asked, referencing the reconstruction he'd just watched. "Will they hurt her?"

"They won't come back while I'm here," Kett said, which didn't remotely answer either of my questions. "Otherwise, I would have you go to Rose's without me. That is if they have a lick of sense, which is not a certainty given the scene you collected."

As he turned to leave, I grabbed for him, unable to articulate all the things I needed to ask. I expected him to instantly shake me off. He didn't.

Instead, the vampire stepped closer, bowing his head to me.

"Please," I whispered. "Please."

Kett smiled, though there was no warmth in his ice-blue eyes. "No one takes anything or anyone who is under my protection, Wisteria."

"And if they have? If they've already killed her?"

"Then they are even more foolish than they appear to be."

As I tightened my grip on him, his gaze fell to my hand—or perhaps to the unnaturally shiny bracelet at my wrist.

"Shall I offer you assurances based on unverified observations? Falsehoods to ease your fear?"

Reining in the aching terror that felt as though it had been threatening to consume me for the entire day, I let go of him. I'd been gripping his forearm so tightly that my hand ached when I released it. "No."

I stepped back, glancing down at the note I'd left on the table. "Just tell me everything you've picked up from the reconstruction. Every observation that you believe I should have already made."

"Treat you like you are incompetent?"

I laughed harshly, not looking at him. "Yes. For this moment."

"Very well. Three vampires—"

"Four," I interjected without thinking. "There's another male who we saw in the lobby."

Kett didn't continue. I tore my gaze away from the note on the desk, looking over at him.

He raised an eyebrow at me.

"I apologize for interrupting," I said. "I'll share my observations after."

"They are a brood, a shiver, which in and of itself is unusual, especially given their apparent youth."

"How is that different than a nest?" I asked, already having forgotten that I wasn't going to interrupt again.

"These vampires are blood related."

"Siblings?"

"The one Jasmine referred to as Yale is their master."

"Nigel's maker."

"Apparently."

"The target of your and Jasmine's investigation."

Kett didn't answer.

Worried that we were nearing the end of the allotted time for my Q&A session, I blurted out my next questions. "Why kidnap Jasmine at all? If they wanted to talk with you, why not just arrange a meeting?"

"Why do you think?"

"She's a bargaining chip, as Declan said. So that you'll listen, rather than simply slaughtering them."

"They are woefully ill informed."

"Because you don't simply execute any vampire that isn't a member of the Conclave?"

"Did I kill Nigel?"

"You needed him."

Kett eyed me. "If you have steadied your nerves, perhaps we should move on so that the brood will return to retrieve your message."

I clenched one fist. And for a brief moment, I contemplated punching him.

He curled his lip at me.

"Caring about Jasmine doesn't make me weak, vampire," I said.

"Wallowing in the fear of what might happen to her does, witch."

Kett's tone was reserved and without heat, but his chiding was clearly articulated nonetheless.

I looked away, carefully squaring the note I'd written so it was centered on the desk. Then I tucked the vampires' note and the reconstruction cube into my bag.

Intending to just walk away, I crossed by Kett. But then I stepped back to catch his eye. "It would be easy, or at least simpler, to blame this on you, Kettil. And the only reason I'm not doing so is that I just want her back. Are you going to help or hinder?"

He eyed me dispassionately for a moment. "Help. If you'll let me."

"If I'll trust you? To side with witches over your own kind?"

"A well-reasoned concern."

"I understand that vampires are rare. Perhaps even more so than the Conclave would allow us to believe. The careful language of the contract in my bag tells me that much."

"And I understand that trust isn't a form of attachment either of us is well versed in."

I eyed Kett for a moment. He gazed back at me, unflinching.

I nodded. Then I strode from the hotel room with an ancient vampire by my side. It was unnerving that he could draw a parallel between us so easily, but that was something to fret about after we got Jasmine back.

Declan was waiting in the hall, leaning back with his foot belligerently up against the wall behind him. I nodded at him, and he offered me a stiff smile. Kett and he ignored each other as we crossed back to the elevators in silent acceptance of the situation.

The odds were stacked against Declan and me—two witches versus four vampires—and we needed any aid or resources Kett could offer. And if Jasmine was tangled up in all this because of a job she was doing for Kett, for the Conclave, then the vampire was presumably almost as invested in sorting it out as Declan and I were.

It was the 'almost' that gave me pause, though. If something else was going on, two witches versus four vampires could easily turn. But into what, I had no idea.

Chapter Six

Rose's home, Fairchild Park, marked the outskirts of Fairchild territory in Connecticut. Even still, the family as a whole owned properties and businesses all over North America, including vacation homes in the Caribbean and Mexico. In one of which, apparently Jasper was currently vacationing in luxury even after everything that had happened.

As children, Jasmine, Declan, and I had once spent an entire day walking the thirty-six miles from Fairchild Manor to Fairchild Park, where Rose fed us chicken and ice cream. Then Jasper arrived to retrieve us. The drive back had taken thirty minutes.

That day, at the age of nine, I'd learned more about myself and the world I inhabited than I ever would again. I learned exactly how quickly my freedom could be snatched away. And I'd also learned that no adult would ever do for me what I was willing to do for Jasmine and Declan. If there were stands to be taken or sacrifices to be made, they weren't going to be taken or made by any of the elder Fairchilds.

So in the space of that single day, I'd learned how to endure. How to place myself between my family and the only two people I loved.

I had learned how to bide my time. To grow strong. To absorb every scrap of knowledge that my family had to impart.

Then I figured out all on my own how to turn that knowledge against anyone who would try to interfere with the bond between Jasmine, Declan, and me.

On that day, the three of us had been smuggling a rabbit sentenced to death in the first of the many cruel training sessions that would shape our childhoods. We'd brought the rabbit to Rose for protection, hoping that she'd shelter all of us from Jasper. But now, as Declan drove the Jeep through the open gates of Fairchild Park and up the drive toward the large white house, death was riding shotgun.

Declan dropped Kett and me at the front doors, pulling the Jeep through the wards and into the garage set back from the house. We had decided on the way over that it was better to approach Rose formally, presenting ourselves and Kett to the head of the Fairchild coven as any visiting Adepts would, rather than texting or calling ahead. But I found it interesting that Declan was already keyed to the wards on Fairchild Park, and that he apparently carried a garage door opener.

Rose and Fairchild Park were considered the Adept authority and power in Litchfield—and, as far as witches were concerned, the entire Eastern Seaboard. As such, the property's perimeter wards were normally simply a warning system, similar to a magical doorbell. Adepts could come onto the property to pay their respects without having to wait on the street. But those wards could be called upon to ruthlessly enforce the property's boundaries if the need ever arose. So attacking a Fairchild on Fairchild land was beyond moronic.

The vampires could come to the house to meet us—as I'd suggested in my note—but if they instigated anything, they wouldn't be able to leave without a fight.

A light rain had started while we were in the hotel, then continued as we made our way over to Rose's. But the bright, almost perfectly full moon broke through the clouds as we were approaching the drive. The house was a well-maintained five-bedroom mansion in the Greek revival style. Thick white columns flanked the well-lit front entrance, while white-painted siding and bold but simple moldings encased the two-storey home.

White-fenced rose gardens dominated the large front yard, with various trees occupying the outer boundaries of the property. From late spring on, the yard would be a riot of color contrasting and playing off the white house and the neatly trimmed green lawn, but the bare boughs and branches were unremarkable in the gloom of winter. Though it seemed unlikely that Kett would give Rose's carefully crafted gardens a second glance either way.

My aunt would have known of our arrival the moment we drove onto the property, but she waited until I knocked to open the red-painted front door. The magical wards coating the house simmered between us. Rose's wide smile dimmed slightly upon seeing the vampire standing to my left. Gazing at Kett, she snugged her quilted pink silk robe around her neck. Apparently, we'd roused her from her bed. The exterior light above the door accentuated her pallid complexion and shockingly thin face. As I'd had to at Grey and Dahlia's, I tamped down on the unease that curdled in my stomach at the sight of whatever was ailing her.

After a moment of taking in the impassive vampire, Rose looked at me expectantly.

"Kettil, executioner and elder of the Conclave," I said. "Rose Fairchild, head of the coven, member of the witches Convocation."

Rose grew even paler at the pronouncement of Kett's titles, but he simply inclined his head, remaining silent. I was already well aware that the vampire was an expert at biding his time.

"We seek respite while we await a message," I said stiffly.

Rose looked aghast. "You don't need permission to enter, Wisteria. This is your ... ancestral home."

"I believe it is best to keep our interactions professional," I said.

Rose looked as though I'd stabbed her in the chest. But then she quickly composed her expression, stepped back, and nodded for us to enter. The invisible wards shifted, creating a pocket through which we could pass unhindered.

Kett swept his hand forward, indicating that I should precede him. He tilted his head my way, looking amused.

I ignored him as I stepped into the entranceway. The library ran to our right, overlooking the front yard. Rose was already crossing through to the formal drawing room to the left. Treating us as guests.

Kett slipped through the wards behind me as I strode after my aunt, noting that she'd updated the interior sometime in the previous twelve years. The white walls and wide moldings were freshly painted, and the wide planks of the dark wood flooring that ran throughout most of the house had been sanded, stained, and satin polished.

The drawing room was situated through an open archway off the main entrance, as were the library and the dining room. The kitchen and utility rooms were at the back of the house. Sliding pocket doors between the various rooms offered privacy, but were rarely used. High ceilings ran throughout the house, and the decor was replete with cozy antiques.

Rose crossed directly through the drawing room, a blazing fire flaring to life suddenly among the wood already stacked up in the brick fireplace. As she passed, my aunt lightly touched one of the two decorative urns on the mantel, both of which contained my grandparents' ashes.

I paused at the edge of the fringed rug, taking off my wool coat and folding it over my arm. An aqua-blue button-tufted sofa I didn't recognize occupied the right wall. A second wide doorway to Rose's right led into the dining room.

Kett stepped just inside the room behind me, casting his impassive gaze over a series of framed miniature portraits on the wall above a round antique table topped with a large bouquet of white-and-pink roses.

My aunt turned to face Kett and me. She looked desperately tired. Saddened. Almost infirm. And for the briefest of moments, I had to stop myself from rushing to her and doing whatever I could to alleviate the burden she carried.

I straightened my shoulders, raising my chin.

Rose grimaced, then sighed.

Even the healer of the Fairchild coven knew how to play games.

My aunt's gaze shifted to the vampire. "We are pleased to welcome an elder of the Conclave. How might I be of assistance? A room? Perhaps some …" She faltered, most likely having been about to offer a vampire a midnight snack.

"I have no requirement of a bed," Kett said, as unaffected as always. "But a computer would be welcomed."

My aunt nodded. "In the library, off the entranceway."

"Thank you." Kett nodded to me, then exited the drawing room.

My aunt frowned, turning to the wide chair nearest the fire. She sat, curling her legs underneath her, watching the fire while she waited.

"Declan is with us," I said.

She waved her hand absentmindedly. "He's already in his room. The one across the hall from him overlooks the gardens and has been made up for you. I waited up for you after I returned from Dahlia's."

"I'm not here for the view."

"I understand that, Wisteria," Rose said wearily. "I assume you wouldn't come here, with a vampire, without further evidence. You have a reconstruction?"

"Of Jasmine's kidnapping, you mean? Or of the four other vampires wandering around Litchfield?"

Rose looked at me sharply.

"Which one surprises you?" I asked.

"Both," she snapped. "As I expect you must already know. I'm too tired for games."

"I see." Once again, I struggled to ignore the concern that her appearance evoked. But I was unsuccessful. "Are you ... unwell? Your magic is—"

"None of your concern. As you made clear earlier."

"Now who's playing games, Aunt?" I posed the rhetorical question softly. I didn't want to get caught up in some loop where Rose and I would display our bruised hearts over and over again for the other person to trample on. Partly because I already knew I would win that contest. And partly because my quarrel wasn't with Rose. She hadn't protected us a long time ago, and I wasn't going to forgive her. But I didn't want to drag it around for the rest of my life.

Rose sighed, closing her eyes. "The only vampire I've seen in at least a dozen years is the one you just presented. Though how you came to know an elder of the Conclave is of great interest."

Not answering her, I slung my coat over the back of the chair I'd kept between Rose and me, untwining my scarf from around my neck to counter the heat of the fire. An elder of the Conclave equaled power. An abundance of power. So naturally, any Fairchild would have had their interest piqued by Kett's connection to Jasmine. And to me.

The fact that Rose, the nominal head of the coven, had no idea who Kett was—and seemingly less idea that there were vampires in Litchfield at all—only reinforced that someone else was possibly working behind the scenes.

More importantly, her honest surprise at meeting Kett confirmed for me that Jasper had inked his contract with the Conclave without the knowledge or permission of his sister.

But none of that was important. Not at that moment anyway. Not until Jasmine was safe.

"Four vampires have kidnapped a Fairchild witch," I said quietly, stating the facts but not passing judgement. "In Fairchild territory. And when Declan came to you, you all ignored him."

"He didn't come to me."

"Would it have made any difference?"

"Of course it would have!"

"I wonder why he didn't come to you, then?"

Rose's face twisted, pained. She started to say something, then checked herself. "How long will you be staying?"

"For as long as it takes to resolve this." I reached into my bag and pulled out the reconstruction I'd captured in the hotel room.

Rose shifted up and out of her seat, crossing to me. I held the magic-filled cube out to her, but she latched on to my arm instead.

"I'll make calls right away, Wisteria," she said earnestly. "I'm sure it's just some terrible mistake."

"Not for the first time," I said, "I wish you were right."

"We will find Jasmine," she said, gripping my arm. "And then can we please talk? We need you. And Declan.

You are the next generation of Fairchilds. It's time for you to take your place among us."

"Me and Declan," I echoed, laying on the sarcasm.

"Yes. We need you both. I'm happy to play intermediary, but it won't be necessary. Because everyone knows this needs to happen."

"Or what?" I whispered. "What is this really about? Jasper?"

Rose dropped my arm, taking the reconstruction instead. "Of course not. I know how you feel."

"Do you?"

She looked up. Wearing just her slippers, my aunt was a few inches shorter than me. Tears edged her bright-blue eyes. "I do. I know what it's like to feel … powerless."

I met her gaze steadily, steeling my heart against the desire for everything she was offering to be true. To even be realistic. "I'm not powerless."

She nodded.

"And if I find that any Fairchild has had anything to do with Jasmine's kidnapping—"

"I heard you before, Wisteria." And as suddenly as the soft-hearted healer had appeared, the head of the coven stood in her place. "I'll review the evidence you have collected, and I will reach out. This will be solved by morning."

Rose strode out of the room, the pink robe billowing after her like a cape of indignation. Misplaced indignation—my family's most unifying attribute.

I retrieved my coat and followed my aunt out through the foyer. While she crossed through to her office situated at the far end of the library, I headed upstairs. I should have checked in with Kett, who was likely attempting to access Jasmine's data online with the password she'd left us in the hotel room. But I needed a moment to myself and I'd most certainly fry any electronics I went near in my current state.

I just needed a brief reprieve from the never-ending onslaught of emotion that came from even thinking of my family, let alone conversing with any of them.

But I would do all this and more for Jasmine. As she would for me.

Halfway up the stairs, a sharp pain shot through my chest, leaving me breathless. I clenched my teeth, suppressing the tears pressing against my eyes, denying the emotion trying to overwhelm me. Clutching the handle of my bag in one hand and the wide wooden railing in the other, I practically pulled myself up the remainder of the stairs. I couldn't collapse where Rose, or even Declan, might see me.

It wasn't the time for despair. There were more clues to collect. I wasn't alone hunting for Jasmine. I wasn't going to be alone in finding her.

I made it to the landing above without faltering any further. I took a deep breath. Rose hadn't changed the decor on the second floor. Glassed sconces lit the wide hallway that led to the bedroom wing of Fairchild Park. The rooms on the left overlooked the back vegetable gardens. The rooms on the right overlooked the front drive and the landscaped yard.

A soft light glowed from within the first bedroom on my right, the door to which was partially ajar. I deposited my coat and bag just inside the door to the left, which was the guest room Rose had prepared for me. My suitcase had been placed on the foot of the bed. Declan must have brought it in from the Jeep. Then I crossed the hall and tapped lightly on the half-open door. I owed Declan an update of my conversation with Rose, at the very least. We had many other things to discuss, but none of them were things I was prepared to broach that night.

No one answered. Assuming Declan was being unresponsive, but that he would be even pissier if I didn't at least offer up some information freely, I pushed the door open just enough to scan the interior of the guest room.

A tall bureau came up to my shoulder on the left. Declan's leather jacket was thrown over a chaise by the paned-glass window. He hadn't drawn the drapes. Through the window, the near-full moon dominated the dark sky above the trees that edged the property. A lamp on the bedside table threw light across the wood-frame bed. The decor was masculine, resembling nothing of Rose's taste.

The shower was running in the main bathroom, which could be accessed by the hall and the bedrooms on either side.

So Declan was staying at Fairchild Park often enough to justify having a room decorated to his tastes, which would also explain the Connecticut license plates on his Jeep. Either that or the decor was one of Rose's less subtle bargaining chips, making him feel as though he might possibly have a home with her. With the Fairchilds. Though he'd seemed just as shocked at Rose's physical state when seeing her at Dahlia's as I had been, implying that he hadn't seen her in a while or that her transformation had been sudden.

The shower turned off in the bathroom.

I stepped back, tugging the door closed with my retreat. But before I cleared the frame, my gaze fell on a hand-turned wooden bowl sitting on the bureau. It was filled with loose change, a money clip, and a single house key at the end of a long chain.

Attached to the chain were each of the tiny reconstructions I'd sent Declan for his last twelve birthdays.

My heart pinched, but not in pain. With hope. An infinitesimal spark of hope bloomed across my chest, flushing up my neck and somehow rooting me to the spot.

Declan stepped from the bathroom, toweling off his hair. Thankfully, he was wearing boxers. But the tight black cotton did little to hide that he was no longer the teenager who I'd tumbled around with in the tall grass, stealing secret moments to learn what pleasured the other.

His shoulders were broader, and the hair on his chest was more abundant. A thin line ran the length of his chiseled abs, disappearing underneath the elastic band of his underwear. The scar I'd glimpsed running down his neck extended out in multiple directions across his shoulder, creating a starburst of healed, puckered flesh. And for one completely irrational moment, I wanted to eviscerate whoever had hurt him that badly—then rush across the room and run my fingers across every inch of him.

Then I remembered how he'd earned that scar.

I closed my eyes, struggling to shove the thought away. But for a single breath, I could practically taste the dank air of the basement, feel the dirt underneath my toes, and the physical pain of holding a barrier between me and the most powerful witch—the most powerful Adept of any sort—I'd ever faced.

"Wisteria?"

I opened my eyes.

Declan tugged a T-shirt over his head, then reached for the jeans slung across the foot of the bed. "You had something to tell me?" Apparently, finding me hanging around in his bedroom doorway hadn't thrown him at all.

"Yes," I said. My voice cracked, but I stepped back into the room, pushing the door open. "I ... ah ..."

"Where's the vampire?"

"In the library, using the computer."

Declan grunted in acknowledgement, crossing back into the bathroom to hang up his towel.

"I gave Rose the reconstruction. She says she'll make some calls."

Declan snorted.

I took another step into the room, so that I could see his reflection in the bathroom mirror. He was halfheartedly running a comb through his hair. I didn't see any other toiletries on the counter, nor were there any signs of luggage in the bedroom. Which confirmed that he stayed at Rose's often enough to leave a toothbrush and a change of clothing.

"Wisteria?" Declan prompted again, brushing past me as he crossed out of the bathroom, then checked the phone he'd plugged in to charge on the bedside table.

"Sorry," I said, achingly aware that I was just awkwardly standing around in his bedroom. "I'm tired. Rose tried to suggest that ..." I trailed off, not wanting to rehash the conversation. "Well, they all play different games, don't they? Rose's is just ... almost heartfelt."

Declan straightened, blocking the light from the lamp on the side table. "We all play games. But yeah, the elder Fairchilds are especially skilled."

I couldn't see his expression, only the outline of him. But instead of that being unnerving, listening to him in the dark was oddly comforting.

"I'm sorry I barged in. I saw the light."

Declan laughed. "You've seen worse. Or better, maybe."

I nodded, offering him a smile. But when I turned back to the door, my gaze fell on the tiny reconstructions attached to his keychain. The single key was from his grandparent's home in New Orleans. Though someone else was already living there by the time Jasper had scooped Declan off the streets, the key was the only personal item he'd brought with him, other than the ragged clothing he wore.

He had attached my reconstructions to the only memento he had of his childhood home. I wanted to reach out and touch all those little bits of magic I'd carefully collected with him in mind.

A tear ran unbidden down my cheek. I hastily brushed it away.

"Wisteria?" Declan's throaty whisper of my name was desperately intimate.

I wanted to spin back into the room, to throw myself into his arms. But the boundaries between us were exceedingly clear. I didn't want to ruin what little connection remained.

"Sorry," I said a second time. "I'm just tired. And …"

"Worried about Jasmine."

I nodded at him over my shoulder. He had stepped away from the light, so that I could see part of his face.

"You kept the reconstructions," I said.

"You think Jasmine would let me trash them?"

The tentative smile slid from my face. I forced myself to turn away.

"That's it then?" he asked. "The vampire is using the computer and Rose has the reconstruction? You don't have anything else to tell me?"

I knew I should have just walked out the door. I knew I should have just left things as they were, because I'd already riled up my family more than was healthy for Declan. But I turned back into the room. The edge was creeping back into his tone, and I was feeling far too vulnerable to simply let it return full force.

"That scar …" My voice caught in my throat, but I forced myself to take another step toward him as I finished the thought. "When I saw you just now, I wondered for a moment where you got it."

His mouth twisted, readying some nasty retort. But I didn't let him speak.

"Then I remembered the bandages," I whispered. "And you lying there in the hospital, so still, with the sheet pulled tightly across your chest. The bandages …" I lifted my hand, not near enough to touch him but indicating his neck and shoulder. "The mundane nurses, the doctors, didn't know what to do with you. The wound kept bleeding …" My voice cracked again, strangling the words. I ignored the tears welling in my eyes, needing to articulate the memory. To own it so that it would stop owning me. "I waited too long to call Rose. But Jasmine wouldn't wake up, and you wouldn't stop bleeding …"

Declan turned away from me, running his hand through his hair. "And they made you bargain." His voice was a low growl. "They made you choose before they would heal either of us."

"They made me … they demanded an explanation. Later, Jasmine told me that Dahlia and Grey came to the hospital, but Rose, Violet, and Slate went for Jasper."

"To see if he still lived."

"I assumed that Rose got him stabilized. And by then …"

"You'd fulfilled your end of the deal."

"No … I … it was never about me going away."

"It was me they were going to banish."

I laughed harshly. "They did anyway, really. All three of us. They sent you to school in Europe?"

Declan nodded, but almost absentmindedly. As though he was thinking of that day so long ago when we'd almost killed Jasper in order to save ourselves.

"But you let them believe it was me who stood against Jasper, not you."

"Yes. They came to their own conclusions about you and I didn't dissuade them. But they never believed that we had anything to stand against at all. Simply that we were … foolish. Careless. And in your case, irrevocably damaged."

He laughed. "They weren't wrong about that."

Silence fell between us. I was suddenly and utterly exhausted. I turned away once more, crossing to the door and keeping my gaze away from the bureau.

"I lied," Declan said behind me.

I paused in the doorway.

"I lied about why I kept the reconstructions."

"I know."

"You really think they would have killed me? That only the belief that I was more powerful than Jasper kept them at bay all these years?"

I shook my head. "That's what I thought then. But I think I was in shock, and desperately scared … about losing you, and about what I'd done."

"You saved our lives, Wisteria."

I shook my head. I couldn't talk about it anymore.

"They wanted us separated," Declan said, as if trying to convince himself of something. "All three of us?"

"Yes."

"But Jasmine …"

I laughed, though I had to push through the pain constricting my chest to do so. "You know what they think."

"That she's weak."

"Yes."

"Even though she was the glue, the mortar. The foundation of Jasper's machinations."

"A useful tool. We all were."

"Except you. Scion." He snarled the title—the function I'd been groomed since childhood to fill within succession of the coven—with spiteful derision.

I spun around to face him, a rush of anger pushing away my weariness. "Why must you be so harsh?"

"Why must you be so poised and perfect?"

"That's … just me."

"There you go."

Utterly frustrated with how the situation was devolving—frustrated by everything I couldn't control—I exited the room. Striding across the hall, I wrenched open the door to my bedroom and ...

No. I wasn't done.

I pivoted, barreling back toward Declan's room only to crash against him just inside the door. He'd been exiting. Perhaps following me.

He opened his mouth to speak, but I thrust my finger at his chest and said everything I needed to say, everything I needed to admit.

"I don't regret it. Not for one second. Not for any moment we've spent apart."

"We almost got Jasmine killed," he snarled. "If we hadn't broken his rules—"

"He was the one who almost killed her! What future do you think we had? What future was he crafting for us?"

"Power. Prestige. No one could have stood against us. The power of three."

"Except Jasper ... " My tone softened as my anger abated almost as swiftly as it had taken hold of me. "He was crafting a weapon. He would have used us until we burned out."

Declan snorted. "We wouldn't have burned out. We never would have faded. Not with you at our center."

I kissed him.

I wasn't sure why. I knew he was angry. I knew he was possibly seeing someone. But desperate to stop talking, I lifted up on my tiptoes, pressing my lips against his hard, unyielding ones.

Placing his hands on my shoulders to push me away, he ended up gripping me so tightly I was certain to bruise.

I wrapped my hands around his face, caressing downward to touch the scar at the base of his neck while wrapping my other hand around the back of his head.

He returned the kiss, practically grinding his mouth into mine. But it didn't hurt.

It felt like home.

Declan pulled me the few steps into his bedroom, kicking the door shut behind us without breaking contact.

I opened my mouth, inviting him to do the same by lightly teasing him with my tongue. He let me in, pressing the tip of his tongue to mine with a soft groan that somehow twisted through me in a rush of pleasure, accumulating between my legs.

Remembering the trail of hair that bisected his abdomen, I tugged his T-shirt up and slipped my hands underneath it, touching every inch of his skin that I could reach.

His fingers worked through my hair, teasing it out of its smooth French twist. Then he transferred his mouth to my neck, nuzzling and kissing me just below my ear as he reached up to cup my breast, flicking my nipple through my thin sweater.

"I've missed you, Bubba," I whispered.

Declan stilled. Then he stepped away from me.

My heart sank into my stomach.

He tugged my hands away from him, holding them together between us. Then after a deep, shaky breath, he looked me in the eye.

"I'm your past, Wisteria. Not your future. You've made that abundantly clear."

"Declan—"

"No." He cut me off sharply. "You don't get to decide when and where you want me."

I laughed sourly. "And all your other women? Do they not come at your beck and call? Isn't it completely fair for me to emulate that behavior?"

He dropped my hands, twisting away from me. I stumbled, the back of my knees striking the bed, and I abruptly sat down.

He yanked open the door, pausing beside the bureau with his hand hovering over his keychain and money clip.

"I always want you," I whispered. "Whenever, wherever. There is no moment of decision."

"I'm not that boy. And I was only him in your and Jasmine's minds anyway," he said fiercely, though his words were pained. "You love a memory."

He met my gaze in the mirror over the bureau, dropping his hand without retrieving his keychain. Then he left the room without another word.

I sat on the bed, listening to him traverse the hall, then the stairs. The mattress beneath me was too soft, threatening to swallow me, to suffocate me. Or maybe it was just that Declan had taken all the oxygen in the room with him. I couldn't even draw a breath to trigger the tears I desperately needed to shed.

I forced myself to stand. Smoothing my sweater, I crossed to the bureau and gazed down at the reconstructions on Declan's keychain. A single key. A key he'd shown up with, wearing it tied around his neck on a shoelace the summer we were all apprenticed to Jasper. A key that opened no door. The locks had been changed on his family home after his mother abandoned him and his grandfather passed away.

I brushed my fingertips across the dozen tiny oyster-shell cubes attached to the chain. One for each year we'd been apart.

He had kept me close. He'd carried me—my magic—with him wherever he went.

"I love you," I whispered to the magic dancing underneath my fingertips. "Past. Present. And whatever time the future grants us."

Then I crossed the hall to my bedroom. Locking the door behind me, I kicked off my shoes and climbed underneath the quilted duvet on the four-pillar bed without undressing. I needed sleep. I needed a blank space within which to rest and rejuvenate. There was nothing else I could do at that moment. Even more emotionally messed up and exhausted, I had no ability to help with any technological aspect of the investigation. Kett or Rose would wake me when and if there was news.

And whatever was looming, whatever hurdles were coming, I was going to need to focus. The past—and everything it represented, including my initial fixation on Jasper—had already slowed me from finding Jasmine. I wouldn't allow it to drag me through tomorrow as well.

Chapter Seven

I slept for an hour and a half, waking somewhat refreshed but exceedingly hungry. I hadn't eaten since the chicken salad I'd picked at on the plane. I splashed some water on my face in the bathroom, then changed into cotton pajama pants and a thick-knit, wide-necked, supremely comfortable sweater that fell down to just above my knees.

Padding past Declan's closed door, I contemplated waking him, pretending that I hadn't practically forced myself on him earlier. Then I could invite him for a predawn snack.

But even as I did, I knew that I would be happier alone. Or at least not so seriously on edge. So I slipped down the smooth wooden stairs and made my way back to the kitchen, regretting not putting on socks the moment my feet met its tiled floor.

Not bothering with the lights, I retrieved some cold fried chicken and potato salad from the fridge. Even after all the years that had passed, I wasn't certain that Rose could actually cook anything else, other than chocolate chip cookies, but I certainly wasn't complaining. My aunt hadn't updated the kitchen—bare wood countertops, white-painted cabinets, pink ceramic plates on open shelves above the apron-front sink—making the echoes of my childhood suddenly threaten to manifest before me in the moonlit darkness.

But instead of ignoring the past, I stood at the counter and literally ate the only good memory I had of my youth—other than the moments Jasmine, Declan, and I snatched together. Though not for the first time, it occurred to me that by refusing to dwell on the bad memories, I also forgot the good. Or perhaps my mind just didn't work the same way as everyone else's, and I was simply better suited to living in the present.

The vampire joined me as I was getting a second helping. He appeared in a pocket of moonlight filtering into the kitchen, gazing out the double French-paned doors that led to the back patio, then into the empty vegetable gardens beyond. The breakfast nook where Jasmine, Declan, and I had spent fleeting moments of our childhood stood behind him, to the right of the kitchen's large, unused brick fireplace.

I scraped and rinsed my plate. After placing my dishes in the dishwasher, I washed my greasy fingers, then crossed to gaze out the patio doors at the vampire's side.

"I have an associate looking over Jasmine's files," he said.

"Jasmine traced the vampire she called Yale to Litchfield?"

"By his credit card."

"Used at the hotel? So she booked a room to sit and wait for him?"

"Apparently." Kett was angry. His rage was subtle, a slight edge to his normally even tone, but it was there.

"Why did she come without you?" I whispered the question, not completely sure I wanted to crack open another tense topic on less than two hours' sleep.

The vampire turned away from the window, gazing at me but not answering.

I kept my gaze on the white-fenced garden beds. "Rose grows berries," I said, filling the not completely uncomfortable silence that settled between us. "Blueberries over there." I lifted my hand, pointing to the far right of the garden. The sleeve of my thick-knit sweater slipped back along my arm, revealing my white-picket-fence bracelet. It glinted with magic, not just moonlight. "Raspberries and strawberries. Jasmine and I often visited for the afternoon. Less so after Declan arrived and we all apprenticed with Jasper."

"I believe Jasmine might have been angry with me," Kett finally said.

"She's not the angry sort."

"No?"

"Not like that, at least."

"I don't understand the distinction."

I turned to look at him. "You were dating?"

"If that is the word you wish to use."

"Having sex, then?"

He inclined his head imperceptibly, allowing but perhaps not wholly agreeing with my word choice.

"And now you aren't?"

"It was enough."

"For you or her?"

"For her. But by my assessment."

I tilted my head, waiting for a more detailed explanation. Kett didn't offer one.

"Jasmine doesn't get angry at that sort of thing," I said. "Breakups, who's sleeping with who. Or, if you prefer, who's having sex with whom, then not having sex anymore. Jasmine ... loves, but she doesn't possess. And she certainly doesn't get any of it tangled up in her job. If she tracked

Yale here without telling you, it just means she thought she could handle it. She was still gathering intel."

"My associate is combing her records for possible places of residence for Yale and his brood, and other patterns that might indicate their movements."

"That makes sense."

"But we will hear from the brood before sunrise," he said.

I nodded, thinking about retreating upstairs for another couple of hours of sleep, then dismissing the idea. "I'll wait up with you."

"As you wish."

Kett slipped back through the kitchen, wandering out into the hall, then into the foyer. I slowly trailed after him, allowing him to pull me in his wake. The fire was still burning in the drawing room, bathing the far corner of the foyer in a warm, flickering light. Kett must have been feeding it. I assumed at first that the drawing room was where we were heading, but Kett turned in the opposite direction, crossing past the stairs into a little-used portion of the house.

The ballroom.

I had indistinct memories of my grandparents throwing grand parties in that columned space, but Rose had left it empty except for the white baby grand piano in the corner. The wood floor was still polished, though, and slick even under my bare feet.

The entire far wall was filled with French-paned doors meant to stand open to the patio in the summer. So that music would spill out into the night while any breeze cooled the dancers within.

Kett crossed to the glassed doors, lifting his face to the moonlight as he'd done in the kitchen. Though he might just have been gazing over the far hedge that marked the boundary of the property and effectively hid the house from the side street.

I trailed my fingers across the exposed keys of the piano, but didn't press them firmly enough to give voice to the instrument. I didn't play. I wasn't certain that any of the living Fairchilds played any instrument. Such magic might have been cherished in my grandparents' day, but it was too subtle—perhaps too much work—for the current elders.

"Why me?" I asked without even realizing I was going to voice the question. "What is it that you … see? You went to Jasmine, at her invitation, I assume. But you'd already crossed her out of consideration on the contract."

Though his back was to me, Kett tilted his head as if considering my query. Then he held out his hand to the side as if he wanted me to take it.

I drifted toward him, slowly sliding each step across the smooth floor. He was even paler in the moonlight streaming in through the window. Almost ethereal.

Yet he was the opposite of delicate. The antithesis of angelic. As was I. And that was why my name remained on the contract. I was certain of that. But I wanted him to confirm my suspicions. I wanted at least that much to be clear between us.

I stood beside him, gazing out at the side yard of the house—the 'park' portion of the estate—but I didn't take his offered hand. Beyond the white-painted patio on the other side of the glassed doors, wide rivers of grass wove through pockets of white-fenced rose gardens. Deep shadows played along the edge of the hedge and around the few winter-bare trees that speckled the yard.

"I wasn't given a choice," Kett said finally, still offering his hand to me without looking in my direction. "And neither was my maker. My grandsire punished his children by forcing them to divide their power, so none would ever stand as strong as he."

The wooden floor was warm where my feet rested, but I could feel the cool air pressing against the glass only a foot or so from me. Without looking, I lifted my left hand, first touching, then trailing my fingers along Kett's hand, which remained suspended between us. His skin was cool. Rougher at the fingertips than I'd thought it would be. And just as unyielding as I'd expected.

"I understand," I said, remembering to breathe.

"I was made in a time when a monster could still hold court, openly embracing power in a remote region of the world. I was bred for the honor of being a sacrifice. The second son of my human family. Unnecessary in terms of the propagation of the clan, but a worthy exchange. Worth my weight in gold."

"You were born to die?"

"Yes."

"But you didn't."

He laughed quietly. "I died. But before that happened, I amused the monster for a dozen years. My magic intrigued him. He took me for his own, for blood, and as his mortal companion. His youngest daughter, who'd held that position for over twenty years, loathed me for it."

I slowly released the breath I'd been holding, concerned I would break the odd tranquility building up around us. We both kept our gazes fixed to the yard beyond the glassed doors.

Kett flipped our hands, tracing his fingers over mine, then up my wrist, as I'd done to him. My skin prickled but I didn't pull away.

"The daughter tried to kill you," I said.

"Yes."

"And in retribution, her father forced her to remake you. Forced her to divide her power?"

"It was more than that. She was relatively young, perhaps only a hundred and fifty years into her reincarnation. Unable to walk during the day, unable to read or control the minds of her victims. But she'd inherited one of her father's gifts. A gift few of his offspring possessed. And by making me, she was unable to access that power for over a century."

"The gift made her valuable to him?"

"Unique. Treasured. It took her many centuries to regain her standing in his shiver."

"He forced her to remake the source of her jealousy."

"Yes. To take me as her companion for the rest of her immortal years. And in doing so, she lost the privileged position she felt was her birthright. For a time."

Kett pressed his fingers against my wrist, feeling my pulse. It was completely steady.

I glanced over at him, allowing myself a moment to trace his profile with my eyes. Looking at him as a man, not a monster. Not a being of terrible power.

He smiled, still not looking at me.

"And now your grandsire makes this demand of you? That you divide your own power? As a punishment? For what?"

"My child will be formidable," the vampire said, justifying his grandsire's demands rather than answering my questions. "A shoring up of his legacy."

"But why me?" I whispered.

"Tell me what happened, Wisteria Fairchild." Kett's tone was warm, inviting intimacy. "What happened to tear you away from your coven? You weaken them by your absence. Why would they bear it?"

He turned, looking me in the eye. I didn't look away, risking becoming ensnared by him. But some part of me wanted to be overwhelmed, to be whisked away from the seemingly endless hollowness of my existence.

Thankfully, the larger part of me was anchored in the present. In the need to protect Jasmine.

"Are you the reason Jasper Fairchild is in that wheelchair?" Kett asked silkily.

"You already know the answer. Or so you indicated when you gave me the contract."

"I had heard rumors. Pieces of the puzzle."

I arched an eyebrow at him. "Guesswork? From the executioner of the Conclave?"

He chuckled, stroking his thumb across my wrist.

"Is that why you want me? Instead of Jasper? Because he's damaged?"

"You are the more powerful."

Dread shot through my chest, but I swallowed it down, determined to continue occupying the present. And at present, I was forming some sort of tentative bond with an ancient vampire. I wanted to be in this moment for a little while longer.

I lifted my hand from his, smiling playfully. "If I tell you all my stories now, what will I have left with which to beguile you?"

He stepped into my space before I'd registered him moving. His breath stirred the hair tumbling across my shoulders. "Forever. You will have forever, Wisteria."

"Stay out of my head, Kett," I whispered. Though I wasn't at all sure that was what I actually wanted.

"Stop inviting me in, then."

"I'm looking for answers."

"I'm amenable to answering your questions."

"Why is my past so important?"

"You make it so."

Closing my eyes, I took the last step that remained between us, turning my face toward his neck and jaw. I dropped my personal shields. An inch away from him, I could feel his magic dancing over my lips. I rubbed them together, relishing the feeling.

He tasted like life.

Which was exceedingly ironic.

"And if I didn't want it to be that way?" I asked, barely giving breath to the question. "If I didn't want to be perpetually controlled by the events of my childhood anymore?"

Kett skimmed his fingers across my palms, over my wrists, and up underneath my arms. Then he lifted my arms to the sides, all the while barely touching me.

"Look at me," he said, demanding my compliance without raising his voice.

Still holding my arms up and out, I locked my gaze to his. Red shards of magic danced in the silver-blue of his irises.

He moved, shifting his hips and tapping my foot back. I stepped back, then to the side at his bidding. He took two more slow steps. Then, touching the small of my back lightly, he spun me around.

Then the vampire repeated the pattern of steps, guiding me gently and touching me no more than was necessary to direct my movements.

He wanted to dance.

With me.

Not knowing where or how I picked up the steps, I curved my body into him, languidly matching his movements. The dance felt like some hybrid form of waltz, but I really didn't know enough about dancing to be able to distinguish it further.

I couldn't hear whatever music moved him, but I didn't need to. In Kett's arms, there was no chance of a misstep.

I settled one hand on his shoulder, allowing my other hand to rest fully in his, extended out to the side. The pace increased, until we were swirling and twisting around the room in perfect sync.

We stirred the air. The floor vibrated underneath our feet, magic whirling in our wake. No one could stand against us, no power would stop us.

We were the music.

Then we abruptly stopped. My hands were clasped in his, stretched above our heads. Throwing my head back, I gasped for air. His mouth ghosted my neck. I clung to his hands as magic and the room continued to whirl around us.

"That's why I haven't crossed you off the list," Kett whispered against my ear.

The room settled. He released my hands. But instead of stepping away, I wrapped my arms around his shoulders and kissed him.

His lips were cold and unyielding.

I'd made some sort of miscalculation.

I broke the embrace, ready to step away, but he brushed his fingers through my loose hair.

"You have mistaken me …" he murmured. "I forget that humans equate so much with sex. And while we might be lovers in centuries to come when you are my equal, or as close as you are likely to be, that is not what I want from you now."

"You haven't explained yourself terribly clearly," I said, taking a half step back so I could give myself some space but not completely break the intimacy of the conversation.

A smile flitted across his face. "Some things are still new to me. It's a novel feeling after twelve centuries."

He paused, allowing me a moment to absorb how old he'd just admitted to being.

"You're still in love with Declan," he said. "With Jasmine. As you've already admitted. You're entangled within your past."

"I will always love them," I said.

"Yes. But when you come to me, you will be ready to move forward. I'm offering you a blank slate, Wisteria Fairchild."

He reached out, delicately tugging Jasmine's necklace free from my sweater and allowing it to dangle between my breasts. He traced his fingers from the tiny reconstructions up my breastbone, pausing at the base of my neck as if watching me breathe. With the lightest of cool touches up my neck, he curved his fingers underneath my chin. Then, applying only the slightest pressure, he tilted my head back.

"When I drink of you fully, you will drink of me. We will be more than lovers. We will … absorb each other. You will die and be reborn through my blood. When you open your eyes, the world will be wholly different. Is that what you want of me now, tonight?"

I drew further away from him. He allowed me to step back.

"Don't misunderstand me, Wisteria Fairchild," Kett said. "I'm offering you power. Centuries of accumulated strength and invulnerability. I don't want to be your lover. I don't want to simply drink your blood. I want to raise you above everything you've never been able to control, everything you've been too weak to fight. Immortality. Dominion over your enemies. By my side for as long as you need to be, but then you will walk the earth untouched, unscathed."

Kett paused. I held my breath, hoping that—uninterrupted—he'd continue. He did.

"As my child, you will answer to no one but me and to the two others tied to me by blood. At this very moment, there are fewer than a half-dozen vampires as powerful as I am. With my blood in your veins, you will walk in the sun. You will choose when and how to feed. The limitations of a typical fledgling won't apply to you. No vampire has ever been born with the power I offer you. I'm looking for an equal, not a lover."

I wrapped my hand around the cubes hanging from Jasmine's necklace, anchoring myself in their magic while trying to absorb everything Kett was saying. "And if I don't accept?"

He shrugged. "I must remake someone. Someone powerful enough to survive the transition."

"The contract stipulates as much," I said, pleased that my voice was steady and firm. "Though the penalty isn't clearly defined."

Kett smiled joylessly. "But the due date is set in stone. I will not be allowed to remain as I am. In terms you will understand, I have collected too much magic. I hold too much, uneasily. When I make you, I will divide my power."

"And hate me for it? As your maker hated you?"

"Hates. As my maker loathes me, still. Even more so, now that I have accumulated enough power of my own to throw off her yoke. She no longer holds sway over me."

"And your grandsire?"

Kett bared his teeth, then chuckled nastily. On another night, I would have flinched away from him. But with the magic generated from our dance still settling around me, I didn't.

"He hasn't tried to call me to heel," the vampire said. "If I resisted him, it would undermine everything he's spent over five thousand years accumulating, by his count."

"So you signed the contract willingly?"

"Faced with losing everything? Yes. If you'd like to call that willingly."

I laughed. The sound was harsh even to my own ears. I pressed my hands to my chest, searching for the stillness I needed to get through this conversation. To get through finding Jasmine, and dealing with my family. "I understand."

"I know you do."

"But you think that somehow, you and I will be different?"

"I never wanted to make another. Immortality is a gift and a curse. You will come to hate me. We will spend centuries together, then centuries apart. And then, perhaps, we will find each other once more."

He brushed his fingers through my hair again, finishing the movement before I'd seen him begin it.

"Not Jade Godfrey? Not Jasmine?"

He smiled. "A part of me wishes that you were asking out of jealousy, except then we would not be well matched."

I raised my eyebrow at him.

He chuckled. "Jade's magic would not be compatible. And I cannot offer her anything she doesn't already have."

I frowned, not completely sure what he meant. Jade was witch-born, and therefore mortal. But the dowser's magic also wasn't any of my business. "And Jasmine?"

"Jasmine is not powerful enough," Kett said. "I believe that the magic I have accumulated would consume her own."

"But not mine?"

"It is always a risk. But no, not you. And ..." Kett paused thoughtfully. "And if I am wrong, if Jasmine could survive the transformation, she might emerge as only a reflection of what she once was."

"That's ... that's a terrible thought."

"Indeed. Even if that were not the case, Jasmine and I would not be able to bear each other for the century she would need to be by my side. She would loathe me, perhaps instantly."

"I don't doubt it. She doesn't like being underestimated."

"Being underestimated is sometimes beneficial."

"Oh?" I asked archly. "Is that your professional opinion?"

"I am not speaking against your cousin, Wisteria," Kett said coolly. "I am only answering your questions and attempting to have a conversation, since I have been accused of being unclear."

I nodded, feeling foolish.

"Allow me to be completely transparent. If I must have a child, I would wish her to be you."

"And if I refuse?"

"Then I will take Jasper. Or perhaps Declan, but I think not."

Despite my resolve to be rational, terror flashed through me. I could feel my face crumpling but I couldn't smooth it, just as I couldn't deny the onslaught of emotion.

"What will Jasper do with all that power?" I whispered, clenching my hands around Jasmine's necklace.

"He will learn the rules. Or risk the wrath of the executioner."

I laughed harshly. "Before or after he kills me?"

Kett wrapped his hand around the back of my neck, cradling my head and pulling me against him. Almost as though he was trying to anchor me, to offer me shelter.

But I didn't know him well enough to accept the gesture. I pushed lightly against his shoulders, nodding to show him I wasn't going to collapse.

He let me go.

I turned away, crossing to the windows and pressing my hand against the glass. I hadn't realized how hot I was from the dancing. From the effort of controlling my emotions.

"You are mine now, Wisteria Fairchild," Kett whispered behind me. "From the moment I chose to not strike your name from the contract. Whatever choice you make, I will protect you. I don't make promises lightly. You will find that living forever comes with that consequence."

I will find ... living forever ...

Kettil, elder and executioner of the Conclave, didn't want my heart. No, he wanted my soul. And while my heart was spoken for twice over, even I had to admit that my soul was in play.

Kett appeared beside me abruptly. His attention was riveted to something beyond the French-paned door.

I flinched, realizing belatedly that he'd been careful that evening to not startle me. Considerate. I followed his gaze.

The vampire in the long mink coat from the hotel and the reconstruction of Jasmine's hotel room took a single step forward from the deep shadows at the edge of the hedge. A hint of red rolled across her eyes as she took in the ancient vampire standing by my side.

Relief flooded through me, followed by sharp, almost triumphant anger. Forget the nebulous nature of the pending future. Forget Kett's offer. Forget the ramifications of not accepting.

This, I could confront. This, I could control.

Flipping the stiff lock, I opened the door, stepping out into the chill of the night mindless of my bare feet.

Question-and-answer period was over. It was time to focus on the present. It was time to find Jasmine.

Forever could wait.

Before clearing the door frame, I brushed my fingers against the wards that coated the exterior of the house, whispering into them, "Declan. Ballroom."

I wasn't certain that I could still stir the magic of Fairchild Park to convey a message to Declan, even though doing so had once been child's play for the three of us. Faced with the vampire standing in the yard and the immediacy of Jasmine's kidnapping, the dark-tinted past that had made sending secret messages to each other a necessity felt distant. Disconnected.

Or perhaps being backed by one of the most powerful vampires currently walking the earth made me bold. When it came to being wooed by ultimate power, apparently I was as susceptible as any other Fairchild.

Stopping at the top of the wooden steps, I curled my toes over the edge. Kett stepped forward on my left.

The female vampire flicked her eyes my way. Then, dismissing me with a smirk, she returned her gaze to Kett.

I lifted my right hand, palm facing up. The moonlight caught on the platinum bracelet at my wrist, a shimmer of blue-tinted magic rolling through its tiny houses, fences, and tree charms.

Kett laughed, low and husky. And I couldn't help but join him.

"Do you know what I am, witch?" The vampire's snarled question was delivered in accented, melodic English.

I regarded her disdainfully. "Do you know who I am?"

"I got your note," she said. "You are she. The Wisteria that the witch evoked before we took her. But now I see you are nothing. Just another witch."

More anger rooted deep in my belly at her blatant admittance of having kidnapped Jasmine. "Let's be clear. All I needed was evidence of your actions, which I have obtained. You kidnapped a Fairchild witch in Fairchild territory. There will be no intervention from the Convocation." I glanced at Kett. "Or from the Conclave."

He nodded almost imperceptibly.

"There will be no trial," I continued. "You are mine to do with what I will. You have no hope of prevailing against me on Fairchild lands."

The vampire lifted her lip in a snarl, revealing her sharp, inch-long fangs. "What are you waiting for, then?"

Declan stepped through the doors behind us. "Me," he said, draping my wool coat over my shoulders from behind.

The female vampire looked momentarily startled at his appearance. The wards on the house would have hidden him from her, sight and sound.

I pushed my arms through the sleeves of the coat.

The vampire tossed her head, and a sudden yowl emanated from the depths of the hedge behind her. The fine hairs on the back of my neck pricked. A matted black cat suddenly appeared, twining itself around the vampire's ankles. Its white eyes reflected the moonlight.

Declan muttered a curse that might actually have been some sort of prayer under his breath. His magic churned, bouncing off the exposed skin of my hands and face.

Kett glanced over to him, grinning. Then he responded in the same language.

Declan laughed, relaxing.

Apparently the ancient vampire spoke multiple languages, including Creole.

"Care to share?" I asked, keeping my gaze on the female vampire and her creepy feline companion.

"Zombie cat," Declan said.

My stomach squelched. "The cat is dead?"

The female vampire laughed darkly. Pulling a small white rectangle out of her pocket, she haughtily stepped toward us across the lawn. Her cat followed, twining around the white-painted fence as its master passed one of the rose gardens.

"Five …" I whispered, enjoying this far more than was professional of me.

Declan laughed quietly behind me. "Four."

"Three … two …"

The exterior wards that normally operated only as an early warning system combined with those coating the house, creating a secondary barrier that reached out and grabbed the vampire. She shrieked in indignation as the protective magic lifted her off the ground, suspending her in midair like a fly caught in a spider's web.

The zombie cat shrieked, tearing back into the shadows underneath the hedge.

That would wake Rose.

The female vampire continued to struggle futilely against the magic that held her. The more she moved, the more the wards suppressed her movement.

A human might drown in that protective magic. But most humans would figure out quickly that they needed to stop fighting its hold.

Kett stepped forward, drawing the vampire's attention. She quieted, still suspended in the air before us—and utterly livid.

"What vampire would be sent to deliver a message to the Fairchild coven, yet be unable to feel the depth of the magic on the house?" Kett's tone was deceptively even. "Have you no understanding of proper protocol? What else does your maker keep you ignorant of?"

"Release me at once," the trapped vampire said, barely able to take the breath that allowed her to speak. "I come bearing a message, and all the protections that affords me."

"It's proper to introduce yourself," I said. "And to wait for introductions to be offered in return before entering another's territory."

"Cite the name your maker gave you," Kett said. "And the name of your maker himself, along with any titles or talent you hold exclusively."

The female vampire curled her lip at that suggestion, throwing herself ineffectually against the wards once more.

"Allow me to demonstrate," Kett said, gesturing toward Declan. "Declan Benoit, extraction specialist, nephew of Rose, member of the Convocation."

The female vampire stilled, casting an intense gaze Declan's way. Then she swiveled her head in an utterly inhuman gesture toward me.

"Wisteria Fairchild, reconstructionist, scion of the Fairchild coven," Kett said obligingly.

I ignored the 'scion' suggestion. I had absolutely no intention of taking Rose's place. The Fairchild coven could die out with the previous generation for all I cared.

The female vampire stopped straining against the magic of the wards. Fixing her red-tinted gaze on Kett, she waited. Sensing her acquiescence, the wards obligingly lowered her to the ground, though they didn't fully release her. From the way she maintained unblinking eye contact with Kett, it was apparent that she had no idea he could ensnare her from where he stood.

"And I am Kettil, executioner and elder of the Conclave."

"I know who you are," she said. "But what of your maker?"

Kett's tone turned low and deadly. "My accomplishments outweigh my blood ties."

She lifted her lip in a sneer. "I'm Amaya, seer of spirits, child of Yale."

"Originally of Ecuador?" Apparently the executioner also had an ear for accents. "A necromancer in your first incarnation? Can you raise anything larger than a cat?"

She didn't answer.

Kett's voice became silky. "And did your master have permission to remake and rename you thusly, Amaya?"

"I have a message," she said, jutting out her chin and ignoring the question. "Release me from the magic that holds me and I will deliver it without retribution."

Kett laughed, sounding completely human.

A shiver ran up my spine. But it was excitement, not fear that triggered it. The executioner laughed like that only in anticipation of having fun. And for a brief moment, I thought about letting go, of meeting the excitement I heard in his laugh. Of matching it with my own.

But then we wouldn't find Jasmine.

"Step back from the wards," I said, kicking into professional mode. "Make your peaceful intentions known and the magic will release you."

Amaya narrowed her red-hued eyes defiantly in my direction.

"Are you incapable of controlling yourself, fledgling?" Kett asked.

"I don't take orders from witches."

"Then what are you doing in witch territory, vampire?" Declan asked.

"Are you Yale's weakest child?" Kett asked. "Is that why he is so willing to sacrifice you?"

Amaya didn't rise to either of Declan's and Kett's attempts to bait her, choosing instead to compose herself and step back from the ward line. The magic protecting Fairchild Park let her go. She looked at Kett triumphantly.

"It's like she has no idea that you could reach over and pluck her head off her shoulders," Declan said conversationally, as if he and the executioner of the Conclave were old comrades in arms.

Kett tilted his head thoughtfully. "It wouldn't require that much effort to end her immortal existence. This Yale has not armed his brood with anything more than words. His blood is weak."

Amaya's expression became irate. The cat returned to her side, yowling for attention. She shifted as if anticipating throwing herself against the wards a second time.

"Shall we move this along?" I asked, ignoring the renewed posturing. "Your message?"

Amaya squared her shoulders, picking up the white rectangle she'd dropped on the grass when the wards had grabbed her. She flicked the envelope toward me. It spun across the yard, bypassing the wards and landing on the bottom step of the patio.

I didn't pick it up, choosing to tilt my head expectantly instead. I had no idea what spells might have been attached to the missive, though nothing overtly nefarious should have been able to pass through the wards.

Amaya huffed impatiently, then intoned, "We offer the witch in trade for a peaceful parlay with the Conclave."

"You stand on witch territory," I said. "If we accept, you will first need to make reparations to the coven. Then, if we allow it, the Conclave will have its say."

Amaya flicked her gaze to Kett. He stood stone-still beside me, offering her no guidance.

She returned her gaze to me, nodding stiffly. "At midnight next. The location will be sent to you by messenger after sunset."

That timing would leave us at least five hours to secure and defend whatever location they'd chosen. "We accept," I said.

She picked up the cat and disappeared. Well, she appeared to disappear. It was more likely she'd just stepped into the shadows, then leaped over the hedge.

Declan swore.

"Unimpressive," Kett said. "Slow. Weak. And ill bred."

"Why did you ask if her maker had permission to remake her?" Declan asked as we continued to stare out at the brightening sky. Dawn was about to breach the horizon.

"Nigel," I said. "The vampire in Astoria. He said he'd been unwilling."

Kett remained silent. But thoughtful, not disengaged.

"And she was a necromancer before?" I asked. "Still capable of exerting her will on the dead cat. Is that unusual?"

Kett nodded.

"How many necromancers would choose to be re-made?" I whispered.

"None." Kett pulled his cellphone out of the invisible satchel he wore, raising it to his ear as he turned back into the ballroom without another word.

"Why?" Declan asked. "Because necromancers speak to ghosts? Raise the dead? What difference does that make?"

"Necromancers can control the undead. All the undead."

Declan scoffed. "Please. If that were so, then …"

"Then powerful necromancers could control vampires," I said, finishing his thought. I wrapped my arms around myself, suddenly noticing how cold I was. Despite the coat that Declan had thoughtfully brought me, I was still outside in bare feet.

"And no vampire would allow themselves to be controlled," Declan murmured. "But why turn her? Instead of simply killing her?"

I looked at him. "Why kidnap a Fairchild witch in Fairchild territory? Why send a vampire to us without any understanding of who we are or what we can do? Why suggest setting a meeting in a way that will allow us time to prepare, to gather the coven against them?"

"He's a moron."

"No." My stomach churned as I put the pieces together. "The cellphone. The necklace. The message at the hotel. He likes to play games."

Declan's face blanched. "Jasmine," he whispered, stepping forward to retrieve the envelope from the bottom step.

I turned away, crossing into the ballroom.

Rose hovered a few feet away from the piano, clutching her quilted silk robe around her neck. Uncertain how long she'd been lingering just out of sight or what she'd heard, I passed her by, ignoring her questioning look. Declan would explain what had transpired with the vampire messenger. I wasn't up for another verbal sparring. There was never any way to really win when it came to my family.

Continuing through the house, I made it to my room with only my thoughts for company.

I climbed back into bed and tried to sleep. Kett would talk to whoever was on the other end of his cellphone. Declan would fill Rose in on the altercation. And Rose would filter the information out to the rest of the coven.

None of that mattered, though, because we really had only until sunset tomorrow to find Jasmine. After sunset, if the coven came into play, I wasn't sure anyone could guarantee my cousin's safety. Once faced with evidence—and a challenge—no Fairchild would sit out a fight.

So there were two options. Either Yale was smarter than he'd appeared so far, and had used Connecticut as a location to draw Jasmine's attention. Because he'd somehow put together that she was a Fairchild witch who might be testy about vampires in witch territory, and who would therefore come to investigate. And this was all about setting up Kett.

Or Jasmine's kidnapping was somehow tied to the Fairchilds. And since Rose had no knowledge of the presence of the vampires in Litchfield, it might still be tied to our Uncle Jasper.

Although Yale might keep his brood in ignorance of the formalities of the Adept world, a vampire strong enough to make four children—including Nigel—and clever enough to stay off the executioner of the Conclave's radar while doing so was definitely not a moron.

But I wasn't interested in playing Yale's games, sitting around and waiting to be told where to go. I might not be able to help with the technical side of the investigation, but I had all the time before sunset to look for more clues. And no matter what Kett turned up or Declan and Rose discussed, I knew where I had to go next.

The connection to Connecticut was too obvious to not be fully explored.

To that end, while Kett had his associates looking for patterns hidden among the vampire's credit-card charges and Rose had the distasteful task of gathering the coven, I was going to Fairchild Manor, whether my uncle was in residence or not. It might have just been all my ingrained instincts that made me suspect him, but I needed to know if Jasper was involved. If he was, perhaps I'd be lucky enough to reconstruct a clue that would lead us to the vampires before they expected us. And if not, we'd move on to the next location and the next clue, until we'd either exhausted the trail or the sun had set.

I wasn't going to gamble on Jasmine still being alive after another day in the custody of the vampires. But I also wasn't going to risk her getting killed in a full-scale battle of witches versus vampires. Not if I could do anything about it.

Kett might have declared himself my protector, but that protection wouldn't necessarily hold for Jasmine. Or even for Declan. And I wasn't actually certain that even Kett could protect all three of us from four other vampires at the same time.

I also wasn't certain—even though Kett was the executioner of the Conclave—that he would side with witches over vampires if that choice ever needed to be made. Especially if my uncle was somehow involved, because that would place Jasmine's kidnapping firmly under the purview of both the Fairchild coven and the Convocation. I had no idea what the rules guiding the executioner's conduct were, or what rules Yale and his offspring would have to break in order to deserve the judgement Kett's title suggested.

I gathered the quilted duvet underneath my chin, suddenly terribly cold. Chilled through, as if I'd never truly be warm ever again.

Jasmine was missing, and I wasn't certain it was remotely within my power to get her back alive. Even if I did somehow manage to get her away from the vampires unscathed, the path that stretched out before me led inextricably to Kett. The vampire might believe he was giving me a choice—a choice he'd never had. But if it came down to Jasper or me, I couldn't let my uncle take the power Kett offered.

Because that power in my uncle's hands would destroy everyone I loved. But becoming a vampire myself would only cost my mortal soul. And I would trade more than that for Jasmine and Declan any day or night.

Exhaustion took hold of my mind, and as I gave into it, it suddenly occurred to me that perhaps vampires didn't know they were so dreadfully cold. So I might have been wrong about never feeling warm again.

Unfortunately, though, I wasn't wrong about where the next steps in the investigation were going to take me.

"Jasper," I whispered, trying and failing to own his name while the dawning of the day brightened my windows. I'd forgotten to pull the curtains.

"Jasper," I whispered again, putting more strength into the evocation and wishing that I could call power forth with just his name. But that talent didn't lie within any of my current abilities, or the abilities I'd abandoned.

"Jasmine," I whispered, closing my eyes against the brightening room. I could feel the faint weight of the chain around my neck, and—if I allowed it—the tiny glimmers of magic in the reconstructions resting over my heart.

"I'm coming for you, Jasmine," I said, bidding the dawn to whisper the words in my cousin's ear.

Then I slept.

Chapter Eight

I could smell the cinnamon buns even before I descended the stairs. Apparently, Rose had brought in breakfast. Forgoing the kitchen, I crossed the foyer into the dining room beside the front drawing room, where a breakfast buffet had been laid on the tall sideboard. Rose was still treating us as guests instead of family, which I knew shouldn't have irked me as much as it did. I'd asked for professional courtesy, after all.

My aunt, dressed head to toe in pink silk and wool, was sitting two chairs from the head of the dark oak table that sliced through the center of the long, narrow room. Declan, in a black T-shirt and jeans, was across from her, though one seat closer to the head of the table.

Rose looked up as I entered, offering me a tentative smile.

"Good morning," I said, crossing to the sideboard and flipping the lid on a carafe of coffee. I leaned over, eagerly inviting the heavy, slightly burnt aroma to fill my senses.

"Good morning, darling," Rose said, sounding utterly delighted. My aunt had a way of putting all confrontation behind her as quickly as possible, whether or not an issue had actually been resolved.

Declan grunted a greeting, then flipped a page of the newspaper he was holding like it might have been a barrier between him and Rose.

He'd cleared his plate. Rose was nibbling on toast spread with red berry jam.

The dining table was set with charger plates, coffee mugs, and utensils. I selected a small white china bowl from a stack on the sideboard and served myself some fruit salad, completely intending to come back for a double helping of the scalloped potatoes I'd spotted in one of the warmers.

"We need to go to the manor," Declan said, not looking up from his newspaper. "I'm not waiting around to hear back from some vampire. Whether or not he's in town doesn't mean he isn't involved."

Apparently, I hadn't been the only one whose thoughts had strayed to Jasper the previous night.

"I know," I said as I picked up the carafe of coffee, then carried it and my fruit salad to the seat across from Declan. I chose to sit beside Rose, leaving the head of the table where Jasper would have sat during a full family gathering vacant.

Rose glanced back and forth between Declan and me. "I haven't collected much information on the vampires. Or contacted some of the out-of-town coven members yet. Give me a few more hours."

Declan closed the paper. Folding it and tossing it on the table, he reached for his half-full coffee mug and settled back in his chair, staring steadily at our aunt.

He looked utterly out of place surrounded by fine china and delicate furniture. And he wasn't actually blood related to anyone in the dining room. For some reason, both observations brought a smile to my face. Declan wasn't a Fairchild.

Rose dropped his gaze, glancing over at me instead.

I carefully placed my bowl of fruit salad on the charger plate set before me. Then I made a show of pouring coffee into the china mug beside it.

"You shouldn't go out without the vampire," Rose said. "This is his issue, after all."

"He walks in the daylight," I said.

"Yes. I see." Rose sounded flustered, but was trying to act as if a vampire not being dead to the world while the sun was up wasn't dreadful news. "Of course."

Declan set his emptied mug on its saucer, then let his hand settle on the table next to it. He tapped his fingers one at a time as if counting down—or perhaps attempting to control his temper.

I leaned across the table, topping up his mug before sitting down. He nodded thanks, still not looking away from Rose.

"Cream?"

"I take it black," he said, not unkindly.

I set the carafe on the stretch of linen-swathed table between us, sitting down to sip the hot, dark brew.

"Is he at the manor?" Declan asked Rose, pointedly.

She played with the sterling silver teaspoon on the edge of her saucer.

I speared a piece of cantaloupe out of my bowl of fruit and chewed it slowly, savoring the sweet juice across my tongue.

"Yes. I imagine … I assumed he'd selected a room in the basement, but now that Wisteria has indicated—"

"Not the vampire, Rose." Declan kept his tone even, but he wasn't as capable as a true-blood Fairchild was of hiding his anger and frustration.

Even Rose's outward fretfulness was something of a pretense. Not that she wasn't worried about what Declan and I were capable of, but she was at least choosing to let us see her concern.

"Is he in residence, Rose? Were you just covering for him last night at Grey and Dahlia's?"

"This doesn't have anything to do with your uncle," my aunt finally said. "This is obviously the vampire's doing, and Jasmine's."

Declan snorted, crossed his arms, and looked at me.

I took a measured sip of my coffee, then set down my mug. China clicked on china, intensifying the tension in the dining room.

"Three vampires are roaming Fairchild territory," I said, keeping my tone politely crisp. "Perhaps four. Jasmine tracked them here."

"Perhaps they followed her home," Rose said. "That would be a far more logical assumption."

Declan snorted again.

"The chance that they're here without permission is exceedingly low. And if you didn't give that permission as acting head of the coven, who did?"

"It's a simple thing to verify, Rose," Declan said. "Is he or has he recently been in residence or not?"

My aunt lifted her chin. "No. But I ... I haven't heard from him this morning."

"I wasn't aware that he was so ... mobile," I said, spearing a sliced strawberry with my perfectly balanced fork. "That the coven permitted him any time in which to answer a summons."

"I tried to talk to you last night, Wisteria," Rose said, laying her hand on my arm. "It's time to put all this behind you. The coven is weakened without—"

Declan stood abruptly, hitting the edge of the table hard enough to slop my coffee.

Rose snapped her mouth closed on the rest of her plea.

Casually removing my aunt's hand from my arm by lifting it, I ate the strawberry.

Declan tossed his cloth napkin on the table, downed his hot coffee in one gulp, then slammed the empty cup into its saucer and strode from the room.

"We'll be heading to Fairchild Manor after breakfast," I said, keeping my tone even despite the way my heart rate ramped up at my own pronouncement.

"He's ... he's on the island ... for his monthly treatment," Rose said, expanding on what my mother had said last night.

The island. She most likely meant the property in Barbados. I glanced over at her, but she was avoiding my gaze.

"So he comes and goes as he wishes," I whispered.

My fruit dish cracked. The white bone china split in half and collapsed to either side, the remainder of my fruit salad spilling out over the charger plate. Evidently, I didn't have myself as under control as I thought. Rose and I both stared at the ruined bowl.

She swallowed. "Please ... it was previously arranged. I'm not strong enough to—"

Declan strode back into the dining room, practically boiling with magic. He placed his hands on the table, leaning across it and leveling his gaze with Rose's. "If I find out that this is you," he said. "If I find out that any of you has arranged for Jasmine to be snatched in order to get Wisteria back here ..."

The promise of utter destruction was laced through every word, but my heart thumped in my chest for a completely different reason.

"Then what?" Rose snapped, shifting back to rise from her chair—and transforming from a simple healer to the head of the Fairchild coven with that single movement. "You'll bring the house down on me, Declan? Destroy the only family you've ever had, flawed as it might be?"

A terrible fierce smile stretched across Declan's face. "Don't allow your snobbery and your misplaced bravado to get away on you, Rose. I'd rather destroy the only family I've ever had than allow everything good and true in that family to be drained away."

"How dare you threaten me across my own dining room table," Rose said. "I will not—"

"He didn't mean you," I said, reaching for the carafe of coffee and topping up my mug.

Rose frowned.

Declan's nasty smile ebbed into a sneer.

"You'll make more phone calls, then?" I asked. "Whether or not he is in residence, I'd like to depart immediately after breakfast."

"Of course," Rose said stiffly. Then she turned to cross toward the foyer.

"And, Rose ..." I called after her.

My aunt paused in the doorway, half turning back to me.

"If Jasper is in any way involved with Jasmine's disappearance ..."—I waved my hand offishly—"... what Declan said holds. There's no point, you see. Jasper has already tried to take Jasmine from us once. If he manages to kill her this time, we won't survive it. One way or the other."

Rose closed her eyes, pained.

I slid my chair back and stood, crossing to the sideboard and serving myself a generous helping of scalloped potatoes from the silver warming dish. "It's the blood connection, of course," I said, continuing as if we were having a casual conversation. "And being raised together under great duress. But it's also what he did to us. How he tied us together. Bound us in power and despair." Then I lifted my gaze to meet Declan's. "And pleasure, unwillingly forced upon us—"

"Wisteria ..." Rose said, chastising me.

"Oh, I know." I added two pieces of perfectly crisp bacon to my plate. "Not a proper topic for the breakfast table. And obviously, you still don't believe me. Or perhaps you just still can't believe that your brother would be capable of molesting—"

"Please. Don't."

Having made my point, I quietly added a mound of scrambled eggs to my plate. Then I carefully closed all the warming dishes and returned to the table.

Rose hadn't moved from the doorway.

Declan was still watching her, not me.

I smoothed my napkin over my lap, picking up my fork. "You know, it didn't occur to me at the time, when I was desperate to save Declan and Jasmine from the coven's wrath, then quickly realized I was going to have to … mitigate the circumstances. But the Fairchild coven could have had the truth, effortlessly. A powerful reader would have shown you all our thoughts. And Jasper's deeds from his own perspective, of course. A reconstruction could have been collected—"

"Multiple reconstructions," Declan said. Still standing, he reached across the table to steal one of my pieces of bacon. "Though who could have been commissioned to collect them without bias?"

Rose didn't respond to either of us.

I took a bite of the scalloped potatoes. They were utterly perfect. Just a hint of onion and garlic, smooth Gruyere cheese, and a touch of salt.

"Of course, any commissioned reader or reconstructionist would have gained too much information about the Fairchild coven," I said musingly, as if I was simply voicing my thoughts as they occurred to me. "How would you have dealt with that? One of my mother's untraceable poisons, perhaps."

"Wisteria … I …" Rose finally broke her silence. "You can't possibly think we would murder someone, anyone, to cover up anything Jasper had done."

The scrambled eggs were fluffy, without a hint of dryness. I looked at Declan, who was watching every little thing I was doing. "Remember that day in the orchard?"

He arched an eyebrow at me, picking up his fork and scoring a bite of my potatoes. "With the rabbit."

Rose flinched as if Declan had slapped her.

"He was seething with power that day," I said, still keeping my tone completely casual. "I'm not sure that it didn't distract him. Disposing of his apprentice's body. Which was how we got off the property without him noticing."

Declan rubbed his neck. "He noticed."

"Eventually."

"He had a lot of apprentices." Declan's tone was deep and deadly.

"But accidents happen," I said, deliberately raising the tenor of my voice over his, light and sweet. "Don't they, Rose?"

Rose didn't answer, choosing to walk away instead. My heart sank as I watched her disappear into the foyer.

I never knew what I wanted from her, what I wanted from any of them. Something I couldn't imagine they would give me even if they were capable of it.

"Did that make you feel better?" Declan asked softly.

Glancing over at him, I noticed that he'd seared his handprints into the linen tablecloth—something he used to do inadvertently when we were younger. So I wasn't the only one letting my magic get away from me.

I caught his golden-hazel gaze with my own, offering him a self-deprecating smirk. "You tell me."

Declan threw himself down in his chair without answering. I filled his mug with coffee, emptying the carafe. He nodded thanks, reaching for it but not drinking.

"Jasmine keeps waiting for them to say sorry," he said, gazing out the windows to my right.

"I never expected an apology. Even at sixteen, I knew what it took to be a Fairchild. Never apologizing is one of their ten commandments."

Declan sipped his coffee, looking at me. The china mug was too small for his large hands.

I nibbled on a piece of bacon, then carefully wiped my fingers on my napkin. "What I did expect was to be protected. I thought we three were worthy of being protected."

"You were worthy."

"No, Declan." I shook my head, knowing from deep within my soul that I was uttering the absolute truth. "The only Fairchild who cherished us stripped our childhoods from us, perverted our affections, then raped and tried to kill Jasmine."

He grimaced. "I'm not sure she sees it as rape."

"We saw it for what it was," I said.

I knew that Declan remembered that day as vividly as I did. We had ripped through Jasper's wards, discovering him in the basement with Jasmine. We'd fought him together, tearing Jasmine from our uncle's grasp.

We saw it for what it was. All of it done in the name of power. All in the name of fortifying the coven.

Declan's face flushed with some intense emotion he couldn't quite keep contained. I wasn't sure if it was anger or regret. Perhaps it was both. "And now they want us back," he murmured.

My voice fell to a soft, fierce whisper. "The only elder Fairchild who ever loved us was Jasper himself."

Declan nodded agreement—though he wouldn't meet my gaze.

"So," I said, "logically, the only Fairchild who would want us back is him."

"Do you think he'd arrange for Jasmine to be kidnapped in order to draw us here?"

"I certainly wouldn't doubt it." I pressed my napkin to my lips, then stood and stepped back from the table. "I'll get Kett."

"He's in the library. I'll meet you out front with the Jeep."

Skirting the table and keeping my gaze steadily focused beyond the door, I pressed my hand to Declan's shoulder. My little finger rested on the warm skin of his neck, just at the edge of his black T-shirt.

He reached up, covering my hand with his own. "Maybe we should finish it today," he said. His voice was thick with emotion.

"Maybe we won't have a choice," I said. "If he's even there."

"We always had a choice."

I laughed mirthlessly. "Jasmine was never negotiable."

"No," he said. "And I haven't blown up a house for at least six months. So, hey, maybe a bonus?"

I threw my head back and laughed. Then I dropped my hand from his shoulder, heading toward the library to recruit an ancient vampire for our mission of vengeance. I had no idea whether Kett would be able to even raise a hand against Jasper directly without breaking the Conclave contract. It was an easy guess that such an action would have consequences, even for the executioner.

But if I was going to storm the manor, I wouldn't want anyone by my side other than Kett and Declan.

Except Jasmine.

If I was going to die, I would want Jasmine holding my hand.

I found Kett sitting at the computer tucked between shelves of Greek mythology and Elizabethan poetry. As he often did during the day, the vampire looked disturbingly human, quickly clicking through files and pictures on the screen.

Rose's library was tiny compared to the one at the manor, and canted toward classical literature. It would be unlikely to stumble upon Keats or Austin, or even Hemingway, under Jasper's roof. But I'd read all those authors in this room whenever Jasper was out of town for more than a day or two, when the three of us had been bundled off to stay with Rose rather than our parents. Otherwise, Declan wouldn't have had anywhere to go, and Jasper didn't want us separated.

The niche that had been built between the bookshelves for the computer was a newer addition to the library, but everything else remained the same.

"Good morning," I said, stepping close enough to see the pictures on the monitor but not close enough to read the text. As unpleasant as the exchange with Rose had been, I had no desire to inadvertently destroy her computer as long as it was a potential link to anything Jasmine had found. "Declan is pulling the Jeep around."

"We're heading to the manor," Kett said.

"Are you guessing, or did you hear us?"

"I never guess."

I laughed quietly in response to his brief smile.

"He's not there," Kett said. "Or he wasn't early this morning. It's unlikely he would deny me entry."

Jasper. He meant that he'd gone to Jasper already. "Since he wants you to remake him in your image."

"Indeed. Though I'm certain he doesn't see it that way." Kett started closing files, but not before I caught a glimpse of a driver's license bearing Yale's picture—and a series of images of the teenagers we'd investigated the previous October, including Ben Vern.

"Vampires have driver's licenses?"

"If they're trying to walk in the mundane world, yes. And credit cards and bank accounts."

"Do you have a driver's license?" I asked. Though I knew Kett drove, I was still oddly perturbed by the idea.

He was suddenly standing beside me. I hadn't even seen him move. "Same picture as my passport." He laughed quietly. "Why does the idea disturb you so, little witch?"

I tilted my head, pretending that he hadn't just startled me. "It's so normal."

He chuckled again as he leaned in to me. "I'm anything but normal."

"And the pictures of the boys?" I asked, drawing back from him and keeping us on the track of the investigation. "Is Ben okay?"

"He's in Vancouver. Teresa has him well under control now that he is fully realized."

That didn't exactly answer my question. "Kett. Is there anything about the investigation you and Jasmine were conducting that I need to know? Anything that could ... affect the outcome of this situation?"

"Nothing confirmed."

"But you suspect ... what? Do you think Yale ... do you think he plans on hurting Jasmine, or turning her against her will? Like he did with Nigel, or even Amaya?"

Kett became utterly still, casting his gaze toward the wall of mythology tomes behind us. "What had drawn my interest was his ability to turn so many in such a short period of time. And for them to have retained some aspect of their Adept powers, suggesting that he himself was an Adept before he was remade."

"The silver or white magic around him …" I murmured, recalling the scene in Jasmine's hotel room. "Suggesting what? Some sort of mind magic? He was a telepath or a reader? An oracle? But how would that have helped the others retain their abilities?"

Kett shook his head. "In the reconstruction, Yale appears to be no older than two hundred years. Yet he has clearly remade three vampires that I know of, and four if the male you spotted in the lobby is his progeny."

"You thought that Yale's youth could have accounted for Nigel's … frailty? Coupled with his lack of magic?"

Kett didn't answer me. I reached out and tentatively touched his forearm. He smiled, possibly pleased at the intimacy implied in my willingness to make contact with him.

"Yes," he said, delicately wrapping his fingers around my wrist. "But then there were the boys, as you call them …"

He trailed off, releasing me, and bemusedly looking at his hand.

He'd been touching my white-picket-fence bracelet.

I grabbed his wrist, tugging it toward me. An outline of the bracelet was seared across his palm. Tiny charms and all.

I looked up at him, aghast. I hadn't even felt any magic shift between us. "I would never … well, I didn't intentionally—"

Kett laughed, the sound filled with warmth and satisfaction. "Armed for vampire," he said, repeating Jade's declaration after she'd tied his magic to my bracelet with seemingly effortless alchemy.

The wound on his hand healed.

I let go of him, stepping back so we weren't huddled by the bookshelf so intimately. I wasn't jealous of the affection he held for the dowser. Whether or not I accepted his offer of immortality, he'd made it clear that what he wanted from me went beyond a temporary infatuation. The fact that he could think in terms of centuries—that he could plan for centuries—was unsettling.

But none of that was more important than finding Jasmine before nightfall.

"What about the boys?" I asked, pulling our conversation back on track and trying to figure out what would still interest Kett in the case. "The fact that they rose at all? With only three pints of blood?"

He nodded.

"So you think … that ability is something Nigel inherited? You said your maker inherited a gift from your grandsire, yes?"

"I did. And perhaps."

"So that makes Yale interesting. Even valuable."

Kett locked his silver gaze to mine, seemingly pleased at my assessment.

"A Fairchild witch would be a valuable ally," I murmured. "For you."

"For Yale," Kett said, correcting me. "I already have connections to the coven. You and Jasper."

"So … with that all taken into account, do you think Yale would try to take Jasmine against her will?"

"I think he'd be a fool to try."

"How foolish do you think he's already been?" I whispered the question, though I didn't really want an answer.

"Quite foolish." Kett brushed his fingers across the back of my hand. Then he was gone.

I wandered out of the library at a slower pace, then climbed the stairs to collect my coat and bag from my room. Too many unknowns were whirling around in my mind.

All the hard evidence pointed toward Kett and Jasmine's investigation being the center of everything, with Yale having come to Litchfield just as part of whatever game he was playing. But still, I recognized that some self-destructive part of me desperately wanted Jasper to be responsible, so that I could immolate myself while rescuing Jasmine from him a second time.

So that I could destroy the Fairchild coven, avenging my childhood in the process.

The sight of Fairchild Manor was still impressive, even though I'd spent almost every day of my life from the age of nine to sixteen effectively trapped on the property.

Not that I had known I was trapped at the time.

I glanced over at Declan as we drove along the sparsely forested western edge of the estate's two hundred and eighty acres. His hands were steady at the wheel of the Jeep, his eyes hidden behind his sunglasses, but tension was etched across his jawline and his thinned lips.

Kett remained a silent accomplice in the back seat, as he had for the entire drive.

I knew that this land didn't call to Declan in the same way it called to me. It never had, even though the manor was more his home than it was mine. I could remember every footstep, every breath of air, every apple blossom in the spring, and every snow sculpture we'd magically coaxed to form in the yard in winter.

My memories of my childhood were few and far between, but I remembered the feel of Fairchild land. The manor grounds were the magical epicenter of the coven, and had been from even before the main house was built in the early nineteen hundreds.

A dozen yards from the front gates, Declan pulled to a stop.

I glanced over at him questioningly.

"Don't want the Jeep caught in the line of fire," he said grimly.

"You think we'll have a shoot-out at the gate?"

"You don't?"

I glanced at the six-foot-high stone wall that radiated out from the gate to encircle the acreage. The manor was situated at the top of a gradual slope, and it was a ten-minute walk from the gates to the front door. "I assumed we'd at least make it to the front yard."

Declan snorted, climbing out of the vehicle.

Kett chuckled to himself, then exited out Declan's open door.

I gathered my bag, buttoning my coat as I followed them. By the time I reached the twelve-foot-high gatepost, Declan had rung the bell twice. Though the day was colder than the previous night had been, it was bright. Kett was sporting his sunglasses-and-baseball-cap look. He'd abandoned the black cashmere coat—or what was left of it after the damage from Declan's blasting rod—opting instead for a dark-blue sweater, a scarf woven in different shades of gray, and dark-blue jeans.

Declan reached toward the buzzer a third time.

"Don't," I said. "If he's here, he'll know we're anxious."

"We're standing by his wards." Declan pressed his finger to the buzzer and left it there as he eyed me belligerently through his sunglasses. "He knows we're anxious."

"Don't punish me, Declan," I whispered. "You called. I'm here."

Declan released the buzzer, looking away from me. "Announce yourself, then," he said bluntly. "He won't turn you away."

I stepped forward, raising my right hand to the impenetrable wall of ward magic that coated the outer edges of the property and could be called forth at any other point on the acreage and used to shield the outbuildings. A separate, even more powerful ward protected the manor itself.

Jasper had often used the centuries of magic embedded within the estate to contain Declan, Jasmine, and me in turn, teaching us to break through that magic. Each time we managed to free ourselves, he had called up another layer with which to contain us. In the end, Jasmine hadn't been able to free herself. We'd been fourteen at the time, and surreptitiously using Bluebell the brownie to slip Jasmine food and water. After three days, I'd freed her myself. Jasper had responded by punishing Declan for a week, confining him to his room and limiting him to one meal a day. Because punishing Jasmine or Declan was always much more effective than simply punishing me.

Pressing my hand to the magic, I laughed wryly at the painful memory, earning myself a quizzical glance from Declan.

That had been the first time I realized that my uncle couldn't track or contain Bluebell. It was also the first time it became clear that I was the most naturally powerful of the three of us.

My hand slipped through the ward with no resistance. Declan muttered something nasty under his breath. I pressed my palm toward the lock at the center of the gates. It released.

"We're expected," I said, not at all surprised.

The gate slowly opened before us.

"Or you're still just tied to all of this somehow," Declan said.

I glanced over at him. "I'm quite possibly about to face the man who destroyed everything I thought to be true and real. Including you, and what I mistakenly thought you felt for me."

Declan set his jaw as if ready to chew through whatever retort he was about to voice, but I cut him off.

"Except for Jasmine," I said. "She's all I have in this world."

"I would do anything—"

"Either you're with me," I said carefully, "or I'll face whatever's to come alone."

"Not alone," Kett said.

Declan's gaze slid over my shoulder as he frowned at the vampire.

"I won't fight you any longer, Declan," I said. "This is too important."

"So I'm just supposed to follow you like a besotted acolyte?"

"There is an in-between," I said. "Make a choice."

Turning away from him, I reached back with my left hand without looking. At my unspoken invitation, Kett threaded his fingers through mine. Then I pulled a vampire through the wards of the Fairchilds' most significant stronghold.

At the last possible second, Declan grabbed my elbow and followed us through the gates and onto the driveway.

We paused as the magic that protected the property from uninvited guests flowed in and around us. The invisible energy tugged at my eyes and hands, as if coaxing me to drop my personal shields.

"Impressive," Kett said.

"You've been here before," I said.

"Not with you." The vampire's hand was still entwined with mine.

Declan dropped my arm as soon as the boundary magic accepted his presence. Though I suspected he could have walked through the ward line on his own just as easily.

I scanned the grounds before us. Extensive, unadorned and gently rolling lawns extended out on either side of the driveway, marking the edges of a broad forest of winter-bare trees. Dogwood, red oak, maple, hickory, poplar, birch, and elms occupied well over two hundred acres of the estate.

Up a slight hill toward the center of the forty or fifty acres that had been cleared around it, the ten-thousand-square-foot, three-level main house had been built by my great-grandparents in the Tudor Revival style—a behemoth English country manor in stone and stucco.

"Can you sense whether or not he's here?" Declan asked.

I didn't respond. Though I'd used the ward magic at Fairchild Park to send a message to Declan, I wasn't about to try to do the same in Jasper's territory.

"It was never a problem for you before," Declan said, somehow picking up on the thread of my thoughts.

"Only a fool would open herself up to magic controlled by a potential enemy," Kett said.

"Helpful, vampire," Declan growled. "And what do your far superior senses tell you?"

Kett untangled his fingers from mine, taking a step away. He slowly pivoted his head, scanning what seemed to be every inch of the property within immediate view, as if he was taking Declan's sarcasm seriously. "No humans currently occupy the lands within the boundary magic," he said. "But the magic is saturated in various places. Impenetrable to casual assessment."

"No humans?" Declan asked. "What the hell else would be here?"

Before Kett gave us a rundown on every woodland creature, rodent, and bird currently nesting on the estate, I interrupted. "The wards on the manor are extensive. Is it safe to assume you also can't penetrate those at this distance?"

Kett nodded.

"You think he's lying in wait for us in the house?" Declan asked mockingly. "Giving us a false sense of security by opening the wards?"

"He didn't open the wards," I said. "They were still keyed to us."

Declan grunted noncommittally.

"We'll have to physically search the house for residual magic," I said. "As well as the orchard and gardens."

"And most of the front yard," Declan said.

"The house wards extend out that far?" Kett asked.

Declan set his mouth grimly.

I glanced at the vampire, ignoring the twist of fear that ran through my belly. "The basement does."

"Let's hope to God that Jasmine isn't in the basement," Declan muttered.

"Even if Jasper is involved," I said. "There's no way he's inept enough to have kept Jasmine here."

"That's debatable," Declan said. "His megalomania could have easily tipped over the edge of insanity."

I glanced at Kett, thinking of the contract Jasper had forged with the Conclave—and what that possibly said about my uncle's state of mind.

Kett nodded almost imperceptibly, as if acknowledging my unvoiced concerns.

I shook off that disturbing thought and began walking up the driveway, focusing on the task at hand. "I'll take the orchard and gardens," I said. "Declan, take the front and side yards, including the pool."

"I'll search the remainder of the property," Kett said. Then he all but disappeared.

Declan swore.

"Remember to look for pockets of magic," I called after the vampire. "We'll meet up at the house."

"I doubt he can hear you," Declan said, stuffing his hands deeply in the pockets of his leather jacket.

"He can hear me."

Declan snorted, then pressed something into my right hand.

I glanced down at the small stone he'd tucked into my palm. It was etched with a single rune I didn't recognize.

"Put it in your pocket," he said. "Trigger it if you get into trouble."

"My magic doesn't play well with—"

"Just put it in your pocket, Wisteria. You can't occupy the moral high ground all the time."

He veered off to the right across the front yard. "Fifteen minutes. Then meet me at the kitchen doors, whether or not you're done."

I tucked the stone into my pocket, more pleased by the gesture than I probably should have been, for the sake of my own emotional welfare.

Declan needed me to find Jasmine. But he'd made his personal boundaries exceedingly clear.

Still, I kept glancing back at him as I continued up the drive. He'd immediately begun to swiftly walk a grid across the front yard, working his way back toward the house.

I focused myself forward, picking up my pace. The manor loomed before me, but I didn't have to tackle that ten-thousand-square-foot magic-infested monstrosity quite yet. First I would check the orchards and the garden. It seemed highly unlikely that any clues would be found underneath the bare grapevines or apple trees, but we'd learned at a young age to never underestimate our uncle.

His brand of evil always hid in plain sight.

Wide stone pathways twined across the property from the back of the manor, crisscrossing through vegetable gardens and stands of Japanese pagoda trees, lilac, and magnolia. They wound through the expansive grape arbors, shooting off toward the apple orchard in one direction, the outdoor pool in the other, and toward the caretaker's cottage and other outbuildings at the back of the property.

Back when Jasper was mentoring, his apprentices had often used a golf cart to come and go across the property. But twelve years ago, Declan, Jasmine, and I had just run free whenever we got the chance.

The gardens were bare now, and not simply because it was winter. They appeared to have been allowed to fall fallow. The grape arbor desperately needed to be hacked back. And as I crossed through into the orchard, I almost turned my ankle on the piles of decomposing fruit littering the ground.

The day was chilly but nowhere near freezing. Normally, the entire estate would be blanketed by snow this time of year, and it was disconcerting to observe its outward lifelessness while feeling the vibrant magic underlying every step I took, urging me onward.

The hutch I'd built underneath the apple trees at the southwest edge of the orchard, then had fruitlessly reinforced every spring in the hopes of attracting rabbits, was still standing after more than twelve years. The magic of the estate settled as I neared the site, whispering to me, brushing against my eyes and teasing the palms of my hands.

I ducked underneath the winter-bare branches that had turned unruly without proper pruning, crossing to hunker down by the empty hutch. From where I crouched, I could see the full extent of the back of the manor through the trees. But when the boughs had exploded with apple blossoms in the spring, then leafed out green and hung heavy with fruit throughout the summer, the orchard had been a perfect sanctuary.

Even after that first spring when I'd built the hutch for an injured rabbit we'd rescued. Even after Jasper had found the three of us secretly caring for the rabbit, and had tried to teach us how to kill with our magic. And even after we'd run away to Rose's and were immediately turned back over to our uncle, we returned to that spot year after year.

I brushed my fingers across the piece of wood I'd angled over a short wall of rocks between two exposed tree roots. It disintegrated underneath my touch.

A wave of shock ran through me. I choked out a sob I hadn't been aware I was holding back.

I pressed my hand across my mouth, stopping any further expression of pain from getting loose. I squeezed my eyes closed, struggling against the tears suddenly streaming down my face.

This wasn't the time to give in.

This wasn't the time to collapse. Wood rotted, returning to the earth. That was just the proper way of things.

The magic of the estate brushed against me more insistently, almost as if cajoling me to play. As if it had missed me, which was ridiculous. That energy didn't have feelings or thoughts. It just existed. It was simply an accumulation of centuries of Fairchild magic. I should be immune to it.

I wrapped my hand over my white-picket-fence bracelet, feeling the tickle of my own magic from the tiny reconstructions nestled among the platinum charms. I touched the tiny cube that held the reconstruction of Declan, then the cube that held the memory I'd collected of Jasmine.

But I didn't have to trigger that reconstruction in order to view it. I was standing in the very spot I'd collected it from.

I opened my eyes.

Jasmine, age nine, was crouched beside me, overseeing the feeding of our rescued rabbit. She threw her head back, laughing at something Declan or I had said.

I squeezed my eyes shut.

I hadn't set any candles. I shouldn't be calling forth magic without a proper boundary. And there was no good reason to be reconstructing that moment again anyway.

I opened my eyes.

Declan, who had just turned ten, swung down from the tree branch above us, landing barefoot in the grass. Jasmine shrieked playfully as she sprang up to defend the sacred space of the rabbit hutch.

With no intent of doing so, I had called forth a reconstruction from the magic teeming around me.

The sequence was already running front to back, as if I'd triggered it simply by walking into the orchard. I knew if I looked down and to the side, I would see myself offering the rabbit a carrot I'd just liberated from the garden.

I was crouched down within my own reconstruction. I was inside my past. And in this moment, we were whole. Undamaged. Free.

Declan had joined us three months previously. We'd just celebrated his birthday and were about to celebrate mine.

But in a few moments, Jasper would find us. With magical power boiling around him, he would cross the orchard grass and teach us the most important lesson of our lives.

Trust no one but each other.

Even now, within the reconstruction, I could feel the magic shifting, preparing for his appearance. It was most likely the sheer power of his residual imprint that made the reconstruction possible in the first place.

Stirring my hands through the magic, I restarted the scene. It swirled around me in a myriad of blues, then

Jasmine was crouched beside me, laughing again. She looked so real that I was almost convinced I could reach over, tug on one of her curls, and watch it spring back.

I lifted my hand, idiotically allowing myself to believe.

Declan jumped out of the tree.

Jasmine sprang away, standing between him and me. Laughter rolled through the fruit-laden boughs around us, echoing back to me with a whisper of magic.

I watched the scene again and again, restarting it each time just at the moment before Jasper appeared.

That moment, that day, was the birth of Betty-Sue, Betty-Lou, and Bubba. And no matter how much the bond between us would be manipulated and conditioned by Jasper over the next six years—in that moment, we were pure.

We loved.

And we believed that we were loved, and even cherished, in return. Even Declan must have thought that Jasper cared for him, having rescued him.

And we weren't wrong.

Not in that moment, anyway.

I replayed the scene, feeding the rabbit, laughing with my younger self, and loving without reservation.

"Wisteria …"

I brushed the voice away, thinking that I'd let the scene play too long and Jasper was intruding.

"Wisteria …"

Someone was trying to call me away … a deep, angry voice. I didn't want to listen. I pressed my hands over my ears.

"Wisteria!"

Rough hands closed around me, pinning my arms to my sides. Then those hands attempted to lift me, trying to pull me away from the magic of the reconstruction.

I shrieked, twisting and kicking out at my captor.

But he was stronger than me.

It didn't matter, though. I had the magic. I was the most skilled reconstructionist in the northern hemisphere. No one could take the magic from me.

I reached for the residual, gathering it toward me. Hoarding it over my heart.

The arms around me tightened, dragging my physical body away. But my captor couldn't have my mind.

At the edge of the reconstruction, Jasper appeared.

I'd lost my focus. I had let him into the scene. He was barefoot, his blond hair long and wild. He boiled with magic, streaking all around him in dark shades of blue.

And we three turned to him, smiling and innocent.

"No!" I screamed. I was sobbing. "No! You can't have them! I won't let you have them!"

My captor gripped my arms even tighter, shaking me.

Then he kissed me, harshly.

My hold on the residual magic slipped.

"Please … please … "

He was pleading. His magic danced against my lips.

"Please, please, Betty-Sue. Come back to me. Please, God, don't leave me again."

"Betty-Sue … " I whispered.

"Oh, yes. God, yes."

Tiny pinpoints of pain rained across my face and neck. Just like the sparks I'd seen cascading from his hand. Just like the fireworks he wielded in the other reconstruction I cherished.

Declan.

Declan's lips. Declan's magic. Declan's touch.

And I was Betty-Sue.

I allowed myself to see beyond the magic I'd collected, meeting Declan's terrified gaze. We were still surrounded by the reconstruction, but all I could see was his golden-hazel eyes. Reaching up, I brushed my fingers across the stubble that covered his jaw.

"I'm here," I said.

He kissed me again, softer this time. Then he swept me up in his arms, lifting me off the ground and somehow buffering me from the magic that seethed across the estate.

I completely lost my hold on the reconstruction. As it collapsed, the blue sky of the late morning came into focus.

Magic didn't have feelings, didn't have moods. But in that brief moment of hazy lucidity, I thought that the estate's magic might have just made a failed attempt to keep me. Trying to collect me, as I had collected the tiny reconstructions on my bracelet.

"I tried," I whispered. "I tried to stay."

"I know," Declan said. "I know."

Darkness closed over me, and I fell into a deep slumber.

Chapter Nine

Cool fingers brushed across my eyelids, pressing lightly at my temples, then releasing. I was lying down with my head and shoulders propped up on something. My legs and torso were tightly wrapped, as if someone had swaddled me.

"Welcome back, reconstructionist." Kett's normally cool voice was edged with frustration.

"I apologize," I whispered without opening my eyes. "I got drawn into the magic." I lifted my arm, palm up, still feeling the power of the estate dancing in and around my hand. "I'm ... having an odd reaction to being here."

"You're letting your emotions lead you," Kett said.

I laughed quietly. "I thought you liked it when I did that."

Declan cleared his throat from somewhere by my head. Blinking, I opened my eyes. I was staring up at the gilded ceiling of the parlor in Fairchild Manor.

Kett was sitting next to me on a green brocade chaise. Declan was standing beside me. He turned away, but I grabbed his hand.

"Thank you," I said. "I'm not sure I could have gotten free on my own."

"Not without wanting to let go," he said.

I nodded, dropping his hand. But not before I noticed the three thick nested rings he wore. Each copper ring held a raw gemstone—a topaz, a sapphire, and a fire opal.

Our three birthstones, imbued with magic.

My magical senses were wide open, which was presumably why I could suddenly see the rings. I assumed Declan must have worn them all the time but kept them magically concealed. It was also why I could feel the magic of the house wards so intensely. I began envisioning layers and layers of my magic building up and around me, calling forth my usually tightly held shields.

"You felt something in the orchard?" Kett asked. "Something that drained your magic? Declan wasn't forthcoming."

So that was the root of the vampire's frustration. He'd found me collapsed on the couch, and Declan had refused to tell him what happened.

"Nothing relevant." I toyed with the tiny reconstruction cubes on my bracelet, feeling utterly stupid.

"But you called it forth nonetheless." Kett's gaze was on my hands. "Without your candles or your circle."

I stopped fiddling with the bracelet. "Yes. Like I said, the magic here is ... intense. Familiar ..." I hesitated, not sure how to rationally explain that the magic of the estate felt as though it was playing with me somehow. "It won't happen again."

I shifted in the chaise so that I was sitting more upright. I had been wrapped up tightly in a patchwork crochet blanket I'd never seen before.

I glanced over at Declan, who was slowly pacing the length of the parlor. The room looked exactly the same as it had the day I left Fairchild Manor, never to return.

Until now. The limestone fireplace was stacked with split wood, ready to be lit. Muted green-printed wallpaper filled the space above chestnut paneling running throughout the main rooms on the first floor. Matching hand-carved double doors led to the marble-floored grand entranceway, while sliding doors led back through the massive dining room to the even larger kitchen at the back of the house.

Kett passed me a glass of water, which I took eagerly, then sipped carefully. I desperately needed to do something with my hands, but was still feeling too depleted to get up and move.

"You didn't have any trouble with the house wards?" I asked.

Declan shook his head. "Kitchen door opened when I was a few feet away. And I was able to invite the vamp … Kett in when he arrived."

"Does the house usually react to you in that manner?" Kett asked.

Declan glanced my way. "Not me."

Kett pinned me with his silvered gaze, and for a brief moment, I felt the brush of his magic.

I eyed him over the edge of the water glass. "Just ask your questions," I said.

"My apologies," he murmured. "It's a struggle to stay out of your head."

Declan muttered sarcastically. "I wonder why."

"Jasmine has told me the story of the rabbit you rescued," Kett continued, ignoring Declan. "Of the origins of your nicknames."

I took another sip of water, not at all surprised that Jasmine had shared the story of that day.

Declan stilled behind Kett. "And why would she have done that?"

"I asked," the vampire said offishly, his gaze still resting on me. "Though that wasn't the story I requested originally.

Was that event the reconstruction you were caught in?" He hovered his fingers over my bracelet. "Is it the one you hold here?"

I laughed sadly, looking up at Declan. "Yes."

"How is that relevant?" Declan asked.

"It is relevant to Wisteria's future," Kett said, keeping his gaze on me.

"It's her past," Declan spat. "The first of many tests we endured."

"Which you failed."

"Until we passed. Until Wisteria passed. It's done. And not remotely relevant to finding Jasmine."

"Do you think we're here because of Jasper?" I asked Kett, untucking my legs from the blanket and swinging them off the chaise so I could sit upright. "Because of the contract?"

Kett shrugged. "I know what you know. Jasmine was drawn home, tracking Nigel's maker. The vampire who calls himself Yale, along with his brood, then kidnapped her. It could have nothing to do with Jasper or the schism within the Fairchild coven. In fact, a connection between Yale and your uncle would be coincidental enough to stretch incredulity."

"What contract?" Declan asked.

"Unless … what if Yale figured out who Jasmine was?" I said, ignoring Declan's question. "He might have approached Jasper for an explanation of her investigation. Only to discover that the Conclave was involved, not the coven."

"Goddamn you both," Declan snarled. "If there's something else going on here—"

"Nothing that has to do with Jasmine's kidnapping," I said, though I wasn't completely certain that was the truth. But I wasn't lying. Not yet. Not unless we discovered there was more to the plot.

Declan's pacing ramped up a notch, circling the room then switching back.

I lifted my palm to the magic I could still feel surrounding us. My personal shields were dampening it, but didn't completely mute it.

"Do you feel that?"

"Yes." Declan and Kett answered in unison.

"Does it feel … lonely to you?"

"No," Declan said.

I locked my gaze to his. "Do you think … do you think the magic is missing us? Or Bluebell?"

"Wisteria," Declan snarled, but then he made an effort to soften his tone. "I know you're still shaking off the residual … feelings brought up from the reconstruction in the orchard, but now is not the time."

"The brownie?" Kett asked.

"Yes …" I whispered, dragging my gaze away from Declan to meet the vampire's questioning look.

I could still remember the lightness that Bluebell's magic brought to any room she was in, whether I could see her—wearing one of the pristinely pressed dresses she had made out of antique tea towels—or not. I remembered how she used to sneak me my favorite treats when I was out of favor with Jasper, her overly large, rough hands brushing away the tears I struggled to hold at bay. The manor was empty without her presence. Dull and displaced.

Then like some deep well had broken open within me, the one memory I'd spent the last twelve years refusing to acknowledge over all others came pouring forth.

"I sacrificed our brownie …" I whispered. "Bluebell, our protector … the only reason we survived our childhoods … I sacrificed her to save the three of us."

I had spent the twelve years since committing that terrible act trying to live a productive life. A good life. Trying to shift the balance. But I could still feel the deep black mark that day had left on my soul. A stain I couldn't ever scrub away no matter how precisely I controlled my magic. No matter how many investigations I helped solve for the Convocation.

"Jasper killed Bluebell," Declan said viciously. "For standing against him. For standing with us. It was the act of defying her sworn master that gave him any power over her at all."

"But I took the magic released from her death." I said it as matter-of-factly as I could. "I grabbed it before Jasper could break us with it. Before he could destroy the bond he'd wrought between us."

"The power of three," Kett said knowingly, as if I was only confirming the pieces of a puzzle he'd already assembled.

I continued as if he hadn't interrupted, needing to purge the past in order to get off the chaise and get on with searching the house for clues. "Jasmine was incapacitated when we found her lashed to a stone altar that Jasper had somehow manifested from the earth underneath the house. The basement is dirt."

"I know," Kett said. "I checked while you were recuperating. No altar."

I nodded, then took another sip of cool water, letting it slip soothingly down my throat before continuing. "Declan fell protecting Jasmine. It was just me ..." Despite my resolve, my voice cracked. "I was all that stood between Jasper and ... destroying everything we'd tried to build, every moment we'd hidden away from him and greedily savored. We'd just been trying to get Jasmine away from him, thinking he'd cool down. He was angry at Declan and me."

"Wisteria." Declan kneeled before me, so that our eyes were almost level. He didn't touch me, though.

I wasn't sure if he was pleading for me to stop talking or offering me solidarity. Either way, something about returning to the manor, about reliving the moment in the orchard over and over again, had loosened my tongue.

"We'd messed up his long-term plan," I said, glancing at Kett sitting silently to my left. "Breaking a purity rule in complete ignorance of why he'd insisted on it in the first place."

"He certainly had no issues with touching us himself," Declan said, more angry than pained. "But Wisteria and I inadvertently cemented the bond between us."

"With Jasmine tied to us both by blood and magic," I added.

Declan touched my knee lightly, then withdrew his hand. "Effectively cutting the powermongering ringmaster out of the loop."

"So he punished us, as he always did. By punishing Jasmine. It was an effective technique. For six years, at least."

"Yeah." Declan hacked out a pained laugh. "Great parenting."

"But then he took it too far. I … I was certain he was going to kill her."

"He was going to."

"And he was too powerful," I said. "He tore through whatever shield we held against him. Until I had nothing left, I was completely drained."

"Of your personal reserves, perhaps," Kett said, inserting his cool logic into the story and keeping me focused on the tale rather than on the emotions connected to it. Perhaps the ancient vampire knew a thing or two about purging the past. "Jasper never taught you how to pull magic from the bond?"

"Why would he?" Declan kept his gaze locked to mine even as he responded to Kett. "The power of three wasn't for us."

"We were to be his weapon," I said. "Whatever spell he planned to use Jasmine for might have been a way to manipulate the bond, letting him control Declan and me again. But we'll never know."

I took another steadying sip of water, then carefully placed the glass down on a side table. "Jasmine and Declan were insensible on the ground behind me. But I couldn't hold Jasper off any longer. He strode toward me, knife in one hand, ready to knock me aside … to drag Jasmine to the altar again. But Bluebell appeared between us. She defied her master multiple times that day."

"We wouldn't have been able to get into the damn basement without her help," Declan murmured quietly, as if he was worried about derailing the story I was weaving.

"In his anger at being interrupted, at being challenged, Jasper stabbed Bluebell with the knife he'd prepped for whatever spell he was planning to work. She fell before me. I caught her, and I tried to pull her out of the way, to staunch the wound. But … he was still coming for me, working magic I didn't completely understand. Bluebell died. I could feel her magic underneath my hands. And before he could harness it for himself, I took it. I took the power released. I took her life essence."

I pressed my hands over my eyes, whispering through the pain and sorrow constricting my throat. "And I broke Jasper with it. I broke him in two. Literally."

Gently, Declan peeled my hands away from my face. But before he could speak, I grasped his wrists firmly. "Then I let everyone believe it was you who'd put Jasper in a wheelchair. I didn't lie. I just didn't challenge their first assumptions."

"What was the alternative?" Declan's voice was edged with wry mockery. "My life?"

"I thought so at the time. Maybe Grey would have stepped up. And Jasmine certainly would have fought for you. Though if she hadn't woken soon enough … she would never have forgiven me if anything happened to you."

"Being sent away to school was a better alternative," he said.

I laughed, pained. "Better than death?"

"Yes. Even though I didn't see Jasmine for two years ... and you for twelve."

"I should have killed him," I whispered. "Then maybe we wouldn't be here."

"It's difficult to kill with magic as your sole weapon," Kett said. "Even with the life essence of the brownie supporting you, your will, your resolve, at sixteen wouldn't have been enough. Stabbing him through the heart after he was down would have been more effective. Or, if you couldn't get through his breastbone, then a slice across the femoral artery in each thigh."

Declan snorted. "Good to know."

I sighed, scrubbing my hands across my face fiercely. "Well ... they say confession is good for the soul."

Declan grimaced, eyeing Kett by my side. "I'm not sure that applies when your confessor is a vampire."

The aforementioned vampire chuckled, apparently finding amusement in Declan's words. Which was good, since the other option was most likely ripping off his head for insolence.

"And you, Bubba," I said.

"Yeah, well." Declan straightened, then stepped away from me. "I witnessed most of it. But I ... appreciate having the fine details filled in."

I nodded, tucking the blanket behind me as I stood, then smoothed out my clothing. "We should recheck the basement."

"While it contains many intriguing pockets of power," Kett said, "I believe I would know if any of them contained Jasmine. And given your ... earlier difficulties, I doubt you want to cast a reconstruction."

"You are extremely correct. I'd rather not."

"However, the secondary house on the property and the three bedrooms on the top floor are shut to me. The grounds are littered with what feel like magical traps, concentrated around the outbuildings. The wards prevent me from getting near enough to look through the windows of the manor, but the cottage appears empty. There was no sign of anyone having lived there in years. I might be able to go through the walls in either case, of course. But I doubt the coven would appreciate me tearing the house down."

Declan laughed. "Always a good backup plan, though."

Kett gifted him with a ghost of a smile.

"That's the caretaker's cottage," Declan continued. "Standard wards. I doubt Jasper has reinforced them in years, same as the house. The pockets of magic are likely traps left over from our training."

I nodded, tentatively opening my witch senses to the magic coating every inch of the estate. "Agreed. The manor feels empty. Underutilized. Is it possible that Jasper doesn't live here at all?"

Declan shrugged, masterfully expressing his never-ending contempt of our uncle's actions and his disdain over his whereabouts in a single gesture.

"We'll double-check the cottage before we leave the grounds," I said. "The bedrooms are likely still sealed with timed wards. Implemented by Jasper in our fourteenth year, to … restrict access at certain times of the day."

Declan glanced at the grandfather clock on the wall opposite the fireplace. "Two forty. We'd be at lessons, not allowed back in our rooms until just before dinner at six."

"We can't just continually wander around the estate looking for clues that might lead back to Jasmine. I can cast a mobile reconstruction. If there's any fresh residual, we'll pick it up quickly."

"Absolutely not," Declan said. "You just put yourself out for three hours after witnessing a stupid memory about a damn rabbit."

"It was never about the rabbit," I said, trying to cover my shock at having lost such a large portion of the day. "And I most likely passed out from expending too much magic too quickly."

Declan threw his hands up in exasperation. "My point is that there's way worse ... garbage to witness, or to relive, in this house."

"I'll set my candles and will stand outside the circle. It was a momentary lapse in judgement."

"While I'd dearly love to witness another round of sibling banter," Kett said, "I have other leads, off the property, to follow up on."

"We aren't siblings," Declan growled.

"From Jasmine's case notes?" I asked, ignoring Kett's obvious attempt to goad us.

He pulled out and referenced his phone. "New credit card charges. A car rental, what appears to be a drugstore, and a few more I'd like to check."

My stomach squelched. "Vampires don't typically need aspirin ... or Band-Aids."

"No. They don't."

"What about the hotel?" Declan asked.

Kett shook his head. "They returned for Wisteria's note, obviously. But as far as I could assess, they aren't staying there. These vampires would need to be underground from sunrise to sunset."

"Like in a graveyard? Really?"

"Anywhere under the earth would suffice."

"Even the one who calls himself Yale?" I asked.

"It would be highly unlikely that he could walk in the sunlight."

"But not impossible," Declan said.

Kett didn't answer. But then, I had the feeling he was catering to me at that moment by answering any questions at all.

"Have you heard from Rose?" I asked.

Declan shifted impatiently. "She's convening a coven meeting. They're gathered at Fairchild Park to intercept the sunset message the vampire promised, and to formulate a response. None of her other leads have turned up anything. Apparently, no one else has noticed four vampires wandering around Litchfield. Without the hotel reconstruction, they probably wouldn't believe us at all."

"It would be unwise for the coven to get involved at this stage," Kett said.

"Which is why we're exploring other avenues, vampire," Declan said testily. "And trying to mitigate the risk to Jasmine."

Kett pinned Declan with his gaze, and for a brief moment, I thought the vampire might have ensnared him. Then Declan glanced away. Not as if he was ceding ground, but more likely because he'd remembered to not look Kett in the eye.

"We'll be fine here," I said. "We'll text if we leave the property."

"You might need to grant me entrance again."

I nodded. "The wards are centuries old."

"So am I." Kett grinned slyly, as if he might be flirting with me. "It is not their age that makes them impressive. It's the accumulated magic they contain."

Then he disappeared.

Declan swore under his breath. "Sneaky bastard."

"Jasmine said the same thing."

"Before or after she started sleeping with him?"

I laughed quietly. "I believe it was one of the many draws."

Declan shook his head dubiously. "No other guy goes around attempting to impress girls with how old he is."

"He's not trying to woo me," I said. "Not that way, at least."

"What other way is there?"

I opened my mouth to answer him, then couldn't figure out how to even begin to explain anything about Kett or the contract with the Conclave. I sighed. "I'll tell the both of you when we find Jasmine. I promise."

Declan narrowed his eyes at me, then nodded begrudgingly.

Exceedingly aware that we didn't have much time, and that the manor might well have been a dead end, I retrieved my bag, then crossed through the parlor in the direction of the kitchen. "I'll start by the back door."

Declan insisted on maintaining contact with me the entire time as I moved my reconstruction circle through each room of the manor in turn. This included the games room, the library, and nine of the twelve bedrooms, scanning each one in search of newer layers of residual magic.

Despite the fact that I stood outside that carefully contained magic, I was grateful for the extra anchor to the present that Declan provided. Brushing away layer upon layer of the echoes of our childhoods would have been emotionally straining without his hand on my back, carefully placed in a neutral spot between my shoulder blades on top of my thin navy-blue sweater.

We progressed painfully slowly, pausing to field text messages from Kett and Rose that seemed to contain more questions than new information. Simply killing time before sunset. On the coven's part, at least.

Though the magic contained within the manor was extensive, most of the residual I picked up consisted of brief flashes of younger versions of Jasmine, Declan, and me, along with moments of Bluebell. The brownie was clothed in her ruffled antique-tea-towel dresses as she bustled around the kitchen or cleaned the house.

As Kett had already indicated, we couldn't enter three of the bedrooms on the uppermost floor—our bedrooms, which pointed to the timed wards still being in place. But other than those unknowns, we ate up another forty-five minutes of our tight timeline and didn't uncover a single current event.

"I can't believe there's nothing here," I murmured. "Nothing for twelve years?"

"Nothing that left a residual," Declan said grimly. "For all we know, Jasper's figured out a way to mask his signature."

I glanced back at him. "That's ... that should be impossible. I'd see the masking spell at least."

Declan nodded doubtfully.

"So ... the upstairs bedrooms," I said. "We could call—"

"No."

"Declan, Dahlia would be able to open them without—"

"I don't give a crap about damaging the house," he snarled. "But I'm not going to admit that we need her to break the wards for us. She doesn't even believe Jasmine's in trouble."

"She'll have seen the reconstruction by now."

"No."

I nodded, letting the subject drop. We were close to an hour away from the bedroom wards opening on their own. But I knew that hour would bring us closer to sunset than I wanted to be without a possible connection between Jasper and Yale—and between my uncle and Jasmine's disappearance.

"We still have the parlor," I said, making my way down the back staircase that led through to the kitchen. We'd ascended by way of the hand-carved marble entrance-way staircase, hoping that the hall and the upper bedrooms might yield something. There hadn't been any residual significant enough to notice when we were in the parlor the first time, though. "Then we should check some of the outbuildings before we go. I'd like to see the caretaker's cottage."

"This is a waste of time," Declan said. "If Jasper is involved, he's kept his scheming off the property, or masked it somehow."

I paused in the doorway to the kitchen, eyeing him. "I can search without you if you're done with this. I'm sure I'll be fine."

He shook his head, pacing past me into the dining room, then the parlor. I followed.

"I don't normally do this part ..." Declan cast his hand about helplessly, echoing my own insecurities at leading an investigation of this magnitude. "I just get brought in when things have gone sideways."

"We're trying to avoid that part." I tempered my tone while I carefully folded the blanket I'd left crumpled on the green chaise. I could understand his frustration. In fact, that frustration was why I was so intent on using the magic I had at my disposal even if it came to nothing. Because that was a better option than simply melting down while I waited to hear from the rogue vampires who had kidnapped the most important person in my life.

"Maybe check in with Rose again?"

"Right." Declan fished his phone out of his pocket, then stalked out into the entranceway. "I'd prefer to blow something up, but I'll make some phone calls instead." He flung open the front door and stepped out.

"I always hated that arbor on the north side of the gardens," I called after him. "It's ugly, and prone to moss."

He stuck his head back through the open doorway, grinning. "Noted."

I laughed quietly, turning back into the parlor and hearing the front door click closed behind me.

Instead of moving my circle with me down the back stairs, I had let its magic ebb. So I went about setting my candles at four points in the room, walking a circle north to west to south to east. I lit the green candle at the north side of the room, then glanced out the front windows as I moved to the blue candle to the west.

Declan was slowly wandering across the front lawn. His phone was pressed to his ear, a smile softening his face.

My stomach squelched. Every smile I'd seen from him in the last two days had been heavy with sarcasm or laced with anger. Tinged with pain. Whoever he was speaking with, it was someone he was completely relaxed around. So not Rose or Grey.

I looked away, lighting the blue candle, then moving on to the red pillar perched on the fireplace mantel. Which was appropriate, since red symbolized fire. It was likely that all the fireplaces in the house were placed on south walls. I'd never thought to check when I was younger, and I hadn't walked these rooms since I was sixteen. But Fairchilds never let anything happen by chance, even architecture, it seemed.

Which once again raised the question of what four vampires were doing in Litchfield, Connecticut. Because whatever Kett thought, I found the idea that they were here by chance all but impossible to believe.

Crossing past the fireplace toward the white candle on the eastern side of the room, I brushed a pocket of magic with my left thigh. It was new. Presumably something I'd called forth while pacing out the circle. I lit the final candle for air, feeding my magic into that circle and snapping it shut. Then I reached for the residual I'd sensed, immediately pulling out a moment from the recent past.

The light deepened in the room, now emanating solely from a pile of blazing logs in the fireplace.

An ash-blond man in a wheelchair sat with his back to me, gazing into the dancing flames. His hair was shorter, thinner than it had been in the glimpse I'd seen of him in the reconstruction. The vision that had almost trapped me in the orchard.

"Jasper," I whispered. My heart thumped once in my chest. Then twice. I squeezed my eyes shut, willing the reconstruction to play out before me so I could watch it front to back instead of in reverse. I inhaled slowly and deeply, trying to settle myself while the magic unfolded before me, unseen.

It was just a reconstruction.

And no matter how much I might have been trying to deflect from it all the time since then, I'd been prepared to see him again since I'd opened the envelope and watched Jasmine's necklace fall onto my kitchen counter.

The magic of the circle shifted, announcing Declan's return. I turned my head, opening my eyes but carefully directing my gaze across at him, through the circle. There was no need to be that careful, though. The reconstruction of the residual was already thinning.

Declan was standing in the doorway to the foyer, his hand pressed to my circle. He met my gaze. There was nothing soft about his face now. He was livid.

"I only caught the end."

I nodded. Then, raising my palms to the circle, I called the collected magic to me and replayed the reconstruction.

Within the circle, flames flared to life in the fireplace. Jasper, in the wheelchair with his back to me, settled his hand on his lap. It was an easy guess that the spell he'd used to trigger the blaze had left the residual for me to collect.

No matter the strength of my resolve, I was glad I couldn't see his face.

"Jasmine Fairchild does not work at my behest," he said, not looking away from the fire. His tone was clipped and precise.

In the green antique chaise perpendicular to the fireplace, a ruddy-haired, pale-skinned man smiled smugly, relaxed.

Not a man. A vampire. Yale.

"So you have no objections to my questioning her?" Yale asked. His Welsh accent was thick and melodic.

"As I said, vampire." Jasper gestured toward the fireplace, drawing tendrils of flames effortlessly to his hand. He let that fire play across his fingers. "But you should speak to Rose. She's the proper point of contact."

Yale straightened on the couch, immediately wary of the implicit threat in Jasper's gesture—casually calling forth and playing with fire.

"Show-off," Declan sneered. "Junior magic."

"Nothing is basic when he wields it," I said.

"Rose?" the vampire echoed with forced amusement. "The healer?"

"The member of the Convocation," Jasper said.

"I understood you to be the power in eastern North America."

"Your information is outdated," Jasper said smoothly. "Something that is no doubt a common occurrence for your species."

Anger flashed across Yale's features, but he quickly smoothed the emotion.

Declan snorted. "Once a Fairchild, always a Fairchild."

"Pay attention to the vampire," I murmured. "He carries himself differently than Kett does. He's more emotional."

"Even if I was inclined to broker a meeting between you and my niece, I'm leaving town tomorrow morning. Plus, Jasmine would never willingly set foot on the estate. Nor would her cousin or brother. Though I have tried to make peace with them multiple times."

Declan laughed harshly. "I wonder where I was for all those offered olive branches?"

"Would you have accepted one?" I asked.

"Of course not."

"I'll take my leave then, Jasper Fairchild." Yale moved from the chaise so quickly that the magic of the reconstruction blurred. He was standing beside Jasper, holding out his hand. "I'm sure we will meet again."

My uncle slowly shifted his gaze from the fire to the vampire looming over him. The side of his face was shadowed, but whatever Yale saw in my uncle's eyes made him drop his hand and nod curtly.

Then the vampire was gone.

Jasper flicked his fingers, sending the flames he'd been playing with into the fireplace.

The fire died. And the reconstruction faded.

I glanced over at Declan. His gaze was fixed on the empty, cold fireplace. His jaw was set, as if he was clenching his teeth fiercely.

"I'm not going to collect it," I said, willing the circle closed by snuffing out the white candle I still stood next to. "It isn't worth the oyster-shell cube."

Declan frowned. "What do you mean?"

"Well, either I just called forth evidence that conveniently absolves Jasper. Or the scene was set up. Playacted for me to find."

"Rose got in contact with Jasper, confirming that he's not in Litchfield," Declan said. "He obviously told her nothing about this conversation. So he might not have colluded with the vampire, but he did nothing to protect Jasmine."

I nodded, systematically snuffing the candles one by one and leaving them to cool and harden. I didn't understand why Declan would have expected anything else from Jasper. Perhaps he held out hope that some sort of mitigating factor would arise that would absolve our uncle for our childhoods.

I kept my tone as casual as I could while changing one painful subject for another. "How long has Rose been sick? Sick enough that she's not the one rehabilitating Jasper?"

"Jasmine thinks his injuries were always beyond Rose's abilities to fully heal," Declan said. "Beyond anyone's abilities, since he's still in that chair. But whatever is happening to her has been getting worse over the last year and a half, maybe."

"And?"

"And she won't talk about it. Even Jasmine can't broach the subject with her."

"Do you think that's what all the talk about us returning to the coven is about? She's dying? And our absence is somehow contributing to whatever has weakened her?"

Declan scrubbed his hand through his hair. "One thing at a time, hey?"

A text message pinged through on my cellphone. I retrieved it from my bag, opening a text from Kett.

>*The second charge from last night is a grocery store.*

"Grocery store? So?" Declan asked, reading over my shoulder.

"Vampires don't eat," I murmured, then hope bloomed in my chest. "They're feeding Jasmine."

Another text appeared on my screen.

>*Shipping labels both track to a FedEx drop box on West Street. Paid for by the same credit card. Dead end.*

"That's only fifteen minutes from here," Declan said. "From the north edge of the property, anyway."

I had no idea how many FedEx drop boxes there were in Litchfield. But understanding that the vampires had been that close to the estate, that close to Jasper—realizing that Yale was making no effort to keep away from the coven—a chill suddenly settled over me.

"The basement," I said, thinking out loud as I clicked the missing pieces of the puzzle together. "Kett said all the vampires, including Yale, would need to be underground. Somewhere with a basement. And Yale knew that Jasper would be out of town."

"I doubt Kett would have missed four vampires in the basement."

"Declan! The caretaker's cottage. It has a basement."

"A glorified root cellar, maybe. But staying on Fairchild land with a kidnapped Fairchild witch? That would be stupidly risky."

But I was already stuffing my candles into my bag. "He likes to play games," I said. "Yale. What better place to hide from Fairchild witches but on unoccupied Fairchild land? Jasper outright told Yale that you and I would never willingly set foot on the estate."

I tugged on my wool coat as I raced for the back door, heading through the dining room and kitchen with Declan shouting behind me as he followed.

"Wisteria! How could they have gotten by the wards?"

"Jasmine's blood," I shouted over my shoulder. I didn't bother to shut the kitchen door behind me as I raced outside.

Chapter Ten

I ran, cutting around the gardens so I didn't need to deal with gates and zigzagging paths. I ran, heedless of the overgrown bushes and branches encroaching on the stone pathways that radiated from the back of the manor, spreading across the rest of the property. I ran, cresting a slight hill, my lungs already burning with the effort of keeping up the pace, though I was barely a quarter of the way to the caretaker's cottage to the north.

Something buzzed by me on the left, shoving me off the path and into the grass. I stayed on my feet—barely—and willfully ignored the fact that it felt as though the magic of the estate was the only thing keeping me steady.

A golf cart slid to a stop a few feet away from me. Declan, in the driver's seat, glared back at me over his shoulder.

"Get in."

In my panic, in my need to be right about Jasmine being on the property, I'd forgotten about the golf cart.

I climbed in, clutching my bag in my lap as Declan zoomed off down the path without another word.

We wove through trees as we crossed the back half of the property, losing much of the sunlight as we did so, despite the fact that the tangle of branches overhead were bare.

"When does the sun set?" I asked.

Declan shook his head. "Soon. An hour? Forty-five minutes? Does it have to be below the horizon for them to … wake?"

"I don't know."

The back of the cottage came into sight. The building was of a later vintage than the manor, and tiny in comparison—though it was still bigger than my apartment by far. And it had a basement. A glorified root cellar, as Declan called it. I hadn't tied it to the vampires because it never occurred to me that they'd be reckless enough to squat on Fairchild property. Apparently, I still had a lot to learn about the motivations and machinations of immortal creatures.

The back gate to the cottage's fenced yard hung open. I barreled out of the golf cart before Declan had even fully stopped, thinking of nothing but how Jasmine might have been within our reach for hours now. And how terrified she must be with the approach of sunset.

"Wisteria!" Declan shouted.

I blew through the gate, managing to not trip over a tangle of dead flower stems and bushes that were trying to overgrow the cracked cement path that led through the yard to the back kitchen patio.

I was four or five steps away from the three wooden stairs that led to the back door, already stretching my arm out for the handle, when magic bloomed beside me. In my near hysteria, I'd triggered a spell of some sort along the path.

Declan slammed into me, throwing me tumbling across the yard. I came to a painful rest, crushing a rhododendron bush.

The spell I'd triggered hit Declan. He pivoted into it, covering his face and neck with his arm as the bulk of the malicious magic splattered across his leather jacket. Keeping his feet firmly planted, he dropped his arm and met my terrified gaze across the small yard.

Red pustules sprang up across the left side of his neck and face.

I moaned and scrambled to my feet, ready to lunge across to him.

"Stay there," he snarled. "Just slow down, Wisteria. Slow the hell down."

I froze.

He rotated his head, stretching out his neck. The pustules faded from red to light pink without bursting.

"Poison?" I asked in a whisper.

"Apparently," he said angrily.

Feeling utterly stupid for not having done so right away, I lowered my personal shields, scanning the yard as I would have before conducting a reconstruction. Jasper hadn't typically used poison as the base for the traps he'd hidden around the estate, all of them set up for us to trigger as part of our ongoing training. "Something by your left foot."

"I see it."

Feeling nothing in my immediate vicinity, I slowly stepped back across the yard until I was within a few feet of Declan. He'd thrown me clear. Then I hunched down, examining the spell by his foot and rubbing my right shoulder.

"I hurt you," Declan murmured. "I'm sorry."

"I was the one running blindly."

"It was uncharacteristic."

I nodded, preferring to drop the topic and focus on getting into the cottage. "I believe you can step back. Or around," I said. "You haven't brushed the edges of the spell yet."

Declan shifted his foot back, then hunched down next to me to survey the path and the decrepit wooden steps that led to the back patio.

"Everything is so … run-down now," I whispered.

"Or we're seeing it all with fresh eyes."

I sighed. "No. We're seeing it after twelve years without Bluebell." I pointed ahead. "I see three more faint purple spots on the path, and the entire second step is spelled with something."

"I see the same."

"I don't think these are Jasper's spells. The placement is too obvious, and his magic is dark blue. What kind of Adept casts purple magic?"

Declan shook his head. "And the wards on the house? Will they allow you entry?"

I straightened. Declan mimicked my movement to tower over me on my left. I carefully navigated the path, stopping just below the steps so I could feel the protections on the cottage.

"The wards feel familiar, like Fairchild magic."

Declan grunted, crouching down to eye the second step. "But the spells don't feel like witch magic. Not entirely."

I stared up at the cottage. "So … they're here, then?"

"It would seem prudent for vampires to lay traps around their daytime resting spot."

I nodded and pulled out my phone, texting Kett.

We believe the vampires are in the caretaker's cottage. The traps aren't witch magic.

Declan eyed me over his shoulder, then glanced back at the spelled steps. "I didn't know vampires could cast."

"Purchased, maybe."

"From who? Your mother?"

"There are other potion masters," I said dryly. "Though I wouldn't be surprised if they bought them from her. I imagine they're expensive spells, and there isn't much of a demand for them."

"Attempted murder is still a crime, even in Fairchild territory. But I would have recognized one of Violet's brews, especially spattered across my skin."

"I'm sorry."

Declan grunted dismissively.

We had all ingested my mother's magic many times over the years. Not enough to permanently harm us, of course. But enough to inoculate us from any potions that might be used against us by potential rivals. Enemies we were born with simply because we were Fairchilds.

A message pinged through on my phone.

>*Wait for me.*

I showed Declan the screen as he stood. He curled his lip derisively, and that was all the encouragement I needed to press forward.

When I reached for the wooden railing, it shifted in my grasp. Slivers of paint peeled off underneath my hand. But hoping it would hold beneath my weight, I carefully stepped up with my left foot. Then I lifted my right foot over the spelled second step, stretching forward to reach the third. Declan's hand hovered around my elbow, but I thankfully cleared the step without incident. I didn't fancy being flung across the yard a second time.

I crossed the four-foot-wide patio, scanning the door and then the windows, through which I could see the empty kitchen and part of the central hall. Declan traversed the stairs behind me.

Another text message came in on my phone.

>*I will be there before sunset.*

I turned the phone to silent, but not before a third message appeared on my screen.

>*Listen to me, Wisteria. I can get you through this unscathed.*

Declan crossed his arms, smirking at me knowingly.

I tucked the phone in my pocket. If we were reading the situation correctly and the vampires were in the cottage, Kett might be able to get me through the coming confrontation unharmed. But I knew the executioner chose his words carefully. And his not mentioning being able to also shield Jasmine and Declan was a deliberate omission.

Declan's smirk turned into a grin. Apparently, ignoring the dire warnings of an ancient vampire was what it took to put me in his good graces.

"Is that something?" Trying to get us back on task, I pointed toward a spot of energy I could feel more than see on the door handle. "Other than whatever that is, the cottage's wards feel receptive to me. But the door looks like it's deadbolted, and we don't have the key."

"I do," Declan said. "Step back. Please."

I took a step back, then instinctively tucked myself behind him. He tossed something at the door, then spun to face me, spreading his coat to the sides and blocking my sight of the house.

I met his golden-hazel gaze questioningly.

Magic exploded. Wood splintered and snapped.

A wide smile spread across Declan's face as he laughed quietly.

"You've just been waiting to blow something up," I said teasingly, ignoring that I would only need to lean forward just a few inches to kiss him. "Though if we were avoiding detection, that just clearly announced our presence."

"Triggering the first spell did that already," Declan said wryly. "Though before I met your boyfriend, I assumed vampires were dead during the day."

He turned to survey the damage to the door. I let the boyfriend comment stand again. As before, arguing the point would have taken far too much explanation.

The wards coating the exterior of the cottage still held the door upright in its frame, but a large fissure had opened across it, from just above the doorknob to the bottom hinge. I couldn't see any hint of whatever spell had been layered on it.

I touched my fingers to the doorknob. The wards accepted me without resistance.

Wrapping my hand around the knob, I tugged forward, pulling the lower half of the door completely away from the frame. Once freed from the wards, Declan grabbed the ruined section, setting it off to the side.

I ducked underneath the top half of the door to slip into the kitchen. It looked clean, though it hadn't been renovated or seen a lick of paint in a decade. Unused.

But when I crossed to open the fridge, it held two loaves of bread and some sliced turkey. All fresh.

"Electricity is on," I murmured. "Is that normal?"

"Most likely," Declan said. "Wouldn't want the place to go musty without any heat." At the sink, he turned on the faucet. Water gushed out, confirming that it hadn't been shut off for the winter either.

I closed the fridge, not bothering to search the kitchen any further. It was already obvious someone was staying in the cottage.

With Declan on my heels, I swiftly crossed out of the kitchen into the dining room, silently pointing out the magic glistening along the edges of the door that led to the cellar as I crossed through. More traps. More confirmation that vampires might very well be slumbering beneath our feet.

Declan nodded silently as we continued on, passing between a teak dining table and a hutch filled with mismatched china.

At the front of the house, the living room was empty. A layer of dust covered every surface.

I passed the front door without bothering to scan it for magic, moving back through the center of the cottage and into the hallway that led to the bedrooms.

Even a dozen or more feet away, I could tell that the closed door at the far end of the darkened hall was spelled. Likely trapped. I didn't bother glancing into the open doors of the bathroom or either of the other bedrooms, instead making a beeline down the corridor in the faint light spilling in from their windows.

"I was afraid they'd have her downstairs," I whispered. "With them. If they're here."

"Too risky. What if she got loose while they were sleeping, or dead, or whatever they do during the day?"

"Right."

I stopped myself from pressing my hand to the door, not sure I could have sensed the interior of the room or Jasmine's presence even if I did. Years ago, I would have been able to touch the wards on the exterior of the house and know exactly who was in the manor or the cottage. But not having practiced for over twelve years, I was rusty when it came to wielding any magic other than reconstruction.

"Let me," Declan said.

I had to force myself to move out of his way as I whispered, "Please be careful."

"I'm not an idiot, Wisteria," he said. "I can be subtle." Then he flicked a small stone at the door.

It hit the doorknob, then burst with a faint pulse of magic—a spell that quickly wrapped itself around the knob, coating it. Then the metal simply twisted in on itself. The mangled knob and its interior components fell to the ground, completely inert.

I stepped forward, brushing past Declan and pressing my fingertips to the door before he could stop me. It swung slowly open.

I found the light switch and flicked on the overhead light without looking. Three of the four bulbs were burnt out, but I could still see inside the bedroom.

Jasmine was naked, tied spread-eagled to a bed that had been moved to the center of the room. Even from the doorway, I could see that she'd been bitten multiple times on her inner wrists, thighs, and neck. Her blond curls were matted and strewn across her face, as if she'd been thrown down on the bed unconscious and hadn't moved since.

For a heart-stopping moment, I wasn't sure she was alive. "Betty-Lou?" I whispered.

Then she turned her head, piercing me through the heart with her sky-blue eyes. She wrapped her hands around the ropes that bound her as she snarled. "They took my phone!"

I laughed, a desperately wild sound. I wanted to run to her, but Declan was holding me back. Tearing my gaze from Jasmine, I scanned the remainder of the room. An old quilt had been tossed on the floor a few feet away from the door, but the room had been stripped of all other furniture.

However, tiny pockets of magic encompassed the brass feet of the bed. And some sort of spell glimmered on the sill of the curtained window, likely another trap and the reason Kett had kept his distance while prowling the perimeter.

"The window and the bed frame is spelled," I whispered, running my gaze across the bare mattress and the ropes that bound Jasmine. "Mattress and ropes look clean."

"Except for the blood," Jasmine said sarcastically.

Declan released his hold on me, hunkering down to get a better look at the magic on the feet of the bed.

"We're coming for you, babe," I said as soothingly as I could.

"I know," Jasmine murmured, squeezing her eyes shut.

Declan gently rolled a series of marbles across the worn oak floor. The tiny beads of glass briefly flared dark blue, then fanned out around the bed. Each came to rest against one of the pockets of magic on the bed frame's brass feet. Then they imploded one at a time, each marble eating whatever spell had been trapping the bed.

It was an impressive casting that didn't earn so much as a second thought from me. Because I was already moving before the last one had triggered. Pushing by Declan and scooping up the old quilt, I threw the blanket and myself across Jasmine.

"Ouch!" she cried, only partially sarcastically.

I reached for the ropes around her nearest wrist, tearing at them futilely with my fingers. Declan paced a quick search around the room before crossing to us. Then he slid a sharp, short blade through the knot holding Jasmine's left arm, freeing her.

"I'm okay," Jasmine said. She flexed her fingers, then wrapped her freed arm around my waist. "I'm okay. I'm okay, Betty-Sue."

Declan circled the bed to systematically cut through the other ropes. His face was etched with pain and he kept his shoulders angled away, carefully avoiding looking at Jasmine.

Once freed, she wrapped both arms around me, clinging to me. "I'm okay." She started sobbing, a harsh, terrible sound. As Declan freed her feet, she curled around me in a fetal position, her head on my lap.

I stroked her hair, avoiding the half-healed bite marks on her neck as I tried to comfort her—but managing only to sob myself.

Declan crawled across the bed, wrapping himself around her from behind.

"Bubba …" She sobbed. "I'm okay. I'm okay. It's just … just … they make you like it, even when I refused. Fucking vampires. They drug you, force pleasure on you against your will. Like Jasper. Like Jasper did. Until you forget you didn't ask for it. Until you forget you didn't give them permission."

"It's still rape," Declan said. His insistence was thick with emotion.

I squeezed my eyes shut. What Jasper had done to us as children, as young adults, had been exceedingly specific and carefully enacted. He'd wanted us bonded to him, controllable by him. He'd manipulated our feelings. Even though we knew it was wrong for him to touch us, to molest us, we wanted to be loved. And even knowing that it was wrong didn't take away the shame of enjoying parts of it.

Our twisted pleasure fueled his spells, and kept us unnaturally bonded to him.

One of the worst things my mother had ever said to me—when I was pleading with her to protect Jasmine and Declan, but before I made the deal that severed me from the coven—was that Jasper had told her I'd never protested. That I'd enjoyed what he taught me.

She gilded over it with the assumption that he'd been talking about magic, when of course he'd been talking about molesting us for the accumulation of power. She'd willfully ignored my declarations of abuse, simply calling my 'stories' feeble attempts to protect Declan.

I'd never spoken about it to anyone, ever again. Never described what it felt like to know I should fight him, but being too scared to do so. Scared for Jasmine and Declan more than myself. And desperately guilty that Jasper could make me feel any pleasure at all.

I had always imagined that Declan and Jasmine felt the same. And though that remained unspoken between us, it only strengthened our bond.

Jasmine rolled onto her back, reaching up and pulling my face within inches of hers. "I knew you'd come. You and Bubba."

"Always," I said. "Always."

She brushed the tears from my cheeks, heedless of the ones still streaming down her own face. "Is it Jasper? Was it Jasper?"

"I don't know yet. It seems to be about Kett. Except ... we found you here."

"Too obvious for Jasper," Declan said, rolling onto his back and slinging his arm across his eyes. "Unfortunately."

"I want him dead this time," Jasmine said. "If it's him, I'll kill him myself."

"If it's him," I whispered, "I'll kill him first."

Jasmine nodded. Then she awkwardly tugged the quilt up, wiping her face with one corner. "I need clothes."

Declan slipped off the bed, crossing toward the door.

"Are the vampires staying here?" I asked. "In the cellar?" I didn't want to press her, but we needed to know what we might be up against.

Declan paused in the doorway.

"I don't know," Jasmine said, shaking her head erratically. "I didn't even know where the hell I was until I realized the ward magic felt familiar. Where's Kett?"

"On his way."

"Then let him take care of those assholes." She clutched the quilt fiercely, but her hands spasmed with the effort.

Declan exited into the hall without another word.

Jasmine watched him go, then looked at me. "I knew you'd come, but you took long enough."

"I'm sorry."

"Well, you were on the other side of the country. And ... you didn't know about the job for Kett."

"It doesn't matter, Betty-Lou. None of that matters now."

"It never does with you, Wisteria," she whispered. "You … your … what could I have possibly done to earn your love?"

Staggered by her question, I could only laugh while more tears streamed down my face. "Don't you know?"

I tugged the gold necklace I'd been wearing for too long already off over my head, then settled it around Jasmine's neck in the same motion.

She brushed her fingers across the tiny oyster-shell cubes with a satisfied sigh. They glowed softly at her touch.

"You're my heart," I whispered. "My beating heart."

"And Declan," she said smugly, as if she'd cornered me into admitting something I wouldn't willingly admit.

I laughed.

" 'And Declan' what?" He strode back into the room with what had to be ten outfits' worth of clothes, dumping everything he'd collected on the bed.

"Whose are those?" I asked.

"Jasper's last apprentice," Jasmine said. "I recognize that shirt." She pulled a couple of the dresses toward her. "This is what you bring me? Floral prints and cotton? I've just been ravaged by vampires."

"Jesus," Declan said, rubbing his hand through his hair, then over his face. "I hate it when you do that. Joke about terrible shit."

"What would you have me do? Wallow in it?"

I quickly sorted through what Declan had gathered, finding a cotton T-shirt, a hoodie, and pink sweatpants. "We'll start with these," I said. "We need to get you to the bathroom, to wash the … wounds. Then to Rose."

Jasmine took the T-shirt and struggled to pull it over her head. She didn't have full control of her limbs yet. Declan was going to have to carry her.

"I'd love a shower," she said. "But the wounds won't fester. He licks them after. All the better to preserve his food."

"He who?" Declan asked—and I heard the terrible promise of death and destruction laced through his words.

"Valko." Jasmine spat the name viciously, but she let me help her with the fluorescent pink hoodie without resistance. "Dark hair, pale skin, accent. Thinks he's hot shit."

"We saw him at the hotel," I said.

Declan snorted rudely, but I ignored him as I zipped up Jasmine's hoodie. She glanced between us. "What?"

"More like Wisteria propositioned him in the hotel lobby," Declan said.

"There's a driveway," I said, getting us back to more pressing concerns. "It runs around the back of the property to the secondary gate."

"More like a wide path," Declan said. "For service vehicles. And the gate will be chained and padlocked."

"Fine, whatever," I said. "I'll go back for the Jeep, then—"

"No!" Declan and Jasmine said in unison.

"Declan, you can hold the room better than I can," I said. "And carrying Jasmine to the front gate, or even to the manor, will hamper you in a fight."

"We've got at least thirty minutes until sunset," Declan said. "We don't split up. We'll go to the manor and you'll seal us in. Text Kett again."

"Jasmine needs Rose," I said. "And most likely a blood transfusion."

"A glass of water would be a good start," Jasmine said weakly, leaning back onto the bed. "And pants."

Declan growled something under his breath, then left the room in a huff.

I grabbed the sweatpants.

"Give me your phone." Jasmine flapped her hand at me feebly.

"Declan has yours." I got the pants around her ankles and started tugging them up her legs, desperately trying to avoid looking at the bites on her thighs and hoping they wouldn't scar.

"Wisteria!"

I looked up at the desperation in Jasmine's plea.

"Your phone. Please."

I looked around, realizing that I must have thrown my bag down just inside the door. I crossed over to grab it. Jasmine wiggled the pants up over her hips, still having issues using her fingers.

As I placed my phone in her hand, she sighed as if she had just been reunited with an old lover.

I shook my head, digging through the pile of clothes for socks or shoes, but finding neither.

Declan strode back in with a glass of water. "The cellar door is still sealed. I think I'll leave a little surprise of my own on our way out."

Though Jasmine waved him off, he held the glass for her, letting her drink while her thumbs flew across my screen.

"A phone." Declan skewered me with his gaze. "You thought a phone was the most important thing right now?"

Jasmine's arms went limp as she finished texting, as if she couldn't hold them aloft any more. She was smiling smugly.

"What have you done?" I asked.

Her grin widened. Then she took the glass of water from Declan and downed the rest of it.

My phone buzzed. Jasmine checked the screen, then chortled.

"Okay, if you can text, then you can move." Declan took the empty glass from her, setting it down, then reaching to gather her in his arms.

As he stood and swung Jasmine around, she shoved the screen of the phone in my face. I caught a glimpse of a series of emoticons, then a single red, angry face in response.

"I wouldn't want to be a vampire on Kett's shit list," Jasmine said, grinning almost manically.

"Christ," Declan said, heading toward the door and out into the hall with me trailing behind him. "You're both dating him? He doesn't seem that hot to me."

Jasmine threw her head back, laughing.

A ruddy-haired, pale-skinned vampire was sitting on the kitchen counter next to the back door.

I glanced at the closed door to the cellar. Whatever magic had sealed it was gone. Behind the vampire, through the window, I could see the first tinge of pink on the horizon. The sun was starting to set.

We could have run for the front door, but it was likely to be trapped, which would slow us down. Plus, I had no idea if the other three vampires were still inert in the cellar or at large elsewhere in the house.

I stepped in front of Declan, who shifted Jasmine in his arms but didn't set her down. Lifting my chin, I channeled every bit of Fairchild haughtiness I could muster while facing down a greater predator. And with a wounded family member at my back.

"You are trespassing, vampire."

"I am," the vampire said, crossing his legs at the ankle and swinging them with childish anticipation. "Wisteria Fairchild, I presume? You may call me Yale." His Welsh accent was heavier than it had been in the two reconstructions I'd collected, as if he was trying to be charming.

"Introductions are not necessary, vampire," I said. "You are none of my concern. If the executioner of the Conclave doesn't take your head for kidnapping an investigator under his protection, then the Fairchild coven will make you suffer for your transgression."

Yale frowned, the expression forced and overly animated. "The witch holds no token from any vampire protector."

"She has her word."

"And I understand she has no standing within the coven."

I deliberately stepped halfway across the kitchen, closing the distance between myself and Yale—and to the shattered back door. Declan kept close behind me.

I met the vampire's moss-green gaze unflinchingly, instantly feeling his attempt to ensnare me. But I brushed his magic away without effort, derisively curling my lip at his feeble attempt. "You understood wrong."

Yale slid to the floor, keeping his hands on the edge of the counter. He was only a couple of inches taller than me. "Which one of you blew the door in half?" His question was eager, as if all his desires could be fulfilled by the answer.

But I wasn't even remotely interested in whatever game he had going on in his head. "My cousin needs a healer."

"Is that your version of a white flag?"

"We're leaving."

Though the cottage wards weren't of my own construction, they responded to my Fairchild blood and the command in my voice. The top half of the back door swung open.

I took a half step, then angled my shoulder to the edge of the counter, placing myself between the door and Yale.

Declan took my hint without further prompting, moving toward the door. I kept my gaze steadily on the red-haired vampire.

"I would have words with the executioner," Yale said, flicking his gaze up over my shoulder as Declan carried Jasmine through the back door, then jumped to clear the patio steps.

"You're about to get your chance," I said. "I suggest you speak quickly."

"You are so deliciously cool." Yale touched his tongue to his lower lip. "What does it take to get your heart racing?"

I flicked my gaze to the window just long enough to see Declan step through the gate, glance back for me, then carefully place Jasmine in the passenger seat of the golf cart.

"You're attempting to take my bargaining chip," Yale said with amusement. "Are you staying in her place?"

He lifted his hand from the counter, but paused in mid-motion when I raised my right arm in response. I tugged the sleeve of my wool coat back. My white-picket-fence bracelet glowed with blue witch magic.

Yale's gaze snapped to my wrist as I curled my fingers into a fist, silently coaxing more magic into the platinum charms.

The vampire grinned. "Oh, good. You're going to fight back. The other witch was a disappointment."

"Allow me to state this clearly," I said. My voice was low and steady. "I'm a valued member within the Convocation. I am the scion of the Fairchild coven. And I am also the chosen of Kettil, elder and executioner of the Conclave."

"You carry no token—"

"His very power is embedded into the bracelet I wear. A bracelet constructed by the most powerful alchemist of our time. As a gift of appreciation."

Yale's gaze flicked to my wrist again. "A pretty trinket."

"It has a name," I whispered, layering my improvised bluff with something I hoped might capture a power-hungry predator's attention. "Vampire's Bane."

Yale laughed, but the sound was full of forced amusement. "I accept your credentials, witch." Then he deliberately turned his head to look out the window. "Of course, I cannot speak for my children."

Over his shoulder, the path beyond the gate was empty. Declan and Jasmine should hopefully have been halfway back to the manor.

"They delight in playing in the shadows of the sunset," Yale said. "And I'm an indulgent father."

I was through the back door before the last words were out of his mouth. I could hear him laughing behind me as I remembered to jump over the spelled second stair, then brushed heedlessly past the other spells along the back path.

The magic of the estate rose up around me, likely responding to my panic. It swallowed the malignant magic I triggered as I bolted through the back gate, then onto the wide stone pathway that led back to the manor.

While I was facing off with the vampire in the kitchen, my heart had been steady. Even sedate. Now it was pounding in my chest in time to my footfalls.

But I was moving so much more slowly than I knew the three vampires would be, visualizing them darting throughout the deep shadows. I crested a shallow hill, expecting to see Declan and Jasmine slaughtered on the stones of the pathway before me.

Instead, all I saw was the endless stretch of trees between me and the manor. And the golf cart overturned at the edge of the path.

I slowed my pace as I approached, then circled the cart. Refusing to allow myself to freeze in terror. My cursory examination didn't turn up any blood or residual magic, which was good. But I also couldn't tell whether or not Declan and Jasmine had been snatched, or if they'd run off into the woods.

I needed to get control of myself, of my emotions. I needed to take control of the situation.

I tugged off my shoes and socks, tucking them into my bag. Then, ignoring how bitingly cold it was underfoot, I stepped off the stone path and onto the dirt. I was thankful that there wasn't any snow.

I might have been out of practice, but I was still a witch standing on her ancestral land—literally. And though the estate's magic might have grown wild or even capricious, it still answered to witches. Not to vampires.

"Jasmine," I whispered, raising my hands toward the shadowed trees surrounding me. "Declan." Decomposing leaves stirred and evergreen bushes rustled around me, though I hadn't felt a breeze earlier. I took another measured step from the path, reaching out with magical senses long atrophied. Seeking some hint ... some presence.

The magic of the land whispered secrets to me, but I didn't understand its words.

I took another step, ready to abandon my attempt to connect with the wild magic of the estate and return to my mad dash for the manor. Then I felt a push underneath my right hand.

I continued walking forward, slowly but steadily. Lifting my hand before me, I whispered again. "Jasmine."

The magic nudged my hand once more and I was running again. I picked up my pace in the direction it had indicated, heedless of the ever-deepening shadows.

Chapter Eleven

Magic exploded against a tree trunk only inches from my right cheek. I twisted away, throwing myself to my hands and knees in the dirt and dead leaves.

"Damn it, Wisteria!" Declan snarled quietly from nearby. "I could have taken your head off."

I crawled forward, weaving through the stands of birch and maple that dotted this section of the estate until I could see Declan standing in a small clearing. His attention was riveted in the direction of the manor. A few feet away, Jasmine was propped up against a tree that looked as though it had been very recently split in two.

My cousin grinned at me weakly, waving her fingers in greeting.

I scrambled to my feet as I crossed the distance between us, then I crouched down again before Jasmine.

"Defensive position," she said.

"Can you stand?" I asked. "If I help?"

"Leave her." Declan was pivoting slowly, scanning the ever-darkening trees around us.

I could see the wide clearing at the back of the manor and the far side of the derelict vegetable gardens over Jasmine's head. Running unhindered, it might take only ten minutes to get there. For one terrible, painful breath, I desperately wished we'd had the type of family we could rely on. Parents who would have believed us without question, putting our safety before their own welfare. But we didn't. And even if we did, they couldn't have gotten to us in time anyway. We were on our own.

Heedless of Declan's orders, I got my shoulder underneath Jasmine's arm, then helped her rise to her feet. "We need to be in the open, out of the shadows."

"The trees are cover," Declan said, as if I were a complete moron.

"They hunt by heartbeat," I said, inching Jasmine along the length of the fallen tree. "Physical barriers, defensive positions, it doesn't matter. They're playing with you, using the shadows to stay out of the sun."

"The rapidly setting sun," Jasmine said.

Laughter filtered in around us. The hair at the back of my neck prickled, but I didn't bother looking around. It was highly unlikely I'd see them unless they wanted me to.

"You think you're scary?" Jasmine shouted into the bare-leafed grove around us. "I've dated scarier."

More laughter followed as Jasmine and I skirted the fallen tree, forced to shuffle deeper into the shadows in order to get to the clearing beyond. My cousin was a dead weight on my shoulder. Though we were practically the same size, I wasn't going to be able to drag her very far.

Declan didn't bother protesting as he kept tight on our heels, rolling marbles that glinted with magic in both of his hands.

"Speaking of Kett," I said, "please tell me you texted him again. That you told him we were being hunted."

Jasmine only grunted, pained. I craned my neck, trying to see her through the matted hair hanging around her face. She had her eyes closed, murmuring something to herself. A lullaby, or perhaps a healing spell she had no actual ability to cast.

I picked up the pace.

As we made it out of the shadows and into the clearing, Declan threw two more of his premade spells behind us. Wood splintered and cracked, but the sinister laughter was the only response.

Jasmine stumbled, silently taking me down with her. Declan glanced over his shoulder, stepping toward us to help pick her up.

I shook my head, pointing back at the tree line. Two shadowed figures had appeared behind us, staying only inches away from where the last rays of sun kissed the clearing.

I scrambled to my feet.

"You aren't wearing any shoes, Betty-Sue," Jasmine mumbled, trying to raise herself onto her hands and knees but failing. "That can't be good."

Ignoring her, I crossed around and grabbed her by the shoulders. Then without thinking any more about it than that, I started dragging her across the grass toward the manor. If I had been a skilled witch, I might have been able to figure out how to harness the magic of the estate in a helpful fashion. If I had been a witch of real power, I probably could have transported Jasmine directly into the manor. But I wasn't either of those things, and wishes weren't going to get Declan and Jasmine to safety.

Declan kept himself between us and the two figures waiting patiently within the shadowed trees.

I fell twice more, eliciting pained grunts from Jasmine that tore at my heart each time.

Halfway across the clearing, I glanced over my shoulder. Valko was standing underneath the grape arbor.

Apparently, the thickly overgrown vines provided enough protection from the setting sun even without their leaves. Blistering rage swept through me in response to the appearance of the dark-haired vampire, and I was glad Jasmine couldn't see him behind us. Gathering all the composure I could muster, I paused to assess our options. My hesitation drew Declan's attention to the third vampire.

We were trapped, hemmed in, and Yale hadn't even joined the hunting party yet.

Ignoring the terror pulsing through my limbs, I carefully laid Jasmine down on the ground. She touched my cheek lightly, trying to smile even though she was struggling to keep her eyes open. I wasn't certain that blood loss was the same as a concussion, but I wanted to shake her awake nonetheless.

We had run out of time, though. There wasn't another moment to worry or fret or be afraid.

I tugged off my wool coat, folding and placing it underneath Jasmine's head. Then I pulled my candles and lighter out, leaving my bag with her.

"We're making a stand?" Declan asked. "Here?"

I nodded, quickly pacing a tight circle around Jasmine and placing the pillar candles at its north, east, south, and west edges. "They've obviously guessed that we're trying to make it to the manor." I glanced at the red now streaking the sky. "We just have to hold them off."

"Until what?" Declan spoke quietly, but it likely didn't matter. If the vampires could hear our heartbeats, they could hear our conversation, whispered or not. "You think Kett can take four of his kind at once? And if you think he can, would he do so for witches?"

I didn't answer. I didn't have an answer. All I could do was try to protect Jasmine, then stand with Declan and stall for time. I didn't know if that was even possible, though the chat in the kitchen with Yale had given me a glimmer of hope.

I systematically lit the candles, saving the green for last. Green for earth. Then with the magic of the estate thrumming underneath my feet and my white-picket-fence bracelet glowing on my wrist, I lifted my hands toward the circle, calling forth magic I hadn't wielded in over twelve years.

As it had at the cottage and on the path when I sought for Jasmine and Declan, the centuries' worth of magic tied to the estate responded to my call, pooling underneath my palms. I pushed the gathered energy through the circle.

The candles flared as the circle snapped closed. Now contained within it, Jasmine gasped. This was a protective ward, rather than a reconstruction circle. A simple bit of magic I'd learned before I was a teenager. But I was so out of practice that I hesitated to try to cast a circle large enough to hold all three of us—unwilling to stretch and thin whatever protection I could offer Jasmine.

Even with this smaller circle, a witch more powerful than me would tear through the barrier with little effort, as Jasper had done over and over again the last time I'd attempted to wield such magic. Because we were so tightly bound, Jasmine and Declan could likely move through it without resistance. But bolstered by the magic that now resided in my bracelet courtesy of Jade Godfrey, I could only hope that the circle would hold off the vampires.

At least for as long as I was alive.

"Nice casting," Jasmine said, sounding a little more together than she had just a few moments before. "I can feel the magic."

I offered her a tight smile, turning to face the manor and placing her and the circle behind me. "Watch my back."

"Always."

Declan stepped up beside me.

The vampires had melted back into the shadows, but the sun was only moments away from fully setting. Dusk was upon us.

"If you get a chance to grab Jasmine and run," I said without looking at Declan, "you take it."

He didn't respond.

"Declan," I said. "Don't try to save us both. We're massively outnumbered."

"I heard you."

A quiet rustling came from behind us. I glanced over my shoulder to see Jasmine sitting upright. She had my phone in one hand and was digging through my bag with the other. Seen through the barrier of the protection circle, the collection of reconstructions gathered on her necklace glowed like blue-tinted stars.

I surveyed the tree line, then the edges of the garden and what I could see of the manor. The windows of the house were dark. Nothing stirred in the dusk.

The vampires wanted to play. I expected that they'd show themselves without warning, but given their behavior so far, they would likely ease into the attack portion of their hunt. No point in just slaughtering us. That would curtail the fun too quickly.

"Declan." I brushed my fingers over the top of his hand, feeling all the magic he held at the ready.

"Yes?"

"If I die ... " As I uttered the words, I realized I wasn't scared at the prospect. "If I don't make it through this ... will you remember that you loved me once?"

"I always remember," he said gruffly.

The three vampires appeared without any warning, fanning out between us and the manor. Amaya, the former necromancer from Ecuador. Valko, the dark-haired male who'd bitten Jasmine. And the as-yet-unidentified female, who dressed like a witch wannabe and was likely responsible for the spells around the cottage, unless those were of Yale's construction.

Deliberately ignoring them, I cast my gaze around the clearing again. Some small part of me was still hoping that Kett would sweep in and save us. But Declan was correct in his assessment of the situation. At this point, saving us likely meant destroying one or more of his brethren. And no matter how many witch laws the vampires had ignored by kidnapping and torturing Jasmine, I wasn't sure they'd done enough to warrant a Conclave-sanctioned execution.

This was a witch matter. A Fairchild witch matter. So we witches were going to have to solve it.

I took a half step forward, deliberately drawing the attention of all three vampires. "I've already had this conversation with your master," I said. "You've kidnapped a Fairchild witch, and you are now trespassing on Fairchild lands."

"Who's going to kick us off?" Valko said with a sneer. "Two witches? Against three vampires? That's ridiculous."

"Three witches," Jasmine said tartly from behind me.

Valko snorted. "I already know you, blood whore. You're no threat."

Declan flinched, angrily gritting his teeth and clenching his fists. But he let me continue to take the lead.

"Call your master," I said. "He knows we're not to be touched."

"Killed," the witch wannabe said. "Not to be killed. We can touch you all we like." She flashed her inch-long fangs at us.

Jasmine snorted. "Please. That one calls herself Mania. But they're all so weak, they can't even walk in the daylight."

The three vampires glanced at each other, as if the idea that any vampire could stand the sun was a revelation.

Yale kept his brood exceedingly ill informed.

"Even if they're nowhere near as powerful as Kett, they still think big," I said, speaking to Declan and not caring if the vampires could hear me. "Opting for massive displays of strength or stealth instead of straightforward attacks. They think they're invulnerable. Immortal."

Mania laughed. The sound was creepy, on the edge of insane. "You think differently, witch?"

"I think you were so weak as Adepts, if indeed you had any magic at all ..."—I let my gaze settle on Valko—"... that you had to find your tiny taste of power in darkness. And the deeper the better."

I lifted my right arm, tugging the sleeve of my sweater back and flicking my hand until my white-picket-fence bracelet lay across my exposed wrist. "But we three were born and bred by darkness," I said. "We learned to walk in the dark. We blossomed among blood and despair."

Declan began juggling a number of small, magically imbued stones in his left hand. He had his blasting rod gripped firmly in his right, but held low.

Valko snorted. "That's all you've got? Snark, stones, and a metal trinket?"

"Try us," I said.

He lunged for Declan first. The vampire was fast, but nowhere near as fast as Kett. Declan got the blasting rod up before Valko could touch him.

Magic exploded, launching the vampire halfway across the clearing, his clothing instantly on fire. He hit the ground and rolled, which unfortunately extinguished the flames.

Amaya darted toward me, but then veered off to attack Declan instead—diverting my attention just long enough for the spell Mania flicked at me to liquefy across the exposed skin of my neck.

"Her eyes!" I screamed at Declan. Then I fell to my knees and vomited what little remained of my breakfast.

More magic ignited in the clearing, then Amaya was stumbling back from Declan, shrieking. Her eyes were blackened smudges, blood streaming down her face.

I vomited a second time, then pinned my gaze to Mania, who was obviously waiting for her spell to take me down. "I suggest you do some research before you attack a Fairchild witch."

"No magic can counter my poisons," she said snottily.

"No one rivals my mother's brews."

Jasmine chortled. "We were fed poison for breakfast, lunch, and dinner."

"Let's see you spit this out." Mania grabbed for me, but I'd been waiting for her follow-up attack. I lunged into her path, straight-arming her in the throat. Pain reverberated up my arm, but despite it, I slammed her with all the power held in my bracelet.

The vampire shrieked as the magic seared her neck. Though she managed to shake me off, I took a hunk of her flesh with me as she stumbled back. It crumbled into ash, disintegrating through my fingers.

As I fell to my knees and vomited a third time, Declan staggered toward me. He'd been clawed across his face.

Valko appeared before us. His chest was a puckered mess of fast-healing scar tissue.

Declan got the blasting rod up between us and the vampire, but even I could see that its magic was dim. It needed time to recharge.

"Hey, asshole," Jasmine said. Then she tossed a black rectangle through the protection circle toward Valko.

The vampire caught it, staring stupidly down at what I realized was my phone—but hooked up to a miniature flashlight and a compact mirror I carried in my purse.

Magic sparked all around the device, hitting Valko with some sort of stun spell. He convulsed, then fell to the ground, thrashing.

I glanced back at Jasmine.

She shrugged. "Even vampires have to have some sort of central nervous system, right?"

Valko went still. Mania darted forward and dragged him away from us. All three vampires huddled together, maybe a few dozen yards away. Amaya's eyes were white orbs, already healing themselves from the effects of Declan's magic.

With Declan's help, I made it to my feet, placing myself once again before Jasmine.

"Give me some spells, Declan," Jasmine whispered.

I glanced over my shoulder. She'd laid out various items from my purse in the dirt just inside the protection circle. Lip gloss. The second half of my compact. A pen. Three quarters.

Declan shook his head. "I'd have to take down the ward to work the magic."

"There are three of them and three of us." Jasmine glanced over at me, her tone pleading. "I won't be a liability. Again."

I looked at Declan. He grimaced, then nodded.

I brushed my fingers against the invisible wall of magic protecting Jasmine. It dissolved at my bidding.

Declan hunched over the items Jasmine had laid out, placing his fingers on each of them in turn and murmuring spells. I could feel magic rising and falling at his bidding. On Fairchild land, we had access to large deposits of energy, but even Declan was going to eventually burn out.

"Sorry about the phone," Jasmine said. "It isn't going to make it through that."

"It was time for an upgrade," I said, keeping my gaze on the vampires as Valko regained his feet. "I hear the camera is great in the newest model."

Jasmine laughed. The sound warmed me, even as the vampires regrouped to face off with us for a second round.

"Be careful with these," Declan said, straightening. "They'll trigger the moment they come into contact with … well anything, really. After you throw them."

"I'm not an idiot," Jasmine said. "I've used them before. Which one did you use on her eyes?"

"The lipstick." Declan rotated his blasting rod in his right hand, the runes etched along its length glowing bright blue.

"Lip gloss, you luddite."

"Right. Important distinction, especially in this moment. Thank you."

Jasmine didn't step forward when Declan and I did, and I wasn't sure she was capable of standing upright on her own yet. But she cackled quietly to herself while she sorted through the spells Declan had made for her.

He and I faced the trio of vampires. We knew their weaknesses now. They wouldn't be getting up from a second volley so easily.

They came at us with no warning. One minute, I was standing in the clearing. The next, I was pinned by the neck against a tree with my right arm twisted above my head. Valko had carried me dozens of yards away from Jasmine and Declan.

Red rimmed the vampire's light-brown eyes as he leaned in to where my shoulder met my neck, inhaling deeply. "Witch," he said. "You made me a promise in the hotel lobby that I haven't forgotten."

I tried twisting against his hold, but he simply tightened his grip in response.

"Is that all you've got, Wisteria?" he asked mockingly.

"You don't have standing to refer to me by my first name, vampire."

He laughed. "How cool you are. But I know something you don't. It's a wolf moon tonight. And not even Yale can hold me back during a full moon."

"Fortunately for me," I said. "You won't be around to see it rise."

The roots of the tree Valko had me pinned against coiled around his legs. He glanced down, surprised—and loosened his grip just slightly on my right arm.

"Tree roots?" he snorted. "Seriously?"

"Is this better?" I punched him in the gut.

He flew straight backward, taking a dozen trees with him and vanishing from my sight.

I stared in astonishment. I looked down at my bracelet.

Then I saw Kett standing beside me.

"What ... who ...?" I stumbled through the process of making sense of what had just happened, realizing that Kett must have punched Valko an instant before I would have made contact with him. "Have you just been lurking around in the trees?"

"You engage in far too much conversation, reconstructionist," Kett said. "I've been waiting to see what you do in between the words."

"What? Really?"

"No." He touched my arm lightly. "Go back into the clearing. Draw their master out. I'd like to see all four of them together at once."

He slipped back into the shadows.

I didn't need any further prompting to hightail it back to the clearing. Once through the trees, I could see Jasmine still seated on the ground, the area around her empty. She glanced back over her shoulder at my approach, her face tight with fear.

"Declan?" I asked.

She shook her head, her movements on the edge of frantic.

My stomach squelched with fear, but I kept my expression carefully neutral.

"They snatched you both, leaving me here and useless." She was clutching the tube of lip gloss so fiercely that I was afraid she might trigger it inadvertently.

I crouched down, getting her arm over my shoulder and whispering in her ear, "Kett's close."

"What?" she hissed. "Just watching? Asshole."

I laughed, dragging her to her feet. "Let's go. They lose their advantage if we get to the manor."

"Declan," Jasmine protested, though she managed to stay on her feet.

"Kett will help him. If he even needs it." Then I began to walk toward the manor, dragging Jasmine with me.

Yale wandered out from the wooded area to our left. His hands were in his pockets, and his body language was relaxed.

He paused a dozen feet away, standing between us and the vegetable gardens. He deliberately glanced back at the manor over his shoulder, then turned and grinned. "So close," he said.

Amaya appeared at his side, then Mania. They both looked seriously worse for wear, their clothing ripped and their skin singed.

I almost laughed. Jasmine couldn't stop herself.

Valko appeared next. His chest was crushed—actually concave—and he moved as if in pain. He snarled at me, taking a step forward. Yale stopped him with a raised hand.

The ruddy-haired vampire eyed Jasmine and me in turn, then smiled charmingly. "You cannot keep up this pace. Witches cannot best vampires, especially two to four."

"Three," Jasmine muttered under her breath.

Declan stepped out of the forest to our right. His rune-carved blasting rod swung loosely at his side as he strode across the clearing toward us.

We waited in silence, facing off against the vampires as he joined us. Jasmine wrapped her arm around his waist, taking some of her weight off me.

"Think about where you're standing," I said, breaking the silence. "This is Fairchild land. Witches are never more powerful than when standing on our own land, our own territory. The power beneath our feet is endless. Even if you manage to kill us, you won't survive the assault. Spill our blood here, and you'll never walk away."

That was a heavy bluff. Perhaps Jasper could have commanded that sort of retribution from the land that encompassed the Fairchild estate. But Declan, Jasmine, and I had severed most of what tied us to the coven twelve years ago.

Yale tilted his head thoughtfully, rocking back and forth on his feet. Valko, Amaya, and Mania stood just behind him as evening took hold of the sky above us.

"Unless, of course, I have permission to be here," he finally said.

"I already know you don't," I said. Though that was nothing more than supposition, based on the reconstruction I'd done of him and Jasper, and on Rose not knowing anything about vampires in Fairchild territory. Obviously, they could have been invited by another Fairchild, but that was unlikely. "And even if you did, your guest status doesn't hold any weight over us."

"But like your cousin, neither of you are coven members. Are you?" Yale's tone was taunting.

A chill ran up my spine. The vampire was far too well informed.

"We are more than coven members, vampire," I said coolly. "We three hold more power than you could ever hope to wield."

Yale curled his lip.

I smiled serenely.

"I can feel the power you hold, witch," he said. "It's discordant and disorganized. Underutilized, perhaps." He leaned toward me. The red of his magic rolled across his eyes. "But I'm impressed with how you held off my brood, and I've decided to gift you with eternal life."

Declan laughed harshly, but Yale simply raised his voice.

"With you tied to me, the Conclave will leave us alone." He turned his head, addressing his brood and crowing. "And we shall feast on witch blood for centuries."

"You're completely deranged," Declan said. "First, the Fairchilds would sooner kill us than accept a vampire into their ranks. And second, you can't turn us against our will."

"Can't I?"

"Not when we'd all rather die."

Yale flicked his eyes to me, smiling smugly. "Would you? All of you?"

Declan followed the vampire's gaze, frowning at me.

"It's a moot point," I said.

"And why is that?" Yale asked.

Kett appeared beside me. The estate's magic, rolling underneath my bare feet, had alerted me to his approach.

Yale flinched, then snarled to cover his own reaction.

Kett stared down Amaya, whose eyes had completely healed from Declan's assault. In fact, Yale had stalled us long enough that except for their clothing, none of the vampires bore any signs of our fight.

The former necromancer stumbled through making introductions. "Yale, master of I, Amaya, and of Mania and Valko. Kettil, the executioner and elder of the Conclave."

"I know who he is," Yale sneered. "Am I supposed to bow or something?"

"These three Fairchild witches are under my protection," Kett said.

"You haven't shared blood with any of them," Yale said. "Other than chewing on that one ..." He smirked in Jasmine's direction. "How was I to know you'd claimed them?"

Kett's attention was drawn over my shoulder to Jasmine, who was still sandwiched between Declan and me.

"Hello, lover." Jasmine laughed weakly, but she stepped back from us to stand on her own.

"Jasmine." Kett frowned, stepping behind me and shifting the edge of her hoodie away from her neck. "Who has bitten you? I assume he or she didn't have your permission?"

Jasmine eyed him fiercely. "He did not. I informed them all that I was under contract to the Conclave. And with you specifically."

"Which one?" Kett asked, coldly furious.

A wash of terror flooded through me at the promise of utter annihilation punctuating the executioner's simple question.

"I want to watch," Jasmine whispered.

Declan swore under his breath.

I took a deep breath, grounding myself within the magic of the estate thrumming beneath my bare feet.

"Deal," Kett said. The anger smoothed from his voice as he slipped his hand underneath Jasmine's elbow, guiding her forward to stand at my side.

"You will not touch one of mine," Yale said.

"He touched one of mine," Kett said. "I've seen the reconstruction. Jasmine Fairchild clearly declared her connection to the Conclave and myself."

"Reconstruction?" Amaya asked.

Yale shook his head in her direction. "How was I to know she wasn't bluffing?"

"Read her mind. Or aren't you powerful enough to do so?" Derision twisted through Kett's once-more cool tone.

Yale opened his mouth to respond, but Jasmine lifted her hand, pointing directly at Valko.

The dark-haired vampire snarled at her.

And then he was headless.

I hadn't even seen Kett move.

Valko's body dropped to the ground between us. Blood sluggishly pumped out from his severed neck, appearing almost black in the failing light.

Amaya shrieked. Mania stumbled back.

Kett tossed Valko's head on top of his body. "Your brood is so weak," he said dispassionately. "They aren't even worth drinking."

Yale's eyes blazed red. He swore viciously under his breath in a language I didn't understand.

Kett answered him in the same almost-lyrical language. Then he laughed.

Jasmine threw her head back and joined him.

The combined sound sent another shiver of terror up my spine, but I suppressed my need to shudder.

"Declan," Kett said, switching back to English. "Some fire?"

Declan flicked what looked like a penny onto Valko's headless corpse. His clothing instantly ignited.

The three other vampires stumbled back, Amaya and Mania slipping behind their master. Yale's face was a storm of anger and frustration.

"You'd believe a witch over one of your own," Yale said.

"You're not of my blood," Kett said smoothly. "We hold no alliance. Conversely, my chosen child numbers among the Fairchild coven. Her word, and the word of her brethren, outweighs the word of a rogue whose only talent appears to be in making weak fledglings he abandons at whim."

Amaya and Mania glanced at each other behind Yale's back. Declan darted a look my way.

"You have no standing," Kett continued, playing off the fear the junior vampires were showing. "You can offer your shiver nothing more than your false word. You have no ability to protect them."

Yale jutted out his chin. "But you do?"

Kett laughed again, low and husky. "I killed your maker, didn't I?"

Yale stilled.

For a moment, I could only think about how brilliant Kett was at bluffing. Then he raised his right hand, which was spattered with Valko's blood. "I didn't make the connection when I bled Nigel," Kett said. "But with this one's blood, and with the three of you standing before me, I see the relationship."

"Who's Nigel?" Amaya asked.

"A weakling," Yale spat. "A mistake born out of loneliness."

"A mistake from before you figured out you could make stronger children out of the Adept," Kett said, piecing Yale's history together with confidence. "How did I miss you when I purged your maker, along with the rogues he'd gathered to slaughter the Garricks?"

Yale didn't answer. Amaya gripped his shoulder, but he shook her off.

"Teresa's family?" I asked quietly.

Kett nodded.

The necromancer, Ben's mother, had been the lone survivor of a family of vampire hunters who'd been wiped out over twenty years ago. When she demanded vengeance for their murders last October, Kett revealed that he'd first been appointed the executioner of the Conclave in order to destroy those rogues.

"Were you out of the country then, Yale, sire of the weak?" Kett asked. "Perhaps banished by your own maker for your mistake with Nigel? Or did you flee the confrontation afterward? Ecuador, was it? Where you happened upon the necromancer, and turned her before she could figure out how to control you?"

"Lies!" Mania blurted. Then, gripping Amaya's arm, she repeated it. "Lies …" As if trying to convince herself.

"I have another talent," Yale said defiantly. "Besides remaking children who retain a goodly portion of their magic."

"Show me," Kett said, amused. "If I'm impressed, I'll take you to London. My grandsire delights in breaking the unbreakable."

Magic erupted without warning in the clearing, whirling around me, blinding me to whatever was happening. I cried out, reaching for Jasmine but crashing into Kett instead.

He swept me behind him.

The magic died.

Across from us, Amaya held Declan pinned to the ground by the neck. Mania held Jasmine limp in her arms. Yale stood between them, arms crossed, eyeing us smugly.

I gripped Kett's shoulder, my gaze glued to Jasmine until I saw her chest rise and fall.

"Can you take all three of them?" I asked. I was tired of playing games.

"Yes," Kett said. "Easily."

Yale's jaw dropped with disbelief.

"But not without possibly losing Jasmine or Declan in the process," Kett continued. "I assume you aren't interested in trading one for the other."

"No," I whispered, stepping out from behind him.

"Finally," Yale said. "I have demands."

I lifted my hands to the air, calling the magic of the Fairchild estate toward me. I reached out across every square foot of the two hundred and eighty acres, calling for the wards on the manor and the protective wards that edged the property.

"There will be no bargain, vampire," I said. "No one, not even my own blood, threatens either of the two your brood now hold. The time to talk has passed."

"If it isn't clear to you already, witch," Yale snarled. "I control my progeny, mind to mind. Act against me, and they will snap the necks of your companions. No matter how many doubts the executioner thinks he's sown in their minds."

I didn't bother answering. I didn't have time to answer, because the energy buried deep within the land around me had come to my call eagerly. As if it had been biding its time. It rose up from the ground beneath my feet, filling me as if I was an empty vessel and it was my blood and air. My soul.

"What ...!" Mania tried to scream.

The air shifted around us. The trees along the edges of the clearing bowed toward me. The vampires clustered together, glancing around in panic.

I closed my eyes, building the power up and around me. Pulling more and more out of the estate while I threw my own magic out to meet it. Acting in desperation, seeking Declan and Jasmine's salvation in the very thing I'd rejected.

I'd break every promise I ever made to myself if it gave me any chance to save them.

I opened my eyes. The earth rumbled underneath my feet. Magic swirled around me in a vibrant tornado of blue-streaked energy. I'd lost sight of the vampires, of Jasmine and Declan. The magic I'd called forth, heedless of set boundaries and proper casting, grew impatient. It tore from my grasp, churning all around me.

And suddenly, it was too much to hold. Too much to command.

I'd gambled, acting instinctively and rashly. And I was going to lose. It was too much magic to wield. It was going to consume me.

I threw my arms out, screaming my frustration and pain into the ravaging tornado.

I lost my footing. I was being pulled into the storm I'd created in my ignorance and fear.

Then Kett was behind me, wrapping one arm around my shoulders and one around my waist, anchoring my bare feet to the ground. And thus shielded, I came to understand that the magic just wanted me to command it. It wanted my control.

I was its instrument, its vessel. But it was mine to wield.

My sight cleared.

Declan and Jasmine were sprawled on the ground at the center of the cyclone, as if they'd been dropped when the magic first hit their captors. Both appeared to be unconscious. Still breathing.

The other three vampires were struggling against the magic that bound them, Mania and Amaya too far away to reach their targets. But then Yale hunkered down, clawing his fingers into the ground and pulling himself forward. Close enough to brush his fingertips against Jasmine's outstretched arm.

I whispered to the energy eager to do my bidding. "Protect Jasmine and Declan."

The magic shifted, wrapping around the two of them. It pulled them out of harm's way even as it pressed against the vampires. Yale grimaced against the onslaught. Mania and Amaya flailed. Their mouths moved as if they were shouting, or perhaps even screaming. But I couldn't hear anything but the triumphant song of my ancestral magic.

Jasmine and Declan were lifted, held aloft out of the vampires' reach and cushioned by the magic of the estate.

My footing slipped again. Kett's grip intensified. The magic tugged at me insistently. I was going to be pulled apart if I didn't get everything under control. But the energy was overwhelming. Incalculably strong.

And some part of me wanted to let go. To simply be swept away, to be consumed.

Kett pressed his lips against my throat. My skin felt as though it was aflame. I was burning up, but his cool touch focused me.

He was asking to bite me. But why?

The torrential magic was tugging at him, trying to pull him away from me. Just as it had pulled Declan and Jasmine from the grasp of the other vampires.

But Kett and I were keeping each other grounded. Without him, I would have been lost. I was certain of that.

The magic of the estate and the wards had heeded me, protecting Jasmine and Declan because of the blood in our veins. It was most likely that the vampires had gained access to the property and the cottage wards because Valko had likewise bitten Jasmine.

I understood without asking that Kett hoped my blood would do the same for him. I wrapped my left hand up and around his head, tilting my head to the right and exposing my neck to him.

Kett's fangs slid into my skin with a sharp pinch of pain.

Yale appeared suddenly only a few feet away, continuing to close the space between us despite the storm of magic around him.

Kett drank from me, keeping me grounded and clear-headed within the steel cage of his arms.

I raised my right hand, palm facing Yale. The magic I'd called forth had coalesced around the bracelet on my wrist, manifesting in a hurricane of blue witch magic swirling around my forearm and hand.

Yale latched on to my other arm, trying to use me to anchor himself as Kett was doing. His grip was bruising.

Without raising his head, Kett reached through the whirlwind of magic surrounding the three of us to grab Yale's wrist.

But before he could do anything more, I spoke, intoning my own doom and binding myself to the Fairchild coven irrevocably.

"Every sliver of darkness shall be stripped from this land. We Fairchilds will walk in the light."

Then I slammed the ancestral magic I was wielding into Yale's chest. He flew backward and was ensnared by the whirlwind—which promptly ejected him across the boundaries of the estate. I felt, rather than saw, the moment he passed through the wards.

Mania and Amaya weren't so fortunate.

Backed by the power that resided in my bracelet—Vampire's Bane, as I'd named it to Yale—the magic at my command completely consumed them until they were nothing but ash whirling around us.

Kett licked my neck, murmuring in my ear, "You are magnificent. You are everything I thought you would be, my chosen one."

Then he released me, walking into the magic. The power of the estate didn't touch him.

His voice sounded in my head. *I'll make certain that he stays away.*

Without Kett to anchor me—or perhaps because I'd simply wielded too much power too quickly, exhausting my reserves—I began to lose my hold on the ancestral magic.

Blackness encroached on my vision. The magic I called forth was demanding more from me than I had to give.

I fell to my knees, crawling across to Jasmine and Declan. They appeared to be sleeping peacefully just beneath the still-churning storm. I pressed a hand to each of their chests, feeling their hearts beating soundly against my palms. Relief flooded through me.

They would survive, even if I didn't. They would go on.

The magic abruptly settled around us, as if I'd satisfied it somehow.

The sky cleared. Stars were beginning to appear. A light coating of ash fell across my outstretched arms and hands.

Then everything went dark.

Chapter Twelve

I woke to the sound of murmuring voices. Blinking rapidly, I attempted to bring the bright day around me into focus. I was staring up at a cloudless light-blue sky. The ground was warm underneath my back, though I could see the mist of my own breath.

A shadow moved across my face. A person was hunched over me, peering down with deep concern etched across her olive skin and dark-green eyes.

No. She wasn't hunching. She was simply leaning over to block the sun from my face.

A brownie.

On Fairchild land.

I closed my eyes.

The murmuring intensified.

The day was cold, the temperature easily below freezing. Based on the amount of light in the sky, I'd been on the ground for at least twelve hours. At minimum, I should have had hypothermia, or even have died from exposure. But I felt cozy, well rested. And ... somehow ... whole.

I opened my eyes again, reaching out to the sides and feeling for Declan and Jasmine. They were curled to either side of me, warm and still slumbering.

I sat up.

Three brownies were standing vigil over us. Two females, one younger than the other. And a male to judge by his shorter hair, along with the overalls he wore as opposed to the sleeveless A-line burlap dresses the females wore. They stood less than three feet tall but were exceedingly stout. Their large feet were bare, and their overly large hands were primly folded. They regarded me without blinking.

"Good morning," I said. I should have been sore, completely drained, but I wasn't.

"We heeded your call, mistress," the younger of the females said. Her voice was deep and full of gravel. "We've removed every object of dark magic from the property."

"Oh." Completely baffled by their appearance, I couldn't remember demanding anything of the sort about dark magic.

"I told you we should have clarified," the male whispered. His voice was so husky I felt as though I could feel it reverberate through the ground.

He caught me looking at him, and his deep-brown eyes widened. He murmured as he nodded his head in a gesture that looked suspiciously like a bow. "The Fairchild."

"We've been awaiting your return," the young female said. "I'm Lark. This is my grandmere Tulip and my nephew Jim. We have taken the items we've confiscated to our cousin Blossom, who attends the alchemist, the treasure keeper, and the far seer."

Disbelief rolled through me—followed by intense panic. I pressed my hands to my face.

The brownies had reclaimed Fairchild Manor.

At my command, they had stripped Jasper's dark artifacts from the estate. Then, as far as I could figure from the titles Lark had listed and those titles' connection to Jade—aka the dowser, aka the alchemist—the brownies had given those dark artifacts to the guardian dragons. The consequences of that action were unquantifiable. Or at least they were for me in that moment.

I forced my hands into my lap. "That … that … thank you."

Lark placed her hands at her hips proudly. "It's our pleasure to serve the real Fairchild."

I nodded. Then I continued nodding, as if I understood what they were saying. Which I wasn't completely certain that I did. "But … but … Bluebell," I whispered. "She's dead because of us. Because of me."

Tulip nodded sagely. "Bluebell made her choice. As we have."

Lark patted my shoulder awkwardly. "You are the Fairchild now. I will serve you."

Declan groaned.

The three brownies disappeared.

He sat up abruptly. With a pained expression, he pressed his hand against his head. "Wisteria. What the hell have you done now?"

Ignoring him, I knelt beside Jasmine, touching her cheek lightly. As her eyes fluttered open, I let out a relieved breath.

Declan swore.

I glanced back.

He was pressing his hand to the frozen ground on which he was now kneeling. He looked up, catching my eye. "Tell me you didn't tie all three of us to Fairchild land."

I opened my senses to the magic embedded in the earth beneath me. It hummed sleepily, almost as though it was utterly content. I swallowed, feeling a little ill as the ramifications of what I'd done hit me. That was why the magic had settled after I'd laid hands on Declan and Jasmine.

"It seemed like a good idea at the time."

"Damn you, Wisteria," Declan hissed. "If I wanted to be a Fairchild, I would have stayed."

"Shut the hell up, Declan," Jasmine snapped. "Wisteria just saved both our asses. Again." She struggled to prop herself up, glaring at her brother. "You going to whine about it for another twelve years?"

Declan opened his mouth to make some angry retort, but then stopped himself. Instead, he cast his gaze my way. "That depends."

Jasmine sighed, shaking her head. Then she grabbed my shoulder, beckoning to Declan with her other hand. "All right, Mr. Grumpy Pants, care to help me up?"

Declan swept Jasmine into his arms as he stood. Then he strode off toward the manor without another word.

I stood, following Declan and Jasmine at a more sedate pace. Glancing around as I crossed through the gardens, I realized that the vibrancy that had felt like it had been missing had returned to the property.

I trailed behind Declan as he carried Jasmine through the back door to the kitchen, feeling the wards of the house slide across me like a caress.

"Did you feel that?" Jasmine murmured.

Declan grunted in response.

Previously, the magic tied to the estate had felt as though it was trying to connect with me. To cajole me and guide me. But now it felt settled. Present, but content.

Jasmine dropped her hand from Declan's shoulder, trailing it across the well-worn wood-block kitchen counter as they brushed past it. Then she rubbed her fingers together.

So I wasn't the only one who could feel the shift in the estate's magic.

Declan strode forward into the dining room, then the parlor beyond, leaving a trail of dirt and other debris behind him. His leather jacket and work boots were streaked with dried mud.

I paused by the dark oak table in the dining room, glancing down to note that every item I was currently wearing was smeared with ground-in dirt as well. My sweater and pants were ripped. I'd left my coat and my bag somewhere in the clearing, along with my socks and shoes.

I reached up and brushed my fingers against my neck, remembering where Kett had bitten me. The skin there was smooth and didn't feel bruised.

Through the open doors to the front parlor, Declan settled Jasmine down on the green chaise, then looked back at me. His gaze settled on my hand still touching my neck.

He frowned as he reached up to touch his face. The wound he'd sustained in his struggle with Amaya had healed. He shook his head as if trying to wake himself or recall a memory. "Was it the estate's magic that healed us?" he asked. "And what the hell happened with the vampires?"

I dropped my hand. "Kett went after Yale," I said. "The estate's magic … consumed Amaya and Mania, then healed us."

Declan muttered something under his breath. It sounded like vicious satisfaction.

"Or the brownies, maybe." I continued through into the parlor. "Bluebell used to heal our minor cuts and bruises."

"Against Jasper's orders," Jasmine said, settling her head back against the arm of the chaise with her eyes closed.

"What brownies?" Declan asked.

I brushed my fingers against Jasmine's curls as I crossed around the chaise. Not even thinking about it, I flicked my fingers toward the stack of logs in the fireplace as I sank down in the chair across from my cousin. A fire I shouldn't have been able to summon so effortlessly flickered to life.

Apparently, claiming the estate's magic came with side benefits. I just didn't want to think about the unfortunate consequences yet.

Jasmine laughed, quietly pleased.

"So you're back to not answering questions," Declan said.

I smiled at Jasmine, simply wanting to sit by the fire with my best friend for a moment of respite. "No," I said. "I'll answer anything you wish to ask me."

Declan nodded. But then he stayed silent, apparently satisfied for the moment.

"I think we should go out for breakfast," Jasmine said perkily.

"You can't even walk," Declan groused.

"I just need a cup of Aunt Rose's tea," she said. "Will you see if there's any here? And boil some water?"

Grumbling, Declan tugged off his jacket, throwing it over the back of a dining room chair as he retreated through the house and into the kitchen.

"Nice that the family is so concerned for us, hey?" Jasmine said sarcastically. "Rushing to our rescue and all."

"I'm sure Kett texted Rose," I said, hoping I sounded diplomatic.

"Right. Because the executioner is so considerate like that." She closed her eyes, pressing her head back against the arm of the chaise. "Don't try to fix it, Wisteria. I know it's always been broken. I'm just finally ready to admit it."

I didn't answer. Instead, I leaned forward to reach for a fringed wool blanket that I was certain hadn't been on the back of the chaise a moment before.

"Brownies, huh?" Jasmine asked.

"Apparently." I tucked the blanket around her legs.

She grabbed my hand before I could withdraw it, pressing a kiss to my palm. "Betty-Sue," she whispered. "Don't leave us. No matter what they say after all of this. No matter what they threaten. Don't leave us again."

I brushed the curls away from her face. Her neck was still a mass of bruises in various stages of healing. "I'm not sure I could leave, Betty-Lou. Not now."

She gripped my hand, almost harshly. "Because you don't want to? Or because you don't think the coven will let you go?"

Declan strode back through the dining room, leaning in the doorway to the parlor with his arms crossed.

My anxiety spiked as the consequences of claiming the estate for myself, and for Jasmine and Declan, threatened to overwhelm my already beleaguered brain.

Jasmine squeezed my hand again, anchoring me back in the present.

"I'm not sure," I said. "Except I don't think voluntarily walking away is an option now. For any of us. We're tied here, even deeper than before."

"Well, it never was an option for me," Jasmine said, dropping my hand. "So it's just you and Bubba who are going to be babies about it."

A comfortable silence settled around us, lasting until the faint whistle of the kettle emanated through from the kitchen.

Declan pushed away from the door. "I'm good with it." He crossed back into the kitchen.

"So that just leaves you," Jasmine said.

I glanced down at my cousin, who was lounging back in the chaise with heavy eyes and a smug smile at her lips. I tugged the blanket up, covering her arms and shoulders.

"What kind of breakfast do you want?" she asked sleepily.

I laughed. "Anything with cheese. And bread."

"I know a place."

"Of course you do."

Instead of heading upstairs to a bedroom, Declan stole a cushion from one of the chairs and crashed on the floor beside Jasmine. He fell asleep almost instantly, snoring quietly.

I listened to the two of them breathing for a few minutes, then began to get restless. I wasn't a fan of sitting around and dwelling on the nebulous future, and I was far too invigorated to take a nap. Though it was slightly relieving that it wasn't the past that was currently unsettling me.

I wandered up to one of the guest rooms overlooking the front drive, finding my miraculously clean bag hanging in the walk-in closet, along with my pristinely pressed three-quarter-length wool coat. My four pillar candles occupied an empty shelf. Either Lark was brilliant at anticipating my actions, or she moved far quicker than I could up the stairs and through the house.

I wasn't interested in reclaiming the bedroom I'd spent seven years of my life in. In fact, I might ask Lark to refurnish it. If I was going to be staying at the manor at all.

I shoved that thought away, opting to focus on stripping off my grubby, torn clothing and standing in a scalding shower for far too long. I took my time drying and pinning up my hair—and, of course, found all my clothing cleaned and repaired when I was done.

I wandered back through the house, checking that Jasmine and Declan were still sleeping, then finding myself in the ballroom overlooking the side patio and the empty pool.

The square footage of the manor's ballroom was twice that of Fairchild Park's, but there was no piano here. The oak floors gleamed as if they'd just been polished, though—and given the brownies' declaration of having stripped all the darkness from the estate, it was likely they had been. Not a single hint of our long years of spellcasting practice was evident. Declan had set the ballroom's floor-to-ceiling gold brocade curtains on fire at least three times.

Crossing the length of the room, I systematically tugged the heavy curtains away from the windows, allowing sunlight to pour into every corner of the room.

The house wards shifted around me. Then a vampire was suddenly standing before the windows, gazing out at the empty pool.

I laughed instead of flinching. Apparently, Kett couldn't sneak up on me in the manor.

He glanced over at me, grinning. Then he held out his hand.

I wandered back across the expansive floor but didn't take it, choosing instead to stand shoulder to shoulder with him.

"Your magic has settled," he said, allowing his arm to rest at his side. "As I predicted it would."

I laughed. "Yes, Kett. I completely believe that you contrived the entire situation just so I would claim the ancestral magic of the estate." But though he chuckled, my own tone turned serious. "I don't believe you would have put Jasmine in harm's way."

"No. That I didn't knowingly do." He angled his shoulders toward me. "But it was my fault nonetheless."

"And Yale?"

"Contained. I'll take him to London."

I met his silvered gaze. "Will you take me to London?" I whispered.

Some emotion flitted across his face that I couldn't identify. "We will avoid London for as long as possible. But we will not be able to avoid it altogether."

I nodded, letting the subject drop. "The three of us are going to breakfast ... well, brunch now."

"Before you go ..." The vampire held out his hand to me again, offering a slight smile.

I placed my right hand in his without hesitation this time, realizing he was being careful to not move too quickly around me. He rotated my hand palm up, brushing his fingers from my wrist to my fingertips. The gesture was contemplative, as if he were the one who was hesitant.

"I understand ... more so now ... that you've had much taken from you." He shook his head as if rethinking what he wanted to say. Then he lifted his gaze to meet mine. "I would ... I offer you a drop of my blood."

"What does that mean?"

"It identifies you as mine to any other vampire. It declares you to be under my protection."

"The token that Yale kept mentioning?"

"Yes."

I didn't question him any further. It was enough to simply think through the implications of his request.

"I've never offered such a thing to anyone before," he said quietly. "I've had my blood taken forcibly, of course. But I've never given it willingly."

"You thought ... in the graveyard, you thought a single drop might possibly kill Ben."

"But not you, Wisteria."

Ever so slowly, Kett lifted his hand from mine, giving me space to step away if I desired. Then he brushed his fingers against my neck, caressing the skin he'd punctured when he bit me.

A wash of euphoria ran down my neck and through my chest, settling in my belly. My nipples hardened. I involuntarily gasped.

Then I took a step back.

"That … I …" I pressed my hands to my flushed cheeks, taking a moment to organize my thoughts. "You said that … vampire venom … with Nigel …"

Kett rescued me from my incoherent attempt to question him. "Yes. Vampires' venom contains certain euphoric properties."

"But when you bit me, I didn't feel … that … what you just made me feel when you touched me."

"You were rather preoccupied," he said, smiling wryly. "But since observing you in your childhood environment, I have come to understand that I might have assessed our potential relationship erroneously."

"Meaning?"

"Meaning … I'll give you whatever you want, whenever you want it." He arched an eyebrow at me. "And if that means going into competition with Declan for your affections, I'm up for it."

I laughed despite myself. "Oh, you are, are you?"

"I was perfectly content to build that part of our relationship. From master and child, then perhaps to lovers. But if it will help you make a decision, if it will sway you …" He gestured his hand offishly. "I'm willing to progress at a quicker pace."

I stared at him. "So you're offering me immortality, invulnerability, and …"

"Pleasure."

"And did you offer the same to Jasmine?" I whispered the question, knowing it was out of bounds and that it was unlikely the vampire would answer me.

He stilled. "You know I did not."

"And if you had? If you offered her a drop of your blood?"

He looked surprised, as if the idea hadn't occurred to him.

"Wouldn't that have protected her from Yale?"

Kett tilted his head. "Perhaps. Though it likely wouldn't have made a difference. Yale wanted to play games with the executioner of the Conclave. To triumph over the vampire who destroyed his sire."

"And she wasn't powerful enough to protect," I said, ignoring Kett's justification—and surprised by the sudden anger in my statement.

"Or perhaps Yale had another reason to get my attention. Another motivation yet to be revealed."

Dread replaced the anger as quickly as it had come, though. I voiced the lingering doubt I'd been carrying with me for days now. "An alliance with the Fairchild coven. With Jasper, specifically? Did he say so? Did you ... did you drink from him?"

"I quelled him," Kett said smoothly. "Further investigation into his involvement will have to wait until he has recovered from your assault. His reserves were rather low."

"And you wouldn't want to destroy him," I said sarcastically.

"Indeed. A waste."

"Because he remakes vampires easily."

Kett nodded. "And you noted how each of his brood retained a large portion of their Adept abilities."

"I did ... specifically while I was vomiting the results up."

Silence fell between us. I turned to stare out the windows, though I could still feel the weight of Kett's gaze and his question.

"I had another reason," he said. "For not making Jasmine the same offer. I thought it might ... displease you."

"Jasmine being protected would never displease me."

"And I was concerned ..."

"About?"

"The ... internalized darkness."

I glanced over at him. He'd returned his attention to the view, his hands clasped behind his back.

"I don't know what you mean. Jasmine isn't … dark. If anything, I'm the one steeped in darkness. I thought that was what you …" My voice trailed off.

"What drew me to you?"

I nodded.

Kett lifted his hand, turning it before us as if it were an object he was examining. "The transformation is never the same from vampire to vampire. I have seen its effect numerous times. And even for those it doesn't kill or consume, it changes them. Often latching on to innate characteristics and amplifying them."

"So Jasper wouldn't make a good vampire, because he's …"

"Set in his ways. Mired in darkness. Too close to the edge. I might remake him, expending my own magic to do so, only to end up destroying him when the transformation drives him to madness."

"And that would be a waste."

"Do you doubt it?"

I shook my head. I was allowing myself to be angry, and therefore irrational, when I should be listening carefully. "Then why cross Jasmine off the list and not me?"

"You acknowledge the darkness," Kett said. "You fortify yourself against it. While Jasmine …" He shook his head. "Even a single drop might alter her, turning her from something lovely and vibrant to something … not."

"And if you remake me? I won't change?"

"You will change. I cannot say how. Only that you are strong and fierce. You won't be manipulated by internal or external forces." Kett laughed quietly. "And you are calm, collected, and poised when you should be terrified."

"Some would call that a psychosis, rather than an attribute," I said wryly.

He didn't answer.

I shifted my gaze out to the empty pool, pressing my palm to the window. It was colder outside than it had been for the last couple of days. Cold enough to snow if there'd been any precipitation.

"When we were younger," I said, "Bluebell used to freeze the pool in the winter so we could skate on it. When Jasper was away for a few hours, of course. We could have used spells, but instead we strapped on old skates that we'd convinced Rose to buy us from a thrift store. The skates didn't really fit us properly, but ..."

"You could be Betty-Sue, Betty-Lou, and Bubba for an afternoon," Kett said.

"Yes," I whispered. "Normal."

"You will never be normal, Wisteria. Remade or not, you will be yourself, but never normal."

I nodded, not looking at him. "Still. I wish it was snowing."

"That I cannot give you," Kett said quietly. "Though I could take you to the snow."

"After you take Yale to London," I said wryly, dropping my hand from the window.

He chuckled. "Yes. Perhaps best to keep you two separate for some time. A few decades should do. That is, if my grandsire ever allows Yale his freedom again."

I nodded, though I was still largely incapable of understanding ideas or plans presented in terms of decades or centuries. Other thoughts and emotions churned around in my mind, but none of them were currently within my ability to articulate.

"You're wrong," I finally said.

"A rare but possible occurrence."

I laughed, looking over at Kett. He was smiling to himself. The sunlight streaming in through the windows lent a golden kiss to his skin. He looked human. Dangerously, deceptively human. And obtainable.

"You're wrong about needing to compete with Declan," I said. My heartbeat ramped up, settling only after I glanced away from him.

"Declan the younger, then," Kett said. "If the elder is using your shared history as justification of his own cowardice."

I snorted. "Cowardice isn't a word I'd associate with Declan."

"We all have things that we allow to hold us back."

"And what holds you back?"

Kett laughed again, but it wasn't a warm sound this time. "Besides humanity?"

I didn't answer, wrapping my left hand over the bracelet on my wrist and feeling the tiny whirls of magic from the reconstructions attached to it.

"Drink from me, Wisteria." Kett whispered the words against my neck, causing me to shiver with pleasure once again. I hadn't seen him move closer.

I shook my head, then softened my refusal. "Ask me again when I'm not so angry."

"I will."

Then he was gone, once again leaving me with unanswered questions. The wards shifted, informing me that he'd left the property.

I pressed my hand to the window again. The chilled glass was fortifying, invigorating. But … this wasn't my home, at present or in the future. Whether or not I took Kett up on his offer, it wasn't my place to attempt to build a life in Jasper's domain.

I dropped my hand, turning toward the warmth I knew the fire in the parlor would offer. Hopefully, Jasmine would be awake soon and feeling well enough to eat.

Chapter Thirteen

Contrary to Declan's concern, Jasmine's phone was not a clone. My cousin had an extended fit of laughter over the idea that the vampires would even know what cloning a piece of technology entailed, let alone that they'd be capable of doing so. The bite marks left over from Valko's repeat feedings continued to fade, but Jasmine's emotions remained close to the surface. Even more so when she discovered that the magic I'd called forth from the estate had ruined her and Declan's cellphones as thoroughly as she'd ruined mine.

Thankfully, Jasmine's computer, satchel, and clothing miraculously appeared in her room at the manor while she was showering. Lark must have found them in the cottage. And conveniently, there was an Apple Store in West Hartford, Connecticut—only forty-five minutes in the wrong direction on the way to brunch, which then turned into lunch.

Jasmine bought three new phones, grumbling about billing the Conclave for the replacements. Then she obsessively booted each of them through her laptop and iCloud, all the while directing Declan back into Litchfield to the Saltwater Grille for lunch.

The restaurant was situated in a tiny red house tucked between two larger buildings in a retail-dominated area, with white trim and French-paned double front doors. Before we'd even sat down at the table tucked beside interior red-painted French doors that led to the currently closed back patio, Declan had ordered the steak sandwich—a rib-eye with grilled onions, peppers, and mozzarella, along with fries, of course.

Quickly scanning the menu as I settled at the far side of the smooth wooden table, I opted for the shrimp scampi pasta—sauteed shrimp and sun-dried tomatoes in a white-wine garlic sauce over fusilli. Hopefully it was served with a generous topping of Parmesan. Jasmine ordered the fish and chips without even glancing at a menu or up from her phone. Though she needed sustenance more than Declan or I did, food wasn't currently a priority for her. And that, more than anything else, said a lot about her state of mind.

We didn't talk much, opting for casual conversation about the weather and news, then digging into our food. But the third time I caught Declan staring at Jasmine's bowed head with sorrow etched across his face, I reached across the table and touched my fingertips to the back of his hand.

I knew that fiddling with technology and exercising her magic were simply Jasmine's first steps toward healing herself emotionally. Declan nodded at my unspoken assurance, then withdrew his hand from the table. "Eat more," he said to Jasmine.

She dutifully broke off a piece of battered cod, dipping it in tartar sauce and popping it in her mouth without looking up.

"What did that damn vampire mean, calling you his child?" Declan finally asked while scarfing fries. He'd already inhaled his sandwich.

"What?" Jasmine said, looking up. "When? Where was I?"

"Taking a nap, apparently," Declan said. Then, relenting, he added, "That whole 'chosen child' thing. He was referring to Wisteria."

"What the hell, Betty-Sue?"

"Right," I said, popping the last piece of shrimp in my mouth. "I guess I'd better tell you." I tugged my bag into my lap, pulling out the Conclave contract.

"Oh, we get to be in on the big secret, do we?" Declan said mockingly.

Jasmine kicked him under the table.

"Ouch."

"Watch your mouth," Jasmine snarled, only half playfully.

Ignoring them, I unfolded the contract, flipping to the final page. My gaze instantly snagged on the list of handwritten names in the *For Consideration* addendum.

Declan's name had been struck out and initialed with a blood-red letter K.

Relief, followed by a spike of fear, rushed through my body. I exhaled heavily.

"What is it?" Jasmine whispered.

I looked up to meet her fearful gaze, then glanced over at Declan, whose face was impassive.

I reordered the pages, then slid the ream of parchment across the table toward Jasmine. "I've had a lawyer look at it. It's … it's binding, unbreakable."

Jasmine picked up the contract, setting it down on the other side of her plate and angling it toward Declan. They both bowed their heads over it, reading it together.

I picked at my plate, waiting with a hollowed stomach that should have been comfortably full of scampi. Then I decided it wasn't worth ruining great food over a pending decision.

The world wasn't ending. I simply had a choice to make. And I would approach that choice with the same efficiency I used for every decision, major or minor. It would help, at least emotionally, to have Jasmine and Declan as sounding boards.

Jasmine flipped to the last page.

Declan let out a string of curses under his breath as the true nature of the contract became clear to him.

A contract inked and signed by our Uncle Jasper. With my name being the last on the list *For Consideration*, other than Jasper himself.

"In his defense," I said, anticipating their reactions, "the Conclave insisted on that list. I doubt Jasper thought there was even a remote chance of any of us actually being in consideration over him."

"In his defense?" Declan echoed, incredulous.

"Poor choice of words," I said.

"He's in a goddamn wheelchair," Declan said fiercely, leaning across the table toward me while jabbing his finger on the contract. "And you ... you put him there. At sixteen. What were the chances the damn vampire wasn't going to want you?"

Jasmine reshuffled the pages in order to read the contract a second time, front to back. Her movements were jerky.

"Well ..." I said, trying to maintain some composure. "How was he to know that Kett would find that out?"

Declan slumped back in his chair, looking at me in disbelief. "You told him. In the manor, after getting caught in that damn reconstruction with the fucking rabbit. To what? Keep yourself in contention?"

"Declan!" Jasmine snapped. Then she glanced up at me. "Kett already knew."

I nodded. "He'd picked up something while he was investigating everyone," I said. "Though I'm not sure he knew the fine details."

"Plus he … he wants something," Jasmine murmured, dropping her gaze to the final page again. "Something he thinks only you can give him."

"The guy is a complete asshole," Declan said. "Trying to have both of you at once."

Jasmine eyed him angrily. "What makes you think I didn't proposition him? What makes you think he wasn't completely clear about the parameters of our relationship? You think I'm some fool? Maybe with an older uncle complex?"

Declan's anger crumpled. "Hey, hey. No. But he is a bloodsucker, and—"

Jasmine swiftly slid the black phone she'd been programming across the table toward him. He barely caught it before it hit the ground.

"Copper," she said nastily, "is trying to get hold of you."

Declan glanced down at the phone, pressing the home button with his thumb. Even from across the table, I could see the notifications lined up on his screen.

"Jasmine," he said, pleading.

But his sister turned her fierce gaze from him to me. "So … you'd leave us?"

I looked at her, then I glanced at Declan. He pushed his uneaten fries away and didn't meet my eye.

"What would you do?" I whispered. "If you were the only thing standing between Jasper and immortality?"

Declan stood up abruptly, walking away from the table with his phone pressed to his ear.

"Well, we know what Declan would do," Jasmine said wryly.

"Don't be upset with him," I said. "He … it's a lot to deal with."

"Don't try to play peacemaker." Jasmine's tone was harsh, though she reached across the table to brush her fingers across my wrist and bracelet.

"No," I said softly. "That's your role."

"I didn't know Declan was living with her. Copper." Jasmine scooped up some of her coleslaw viciously with her fork, then chewed it thoughtfully. "Not until Christmas. She's a witch."

"He's not ours to own," I whispered. "Not mine." Though a sharp pain lodged in my chest, just over my heart, at the confirmation that Declan was in a serious relationship.

"He'll always be ours," Jasmine said.

I nodded, not wanting to fight about semantics with her when she was injured, her soul bruised.

"Kett thinks Declan and I aren't powerful enough," she said, changing the subject so swiftly that it took me a moment to follow her. "Like with Ben. Something about his blood, and all the power he's accumulated. Except you, apparently."

"He told you?"

Jasmine tapped the contract that still lay open before her. "It's in here. And, yeah. He doesn't talk much, but occasionally he'd trade, secrets for secrets. Like it was a game." She twined her fingers through mine, steadily holding my gaze. "I'm not in love with him, you know."

I nodded, though I hadn't known that for sure.

"I mean, he's a fun ride and all. But it's easy to lose track of your life around him." She withdrew her hand from mine, carefully refolding the contract before handing it to me. "I guess that won't be a problem for you, if you accept."

"Because I'll be dead."

"Remade, yes. But … I don't think we'll be getting brunch or lunch together …" Her voice cracked.

Spotting Declan returning from across the restaurant, I quickly whispered, "What would you do?"

"You know what I'd do," Jasmine said. "Same as you. Protect the other two. At all costs."

I nodded, brushing away the stray tear that had made it past my resolve to be focused and rational.

"I tried to pay, but my credit and bank cards are useless," Declan declared as he neared the table. "Fried. Same as the phones."

"I'm still eating," Jasmine said snottily. And without offering to pay with the credit card she'd used for the new phones.

"There's a branch of my bank down the block," I said. "I'm sure a teller can issue me a new card and some cash."

"I'll go," Declan said.

"Let Wisteria go," Jasmine said. "We need to talk."

I chuckled despite myself at the look of horror that flitted across Declan's face at this pronouncement. I tucked the contract back in my bag, pulling my wallet out instead.

Declan sat down with a heavy sigh.

I stood, weaving my way out of the restaurant but turning back at the front door to catch sight of Jasmine and Declan across the room.

My cousin threw her head back, laughing. Declan was leaning into her, smiling. Their body language was open and caring.

I should have been heartbroken at the confirmation that Declan was seriously committed to someone else. I should have been worried for Jasmine and all the healing she was going to have to live through. Again. I should have been frightened of how the future seemed likely to unfold.

Except I wasn't.

I had them back. Both of them. It was fractured and tentative, but the two of them made my heart full, not heavy.

It didn't take long to get things straightened away at the bank. While I waited for the clerk to return with a temporary card and the cash I'd requested, I stood at the rounded, chest-high reception desk, watching as traffic slowly rolled past the front windows.

An older man approached to my right, moving slowly, then pausing when he reached the edge of the counter. He was looking at me as if he knew me, so I glanced his way.

It took me a moment to recognize him.

Jasper.

Back from his island retreat—if he'd been there at all—and using a cane, not a wheelchair.

He stared at me, magic dancing in his otherwise expressionless blue eyes. "Wisteria," he said, once he had my full attention. "I've been meaning to get in touch with your mother."

"She's easy to reach," I said coolly. "Same address and everything."

"I see."

I turned so I could really look at him, scanning him up and down. I wasn't surprised I hadn't recognized him at first glance. His hair had thinned and lightened, and he wore it shorter. His face had sagged and thickened, though he didn't seem to be carrying any extra weight. Whatever he'd done to get out of his wheelchair must have involved some nefarious magic, but I couldn't assess such things simply by looking at him.

And I certainly didn't want to know how he'd tracked me down, because bumping into each other at the bank was an impossible coincidence.

I could inform the Convocation of my suspicions easily enough, though. Telling them that he was walking again. Asking them to open an investigation into what kind of dark magic might have fueled such a miraculous transformation.

If I wanted to get tangled up in the Fairchild coven once again.

Silent tension built up as the bank clerk returned, glancing uneasily between us.

I reached over the counter and plucked the card and cash out of her hand. "Thank you."

"You're very welcome," she said, overly cheerfully. Then she grabbed a stack of papers and bustled away.

I met Jasper's gaze. He was laughing at me without smiling, thinking he could dominate me by his mere presence. "I heard you were in trouble."

"And you flew in to help."

"You are my beloved niece."

"You look old, Jasper." I sneered his name, making it an insult.

"You look weak, child."

I smiled, feeling dark-tinged laughter burbling up from my belly. I pinned my gaze to his washed-out blue eyes, deliberately placing my right arm on the curved counter between us.

His gaze flicked to the bracelet teeming with magic on my wrist, then back up to my face.

My perfectly pleasant smile morphed into a vicious baring of my teeth. Something beside me crackled. Then the computer sitting on the desk below the counter began to smoke.

"Look again," I said. My heartbeat was steady and sure.

My uncle blinked. Once.

I turned and walked away, not looking back.

He had no power over me now.

Acknowledgements

With thanks to:

My story & line editor
Scott Fitzgerald Gray

My proofreader
Pauline Nolet

My beta readers
Terry Daigle, Angela Flannery, Gael Fleming,
Desi Hartzel, and Heather Lewis.

**For their continual encouragement,
feedback, & general advice**
SFWA
The Office

Meghan Ciana Doidge is an award-winning writer based out of Salt Spring Island, British Columbia, Canada. She has a penchant for bloody love stories, superheroes, and the supernatural. She also has a thing for chocolate, potatoes, and cashmere yarn.

NOVELS
After the Virus
Spirit Binder
Time Walker
Cupcakes, Trinkets, and Other Deadly Magic (Dowser 1)
Trinkets, Treasures, and Other Bloody Magic (Dowser 2)
Treasures, Demons, and Other Black Magic (Dowser 3)
I See Me (Oracle 1)
Shadows, Maps, and Other Ancient Magic (Dowser 4)
Maps, Artifacts, and Other Arcane Magic (Dowser 5)
I See You (Oracle 2)
Artifacts, Dragons, and Other Lethal Magic (Dowser 6)
I See Us (Oracle 3)
Catching Echoes (Reconstructionist 1)
Tangled Echoes (Reconstructionist 2)

NOVELLAS/SHORTS
Love Lies Bleeding
The Graveyard Kiss
The Graveyard Kiss (Reconstructionist 0.5)
Dawn Bytes (Reconstructionist 1.5)

For recipes, giveaways, news, and glimpses of upcoming stories, please connect with Meghan on her:
Personal blog, www.madebymeghan.ca
Twitter, @mcdoidge
Facebook, Meghan Ciana Doidge
Email, info@madebymeghan.ca

**Please also consider leaving an honest
review at your point of sale outlet.**

OTHER BOOKS BY MEGHAN CIANA DOIDGE

Dowser Series · Book 1

CUPCAKES, TRINKETS,
and other
DEADLY MAGIC

MEGHAN CIANA DOIDGE

Dowser Series · Book 2

TRINKETS, TREASURES,
and other
BLOODY MAGIC

MEGHAN CIANA DOIDGE

Dowser Series · Book 3

TREASURES, DEMONS,
and other
BLACK MAGIC

MEGHAN CIANA DOIDGE

Dowser Series · Book 4

SHADOWS, MAPS,
and other
ANCIENT MAGIC

MEGHAN CIANA DOIDGE

Dowser Series · Book 5

MAPS, ARTIFACTS,
and other
ARCANE MAGIC

MEGHAN CIANA DOIDGE

Dowser Series · Book 6

ARTIFACTS, DRAGONS,
and other
LETHAL MAGIC

MEGHAN CIANA DOIDGE

ORACLE SERIES · BOOK 1

I SEE ME

MEGHAN CIANA DOIDGE

ORACLE SERIES · BOOK 2

I SEE YOU

MEGHAN CIANA DOIDGE

ORACLE SERIES · BOOK 3

I SEE US

MEGHAN CIANA DOIDGE

WWW.MADEBYMEGHAN.CA

www.ingramcontent.com/pod-product-compliance
Lightning Source LLC
Chambersburg PA
CBHW07065518060626
46817CB00006B/2381